CASSANDRA VEGA

Die For Me

Copyright © 2024 by Cassandra Vega

All rights reserved. No part of this publication may be reproduced, stored or transmitted in any form or by any means, electronic, mechanical, photocopying, recording, scanning, or otherwise without written permission from the publisher. It is illegal to copy this book, post it to a website, or distribute it by any other means without permission.

This novel is entirely a work of fiction. The names, characters and incidents portrayed in it are the work of the author's imagination. Any resemblance to actual persons, living or dead, events or localities is entirely coincidental.

First edition

Cover art by Turning Pages Designs
Editing by Andrea Halland

This book was professionally typeset on Reedsy.
Find out more at reedsy.com

For the ones who love their fictional men morally gray with a very big scoop of dangerously obsessed, this one's for you.

Disclaimer

Your mental health is important. There are some very heavy topics in this book. Please check the trigger and content warnings on my website: https://authorcassandravega.com/faq

"You don't love because, you love despite; not for the virtues, but despite the faults." — William Faulkner

Hana

I hurriedly walked up to our new apartment in a lush condo building located right in front of the Williamsburg waterfront. The mid-April spring brought a slight chill as I walked up the steps into the lobby. The views from our place were amazing—from our living room, you could see the Williamsburg Bridge and the Manhattan skyline. It was only eight or nine blocks from mine and Billie's apartment, but it felt like I was a thousand miles away. I hadn't seen or talked to her in six weeks, not since the night I left Michael alone in that hotel in Jersey City. My life had changed drastically since then. I had talked to Emily only a handful of times, mostly to convince her that I was okay, that I had left with Jack willingly, and that I was really fucking happy living my new life as Mrs. Jack Maynor.

And that was mostly true.

I *was* okay. I was pretty happy, considering the circumstances that led me to this. I did not leave Michael willingly, but I had to pretend I did. That was the only way I could accept that I would never see him again. I pretended it was my decision—that I *had* to let him go. Now he could move on and live a happier life with a level-headed person that wouldn't always have a violent homicidal maniac hunting them down.

HANA

Of course, Jack wasn't that way all the time. He had been a loving and caring husband in the previous six weeks. He let me pick out our place. He brought home flowers and took me on romantic dates. He continually supported my creative ideas, gave me massages while we watched cheesy movies, and made me feel like the most important and special person in the world. He gave me the freedom to wander the streets of our neighborhood, but still reminded me that he would always know where I was. He hadn't laid a hand on me, except during sex; then he still liked to slap me around, bruise me, choke me, spit on me, call me his whore. And I still liked it.

But it left me with a little problem: I was potentially pregnant. I couldn't remember the last time I had gotten my Depo shot—was it before Michael and I got together? Was it after we were engaged? That time was all fuzzy in my brain; I think it was a coping mechanism. I was starting to forget his touch, his voice, the look in his eyes when he told me he loved me.

I couldn't even remember the last time I took my meds, or saw my therapist or psychiatrist. Jack wouldn't allow it. He liked me unmedicated and not talking to anyone without knowing exactly what I was saying. I think he worried that I would tell someone everything that had happened between me and him. I didn't want to talk to anyone, though—I was *fine*. I had been perfectly content and hadn't had any obvious hypomanic or depressive episodes. So clearly, something was going right.

However, when I realized I hadn't had my period since before we moved into our new apartment five weeks ago, I started to panic. *It could be nothing.* But I wanted to make sure. Because if I was pregnant, I didn't know if it was Michael's or

Jack's.

I threw my purse on the couch, set down some bags, and hurriedly went into the bathroom with my pregnancy tests in my coat pocket. I didn't want Jack to know that I might be pregnant. I needed time to think about how to tell him. Jack had installed cameras on the outside of the front door and in the living room. I knew he was always watching me if he was out—he was still paranoid that I would try to run away again. Which was fair enough, but I knew I would never try to leave him again. It was too dangerous. And, for some reason, I didn't want to.

I quickly put the little box into the back of the cabinet under the sink next to some makeup remover wipes and a big bottle of shampoo. I didn't think Jack would be interested in snooping around back there.

And then I was back to decorating our apartment. Our place was beautiful—definitely fancier than my last Williamsburg apartment. The floor-to-ceiling windows in every room provided a beautiful view of Manhattan and the waterfront. The kitchen had brand new appliances and granite countertops, and the light fixtures were modern and artsy. The small dining area sat a small rectangular black table with four chairs around it; Jack always got me fresh flowers for it. Outside of the dining area, there was a little balcony where I had set up a cozy outdoor couch with white lights lining the railing. In the living room, parallel to the kitchen and dining area, sat a huge gray L-shaped couch in front of our big-screen TV.

I unloaded my bag of useless things that I acquired at an antique store nearby, wanting to fill our apartment with things that didn't remind me of the past. At least not *my* past. I set down a bronze pitcher in the kitchen, a cat salt and pepper shaker set on the dining table, and a pretty little glass picture frame on a bookshelf near the TV. I sighed as I put my hands to my hips and looked out the living room windows; it was such an amazing view of my beautiful city. The sun was starting to set, and I had hoped that Jack would be home soon so we could walk to the waterfront and watch the sunset, as we often did. It was a cute little routine we had that I was starting to enjoy. I took time to appreciate all the small things I could in this new life of mine, and at the top of my list was watching the sunset next to my handsome husband—even if I hadn't chosen him.

As I started for the kitchen to see if we had anything to make for dinner, my phone went off with a text. It was a special tone reserved for Jack—I knew if I heard it, I needed to get to my phone immediately.

Hello love. I miss you terribly. How are you doing?

I smiled as I read it and texted back: **I miss you more. I'm just getting the place all set up. Will you be home soon?**

Maybe I could take the pregnancy test quickly and get that out of my mind.

As I looked up at the setting sun, the pinks and blues around the clouds swirling together, my phone went off again: **Yes, sweetheart. Within the next couple of hours. xx.**

I stared at my phone. Jack was in the Lower East Side at his loft working on some paintings. Even if he left now, I would still have time. *I can do it now. Just get it over with. Just go fucking see.*

Before I could change my mind, I tossed my phone on the couch and headed for the bathroom in our room. I shut the door behind me, locked it, and opened the bottom cabinet. My hand shook as I reached behind all of my bathroom bins and found the box. I held it up, quickly read the directions, and then tore it open.

I set the pee stick on the counter and nervously started the five-minute wait. I had no idea what it would mean for me and Jack if I were pregnant. What if it was Michael's? Would Jack make me get rid of it? *What if it's Jack's? Isn't that worse?* Did I really want to give this man a child? Did I want to give him one more thing to hold over my head so that I would behave? But isn't this what we had planned for our life? To live in my favorite neighborhood in New York City with little children running around as I cooked dinner, as Jack...*god, I can't imagine Jack with a child. Would he be jealous of this baby of ours? That it was taking up all of my time? Do I even want children anymore?*

The timer on my watch went off, and I held my breath as I slowly turned to look at the test.

It was positive.

Jack

My plan had worked—I had gotten Hana pregnant. The first time we had sex, she told me she took the Depo shot as birth control. When I took her, I deleted the reminder on her phone and canceled her follow-up appointment in late February. It happened a lot sooner than I thought it would. Now Hana was even more bound to me; I knew she wanted children and I was on the way to giving her one. Now she could never leave me, even if she wanted to. That was my child and there was no way she could take that away from me.

I watched through the camera as she took all of the tests to be sure of the positive. She started cursing to herself—perhaps she had changed her mind about wanting children. I would never let her get rid of it, though. I was going to make sure she was well taken care of and that she and the baby were as healthy as possible.

She wrapped the tests with toilet paper and stuffed them at the bottom of the bathroom bin. Was she trying to hide it from me? She stared at herself in the mirror for a long time; I wondered what she was thinking. I wondered if she would tell me when I got home. How could I let her know that I knew without telling her? Perhaps I could find the tests in the bin. She wouldn't be surprised at me snooping in the trash, looking for any evidence of wrongdoing.

So many questions ran through my head as I cleaned up my work space, getting ready to head home to my pregnant wife. Would I be a good father? All I had to do was provide a safe, nurturing home for this child. I didn't plan on killing myself and letting my child find me, like my father had done to me. I wouldn't fuck up my child's life and leave him with abandonment issues. I would provide love and security, like I was doing with Hana. I would never lay a hand on my child—I was getting better about that with Hana. I hadn't gotten angry at her since she came back to me, and I didn't intend to hurt her again. She still liked it very rough while having sex, which gave me a release for the urges I had every now and then. When she begged me to hurt her the night of our wedding reception, I felt like a fucking god. It was the most incredible night of my life. I felt guilty afterward, but she had literally asked me to do it—she *begged* for it.

I started getting hard at the thought. I knew it was fucked up of me to enjoy myself that much, but I loved that I bruised her and claimed her body as mine. It was fucking *thrilling*.

I knew I wanted to rough her up a little bit that night during sex. The thought was in my head too much now. Even pregnant, she could handle a little bit of my roughness. I just needed to not get too carried away. I couldn't do that to her anymore.

Fuck, concentrate! I caught myself daydreaming and fantasizing as I stood at the door of my loft. The loft had given me such precious memories; it's where I made Hana mine. I don't know how I got away with it, but I did. I had made Hana realize that she loved me, that she needed to be mine as much as she needed to breathe. And now she was mine forever.

JACK

* * *

I texted Hana while on the train, letting her know I was on the way home. The edges of my lips lifted when I saw the little bubbles pop up immediately, alerting me she was responding. I knew she was deeply in love with me and as codependent as I was. I couldn't believe she didn't run off to the police when she had first left me. That's how I knew she was really in love with me. It was so easy to lure her back; she knew she needed me. She knew she didn't belong with Michael. She belonged to me. It was obvious that I was obsessed with her, and she liked that. I would do anything it took to make her happy, including making sure she would never leave me again. She would never be happy with anyone else, especially that twit Michael. I did her a favor by cutting her off from that boring, mundane life. She didn't even really ask to see Emily or Billie, not that I would let her, not without me.

Once she was mine again, she never took her hands off me. I knew how fucking wet I made her—I could tell by the way she looked at me when we "accidentally" bumped into that coffee shop twelve weeks ago, the day before I brought her to the loft. I could tell by the way her cheeks reddened when she looked at my toned arms—which I had worked really hard for, just for her—and by the way she bit her lip every time she looked longingly at my lips. It was so fucking obvious that everything I had been planning was the right thing to do.

I smiled down at my phone while reading her text: **I can't wait to see you. I've missed you all day.**

I'd missed her as well, even though I had been watching her nearly all day while finishing my work.

Someone called out my name as I exited the train at my stop.

I turned around and there was that tenacious fucking cousin. I gave her my best fake smile.

"Emily."

Emily

Seeing that fucker Jack boiled a blind rage inside of me. I noticed him as we exited the train, his stupid fucking smug smile on his face while he looked down at his phone. I couldn't believe he had tricked me, and even his best friend, into believing he was some sweet, hopeless, helpless romantic. He was a literal monster in sheep's clothing.

I had been trying really hard to get back into Hana's life after she left Michael. However, I knew Jack was controlling her, keeping her to himself and brainwashing her even more than she already was. I had only seen her three times since then. Once by accident when I was on my way to work at a bar in Williamsburg—but we didn't get to talk much because of Jack, of course, and another time when she and Jack came by the apartment to say happy birthday to Adam. They stayed for five minutes before Jack whisked her away from me again.

I had last seen her at Easter brunch when her parents came into the city and, luckily, they invited me along. Jack was his sociopathic self, being charming and even making Uncle Dan laugh at some stupid joke he made. I sat across from Hana at the table where she sat next to Jack, and she seemed like her normal, happy self. She looked relaxed, she smiled easily and cracked jokes with me like old times. I didn't know if she was too far gone now. I didn't know if I could still save her from Jack.

She kept dodging my attempts to hang out with her. She never answered the phone anymore—she only replied by text. I had no idea if I was really texting Hana, or if Jack hijacked our conversations. But now I finally had the chance to stick up to him again like I had all those weeks ago…only this time I wouldn't fail miserably.

"Jack," I called out after I stalked him for a few seconds.

He turned around, and his face was blank as he noticed me. Then he plastered on the fakest grin I had ever seen. He stopped, and I walked up to him, feeling brave.

"Emily." His expression seemed tense as he looked me up and down.

"How's it goin'?" I asked casually, trying my hardest to sound friendly.

Jack's eyes widened, seemingly with surprise. "Quite well," he responded blankly.

I had no idea what I was going to say to him; my previous approach hadn't worked very well, so I thought maybe I could at least *try* to be nice this time.

"How's Hana?" I asked curiously. "What brings you around this side of town?"

He looked annoyed. "She's great. Didn't she tell you? We've moved back to Williamsburg. Just near the waterfront," he replied, smiling smugly again.

Fuck. I've been working literally blocks away from her this whole time? I felt angry not only at Jack, but at Hana. I hated that I felt that way.

"No, she didn't." I put on my best fake smile. "But hey—I work just a couple blocks from there, at that bar called The

Pit. You guys should come in, drinks on me," I offered.

Jack paused before responding. "I don't think Hana's up for drinking much lately. But I'll let her know," he said and then turned around and walked away.

Hana's not up for drinking? Since when? Sure, she took it easy around family and she had her meds, but...*did* she have her meds? Michael mentioned her not taking any of that with her when she vanished the first time.

I hesitated only a few seconds before I decided to follow Jack. If he was on his way home, then I could figure out where they lived. And then maybe I could finally get Hana alone.

Hana

I managed to get rid of any evidence of the three positive pregnancy tests. I didn't even have time to let it sink in—once I realized Jack was on his way home, I panicked and started to wrap them in toilet paper and stuff them at the bottom of the bathroom trash. I tossed the empty box back behind the bathroom bins and hurriedly shut the cabinet.

And then I started to bawl.

This was not at all how I envisioned my life at almost twenty-six. I was with a man I loved, but I was still scared. He still scared me, even though he was so sweet to me most of the time, because I knew what he was capable of. I didn't want to have to raise a child with that fear always lingering. And what if it wasn't Jack's? How the fuck would that work? How would I even find out?

I quickly went to the living room, grabbed my phone, marched back into the bathroom, and opened Safari. I was about to search *when is the earliest I can get a paternity test?* when I realized Jack would probably, somehow, find out I had searched for it. I didn't know what kind of spy technology he had on my phone, so I was always careful about what I did on it. Would he be able to know the things I *asked* Siri?

Fuck it. "Siri, when is the earliest I can get a paternity test?"

I asked my phone as quietly as I could.

A few suggestions popped up, and I read that it could happen as early as seven weeks. Not wanting to risk tapping on any results, I immediately turned off my phone and walked out of the bathroom. *When the fuck did I even get pregnant? How far along am I? How can I get an abortion without Jack knowing?* There it was, there was my decision: I didn't want this pregnancy. I had to figure this out somehow.

Suddenly, our front door unlocked—Jack was home. I hurriedly walked into the kitchen and opened the fridge.

"Hana, darling. I'm home," Jack called out, his voice light and chipper.

I put a smile on my face as he appeared in the kitchen. How was it possible that I still got butterflies when I saw him? He was so attractive that all I ever wanted to do was jump on him as soon as I saw him.

"Hi, babe." I smiled, reaching for him.

Jack took me in his arms and lifted me slightly, twirling me around, and I let out a giggle.

"Hello, my wife," Jack said into my ear before he pressed his lips to my neck.

There was that magic touch. I was instantly wet. He knew his effect on me and I didn't try to hide it anymore.

I moaned as I ran my fingers through his hair.

"Mmm, Jack, I need you," I whispered, closing my eyes as I let my head fall back.

"Yeah?" Jack whispered between kisses on my neck. "How badly do you want me?"

Jack tugged down my leggings and quickly put his fingers to my slit. I moaned as he slipped one finger in, the slickness of my pussy easily guiding him.

"Fuck, Hana. I love feeling your wet pussy. This perfect wet pussy is all for me."

His other hand fisted my hair.

"Get on your knees and beg for this cock, Hana," he ordered, releasing my hair and letting me fall to my knees.

I still loved his bossiness. I loved him forcing me and me playing along. There hadn't been a time in the last six weeks that I didn't want him to fuck me.

I placed my hands atop my thighs and looked up at Jack, his eyes eager and lustful.

"Please, Jack. I need your cock," I moaned. His huge erection bulged underneath the fabric of his jeans.

He grinned a little before his eyes turned dark. *The scary Jack.* My stomach dropped, and my heart started thumping wildly in my chest.

"Do you want me to hurt you, sweetheart?" he asked as he started to unzip his jeans.

I hesitated. Were we playing a game like we usually did, or was this real?

"Jack."

I knew I wasn't hiding my terror very well. I knew I wasn't smiling.

"What's wrong, sweetheart? Don't you want to play?" he continued, lowering his boxer briefs and letting his erection spring free. There was absolutely no hesitation or worry in his face.

"Play how, Jack?" I asked cautiously.

Now it seemed he was starting to sense my fear. His grin grew even wider before he grabbed onto his thick erection and started stroking himself. He put his hand to the back of my head and shoved his cock into my mouth, hard and rough.

"Like this, Hana," he moaned over his thrusts.

He was fucking my face, my mouth wide and dripping drool all over me. I didn't know what he was planning but I was still wet, if not wetter than before. He quickly stopped and bunched my hair with his hand again. This time, he pulled me up by the hair and had me standing; I shrieked with pain and confusion. Jack stared right through me, like he was lost in his thoughts and couldn't come back. All I could think was that he knew: He knew I was pregnant and that it possibly wasn't his. He was punishing me.

"What are you going to do, Jack?" I whispered, tears filling my eyes.

Jack wrinkled his forehead. "Don't you *want* me to hurt you, sweetheart?" he asked with confusion, one hand still stroking himself and the other behind my head.

Maybe I did. Maybe this would solve my problem.

"Like the night of our wedding party?" I asked hesitantly.

Jack smiled instantly. "Yes. You loved it, Hana. Don't you want to remember this time?"

His voice was low and gravelly. He seemed like he was lost in a different head space—he was stuck in scary Jack mode.

I wasn't sure if I wanted to feel that pain again. He had hurt me since then, but this was different. This felt like day one all over again.

I blurted it out before I could even think.

"Jack, you can't. You can hurt me, but…I don't want you to hurt the baby."

His face morphed from terrifying to terrified. My Jack was finally back.

Jack

I knew I was getting carried away. I knew I was scaring her, but fuck, didn't I love that? Didn't *she* love that? I wanted to embrace my monster, let him out to play. She still loved me despite him, and it had been too long. I knew I would feel guilty after, but it felt too good in the moment. She would try to stop me if it went too far, wouldn't she? And I knew she wasn't going to tell me about the pregnancy tests. This was my way of punishing her for trying to trick me, for keeping this colossal secret from me.

But then she brought me back.

She told me—she surprised me there. I already had time to process everything, and I wasn't going to lie to her.

"I know, love." I stopped stroking myself.

She shook her head to herself. "What? How do you know?"

I towered over her as she sat back on her ankles.

"I have a camera in our bathroom," I answered, putting my cock away and sitting on the floor in front of her.

Hana looked deeply offended, but she didn't seem surprised.

"Why aren't you freaking out right now, Jack?" Her forehead wrinkled. She looked so beautiful.

I smiled at her. "Because I wanted to give you a child. And I've achieved that. We're starting a family, Hana."

JACK

She still looked confused. "But…are you angry? That…"

Now I was confused. "Why would I be angry, sweetheart?"

Tears started to fill her eyes. She looked terrified all over again.

"I…I don't know," she cried.

She was hiding something. I eyed her as I pulled out my phone. I wanted to see what she was up to while I was on the way home.

"Jack." She put her hand on mine. "Jack, wait. What are you doing?"

"Tell me why I would be angry, Hana!" I shouted.

She flinched—her hand retreating from me—then covered her face with her hands. Why was she so scared? What was she hiding?

I went to the feed from the bathroom after I left the loft. She hid the tests, stared at herself in the mirror, and cried for a long time. I almost felt bad, until I saw grabbing her phone.

"Jack, please." Hana stopped crying and got to her knees.

I had to know what she was hiding. I looked back down at my phone and then Hana bolted for the bedroom. The bathroom door slammed shut and locked.

"Hana!" I got up and followed her.

I was almost worried that she was calling someone or dialing 911, but then I saw her phone lying on the night stand beside the bed. I wanted to wait to react until I saw what she was hiding. *"How early can I get a paternity test?"* Hana's whisper crackled from the video feed. My whole body vibrated with rage. She fucked Michael when they tried to hide in Jersey City? That was the only explanation. Now I really was going to fucking kill him.

"Hana! Did you fuck Michael?" I yelled at the door.

She was crying loudly.

"You weren't even gone for twelve fucking hours and you fucked him! Were you *confused*, Hana?" I went on.

More crying.

"Get out here right now. I have a fucking key to this bathroom, Hana. Either I open it or you do. I'm betting I'll be less angry if you open it."

I didn't hear anything. For a second, I imagined her slitting her wrists. With that thought, I quickly went to the safe in the closet and unlocked it then grabbed the key to the bathroom. When I turned around, she was standing at the door. I could see the terror behind her red, tear-soaked eyes. I was too angry to feel bad for her; she did this to herself.

"Sit on the bed," I ordered, watching her carefully.

"I know it's yours, Jack—"

"Sit the fuck down, Hana!" I shouted.

She didn't hesitate to go to the bed and sit on the edge. I sighed as I stared down at the key in my hand. What the fuck was I going to do with her? What if this child wasn't mine? She would definitely need an abortion then—there was no question to it. My face was burning with jealousy as I stared down at her.

"How many times did you fuck him in Jersey City? Or did you fuck him at Emily's place too?" I spit out.

Hana shook her head. "Just once, Jack," her hoarse voice answered.

"You married me then ran off with another man, and then you fucked him," I explained, as if she didn't know why I was so fucking angry. "I should go kill him now."

"No, Jack! Please!" She was crying again.

"Why? Fancy fucking him again behind my back?" I walked

up to her, my fists clenching.

She shook her head and tried to cover her face, but I slapped her hands away.

"You fucking look at me when I'm talking to you, Hana!"

She started sobbing as she put her hands to her mouth. I was fucking fuming. This was going to ruin everything.

"First thing tomorrow morning, we're going to the doctor and we're going to find out how far along you are. And then we're doing this fucking paternity test. And if it's not mine, you're getting rid of it," I declared, my heart pounding wildly in my chest.

Hana just nodded.

"And I've got a brilliant idea, Hana," I blurted out, my voice softening.

I was hoping we would be able to do this without Hana putting up a fight. Now was the golden opportunity. She thought I would hurt her, but what I really wanted was to hurt Michael. This would hurt him over and over again.

"We're going to make a sex video. Then we're going to send it to Michael."

Hana

My heart dropped to my knees. He wanted to film us fucking and send it to Michael. *That's so fucking cruel.*

"That's awful, Jack," I said quietly, staring up at his big, blue, mischievous eyes.

Jack grinned like I had complimented him. "Exactly. Now get up and get yourself dolled up. We're making a porno."

I didn't hesitate to get up and go to the bathroom, but this time I didn't close the door. *Why bother?* I rinsed my face before I looked in the mirror; I felt like I had aged years in these last twelve weeks. So much stress, so much heartbreak, so much trauma. I didn't know how much more I could handle. Seeing Jack turn into his scary counterpart terrified me, and I had no idea what brought it on. He wanted to hurt me before he even knew of Michael potentially impregnating me. *What the fuck was he going to do now that he knew?*

I was slower than usual applying my mascara and matte-red lipstick. I fluffed my hair around and shrugged in the mirror. This would have to be enough for him.

I walked out to the living room to find Jack had set up each of our phones onto stands with ring lights behind them. He put one directly in front of the couch and another beside it. Had he been planning this? Was he saving this for the ultimate punishment?

Jack looked up at me and grinned. He looked like his sweet, usual self. How could I always forget how cruel he could be? Oh yeah, because looking at his gorgeous face made my pussy wet and made me forget all about scary Jack. His hard dick under his boxer briefs made my knees weak as he started to walk toward me.

"Stunning. Now get undressed," he ordered gently.

I stripped off my leggings, panties, and thin, cotton shirt. Jack eyed me up and down with lust before he gave me another mischievous grin.

"This is going to be so fun, sweetheart."

My heart fluttered. What the fuck was wrong with me? We were about to film a sex tape and send it to the other love of my life. This would absolutely ruin him, and here I was dripping wet.

"I want you to look in the camera and tell him this is for him," Jack instructed, pointing at the phone in front of the couch.

I immediately tensed up, a lump in my throat. "I can't." I shook my head.

I knew he would get angry, but I just couldn't bring myself to do it. Even if he forced me, I was still going to put up a fight.

Jack didn't seem surprised.

"Yes, you can," he snarled. "You fucked him, now I want you to show him how much you love fucking me."

I didn't move or respond. There was no way he could hurt me at that moment: I was potentially carrying his child. I wanted to test him and myself. My sweet Jack had to come through somehow.

"Hana. Either you say it, or I'll go fucking chop his dick off right now," he snapped, now standing only inches from my face.

Tears began streaming down my face.

"Please, Jack. I'll do anything else. Please just don't make me say that." I could barely hear my own voice.

Jack eyed me like he was considering his options. My heart thumped in my chest. I wondered why I didn't feel more scared. Maybe because I knew he was going to make me do something terrible, regardless of if I fought or not.

"Okay, sweetheart." Jack smiled. "I have a better idea then."

I was terrified, not because scary Jack was present…but because sweet Jack was as well.

"What is it?" My lip trembled as I spoke.

He smiled triumphantly. "You'll see, love. Now get on your knees," he ordered, still gentle.

I didn't hesitate as I got to my knees. Jack took the phone that was beside the couch and rearranged the lights. He walked up to me and lowered his boxer briefs, and his thick, long erection sprung free in my face. Jack had my phone pointing down at me as I looked up at him.

"Open, Hana," he ordered, grazing his thumb over my lip.

I opened my mouth wide before he shoved his cock in and immediately began thrusting quickly. Drool fell on my legs and tits. My pussy was practically dripping, the need for him to touch me overwhelming.

"Look up at me when my cock is in your mouth, love," Jack moaned.

My eyes flashed up to him, his darkness starting to seep through again. He took one hand to the back of my head and pushed his cock further down my throat, making me gag and keeping it there while my eyes watered and even more drool dripped down my body.

Jack moaned loudly. "Can't take this big cock all the way, can you sweetheart?"

I moaned as he started to face fuck me again. Suddenly, Jack let go of my head and wrapped his hand around my throat; I gasped for air, trying to catch my breath from him fucking my mouth and now his tight grip around my throat restricting my air flow.

"Open that pretty mouth," he ordered.

My mouth flew wide open and Jack spit at me. His hot spit swarmed around my mouth and went down my throat.

"Who do you belong to, Hana?" His grip tightened.

"You," I croaked out, almost unable to speak.

He squeezed tighter, and I was getting lightheaded, my eyes fluttering shut—then Jack let go quickly and chuckled as I gasped for air.

"Did you like that, sweetheart?" Jack asked, smiling down at me.

Endorphins rushed through me, all of my emotions bubbling up as hot tears streamed down my face.

"Yes." I nodded, my breath hiccuping from the tears.

My nipples hardened and the wetness between my legs slid down my thigh. What the *fuck* was wrong with me? Jack almost choked me to death, and here I was more aroused than I had ever been.

Jack chuckled again. "You like being scared, don't you, love?"

I realized what he was doing now: He was proving to Michael that I wanted all of this, that I was here willingly, and that I enjoyed it.

"Yes," I answered, still staring up at Jack.

"You're such a fucking whore. Get on your hands and knees and let me have a look," Jack demanded, his tone still light.

I turned around on my knees and let my hands fall to the ground. Jack gently grazed his hands on my ass and he moaned; I looked back at him and bit my lip, watching him survey my body. I almost forgot he was filming all of this, but then I saw him pointing my phone to my ass.

"Look at this," Jack gawked then opened my ass cheeks and let a finger slide into my slick pussy. "You're fucking drenched, sweetheart. You're dripping wet for me."

He sounded so pleased and I moaned. The bliss of my blank mind had returned and all I could think about was how much I wanted him inside me.

"Go on, get down on your elbows. Put this pussy in the air so I can eat it."

I immediately dropped down to my elbows, my ass now high in the air. Jack lowered the stand, the phone now mounted as he adjusted the lights again, focusing them on my pussy.

"Mmmm, fuck, Hana," he moaned.

Suddenly, his hot mouth buried into my pussy, his hands spreading me open, and I let out a loud moan. Jack's tongue dug inside my pussy before his thumb started circling my clit. I knew I was going to come; the build was too much to bear.

"Jack, I'm coming," I moaned loudly, my hips pressing back against his face, his tongue and thumb going faster.

"Mmmm," Jack moaned into my pussy, the vibration adding to my pleasure.

I let out loud yelps, the pleasure consuming me and Jack's tongue and finger doing magic as I rode the wave of my orgasm.

Jack slowed down before he grabbed the back of my hair

and pulled; I gasped as I straightened. My back pressed to his chest and his thick cock nestled against my ass.

"I think your drenched pussy can lube me up to slide into your beautiful ass," Jack said into my ear, then pushed me back down to the ground, my hands catching my fall.

Only seconds passed before Jack's thick cock rammed inside of my pussy, his pumps fast and hard. I let out another yelp, feeling a mixture of pleasure and pain, his size always making me question how he even fit inside of me.

"You like my cock pounding you?" Jack muttered.

"Yes, baby," I moaned, driving my hips back against him.

"Tell me!" he ordered.

"I love your cock pounding me, Jack," I cried out. "Harder!"

Jack grunted and his nails dug into my hips, his pounding faster and harder, making me scream. As quickly as he started, he pulled out of me and spit dripped down my ass cheeks.

"No lube today, baby. My cock is so slick from your pussy."

I was still catching my breath and hadn't registered what he was saying. The few times we had done anal, we always used lube. I wasn't sure I could take him without it—he was just too big, too thick.

"Jack." I looked back at him.

His gaze tore from my ass to my eyes.

"You're too big."

He smiled and looked over at my phone, then back at me. "The biggest you've ever had?" His eyes lit with mischief.

Oh, I see—I have to admit to all of this on camera.

"Yes."

"And whose cock is the best you've ever had? The one that's pleased you the most?" Jack was smiling now.

"Yours, Jack," I answered. I had to give him what he wanted.

And that was true, wasn't it? As much as the guilt consumed me, he was right. Michael opened up a whole new world for me; Jack had me consumed in it.

Jack nodded and got up, grabbing my phone again. He also had something in his hand: lube. *Thank fucking god.*

He let a generous amount of lube fall onto his cock then dropped some down on me. I eagerly waited, wanting to come again, needing to feel him inside of me. He suddenly had a finger in my ass and I gasped—what the fuck was I going to sound like when his cock was inside of me?

"Mmm, such a tight little ass," Jack moaned, then stuck another finger in.

I closed my eyes tight and braced myself for more.

"Does my fucking whore wife want more?"

"Yes, baby," I begged, once again forgetting about the cameras and mentally smacking myself; I hated that Michael was going to see all of this.

I gasped as another finger went inside me, wiggling around. My whole body shivered with goosebumps.

"Please, I need it," I moaned, ready to burst.

"What do you need, love?" He had a smile in his voice.

"Your cock." I pushed my ass back, driving his fingers further inside of me.

Jack chuckled then removed his fingers from me. I moaned as I waited, feeling the tip of Jack's cock start to enter me.

"I'm going to destroy your ass," Jack blurted out before he swiftly and furiously pushed his cock all the way into my ass and started to thrust.

"Oh, fuck!" I screamed out, the pain overwhelming but quickly turning into pleasure the more he pumped in and out of me.

"Rub your pussy, Hana. Come for me," he ordered, almost out of breath.

My right hand went up to my clit and I started to move my fingers around, the sensation of Jack filling me up and the pressure on my aroused clit quickly making me come.

"Fuck, I'm coming!" I shouted out, my pussy throbbing with my orgasm.

"That's right, baby." Jack gave me a moment as he stilled his hips. Then he pulled out of me and ordered me on my back.

I lay on the floor, watching Jack hover over me with his cock in one hand, my phone pointed at me in the other. I instinctively opened my mouth, lifting myself up slightly with my elbows, as Jack groaned out and his warm cum shot out all over me—my belly, my tits, my face.

"Fuck." Jack's eyes were closed as he released the remainder of his cum. He blinked his eyes open and looked down at me. "Filthy fucking whore."

He smiled then spit on my cum-covered belly.

Out of breath, my body fell to the floor and I started to softly cry. The image of Michael's jealous, angry, heartbroken face played on loop in my mind. Jack began to sing to himself as he started the shower, not a care in the world.

Emily

Now that I had learned where Hana lived, I planned on camping out in front of her apartment building. There were plenty of benches nearby, and I could go incognito if I needed to. And I had a plan: If I saw Jack leave, I would go inside and nicely ask the lobby staff if they could possibly help me surprise my dear cousin because it was her birthday! If that didn't work, I'd knock on every single fucking door in that thirty-eight story building.

I tried every way possible to avoid Jack before that day. I never went to band practices and I kept my distance at the few shows they had. I only later learned that Hana was at each show, staying far away from the band but keeping close to Jessica. Jessica, that evil fucking bitch that helped her evil fucking brother capture Hana. How could Hana even stand to be near her when she did all of that to her?

The band had gotten signed to a major label, changed their band name to Chaos Catalyst, and Jack and Adam were planning on touring once their album was released in the summer. I hadn't planned on going with them, only because I didn't think Hana would be allowed to see me. But I was starting to have second thoughts. Maybe I would be able to get to her somehow. But it would be even better if I got to

EMILY

speak to her alone before then.

My alarm I had set when I lay down in bed at 4 a.m. woke me up at 7. I would happily skip sleep to free my cousin of the hell hole she was living in.

I quickly got ready, told Adam I needed to go to an appointment, and then I was on my way to Williamsburg. I wasn't very far away—I was living with Adam in Cobble Hill, only about a 15 minute train ride from where Hana lived. By 8:15, I was propped on a bench near the waterfront, pretending to read but actually surveying every face that walked out of Hana's apartment building. Hopefully there was only one exit to that building. *Maybe I should have planned better*.

By 9:30, the lack of sleep had caught up with me, and the sunny fifty-degree weather had me cozy and warm as I bundled up in my jacket. But then I spotted them. Jack had walked out first, in his usual stupid all black ensemble and black boots, trying to look like a badass but in reality he was just bad. *A bad asshole.* I snorted to myself. He held the door open for Hana; she smiled at him, but she looked tired. She had no makeup on and wore black leggings with black Nikes, her body covered in a long, black puff jacket. She quickly put on her sunglasses, and they headed north as they walked hand in hand.

I rolled my eyes as I got up and started following; I knew I needed to keep my distance, so I stayed about 20 feet behind them in between dozens of other people walking the streets of Williamsburg. I realized they were headed into the subway and panicked a little—would I lose them on the train ride? I scanned my Metro pass and followed them to wait for the L train. Hana and Jack didn't speak at all—Jack only looked down at his phone while Hana stared at the ground, seemingly in deep thought. Once the train arrived, I eyed them as they got on first and went to the corner of the train. I got on the other side, keeping my back to them. They only stayed on for one stop before exiting the train toward south Williamsburg. They headed west, past the police station and fire department, past random businesses and brownstones, and then they finally stopped and went inside an unmarked business. I stopped and googled what the hell it was, and bile started to rise in my throat when I realized they were in a fucking OB-GYN office. This could mean anything, but I immediately thought the worst.

Hana is fucking pregnant.

Hana

I tossed and turned in bed that night. Jack had told me he would edit the video of us and then send it to Michael the next day. I glanced over at him watching it on his MacBook, his erection growing as he watched us having sex on the screen. He side-eyed me with his dimples slowly emerging, igniting a mixture of guilt and arousal in my belly; that was a common feeling I had the last twelve weeks. I enjoyed myself with Jack, I enjoyed our life, our banter, our creativity allowing us to paint and write together all day and then fuck each other all night long. I usually forgot about how we had gotten to that point, and then the guilt would start to weigh in again. I felt guilt for staying, for not running that first time with Billie before things got really fucking complicated. Now I knew I was stuck forever, and I knew this because I didn't want to live without him. I needed him as much as he needed me—we were so codependent on each other. And I didn't *want* to leave him. I loved him despite everything he had done. How fucked up was that? How was I ever supposed to live a normal life again after this? I wasn't. My life was always going to be with Jack, and he was far from normal.

Jack somehow got an appointment for us at 10 a.m. the next morning at an OB-GYN office in south Williamsburg. I was terrified and could hardly speak or think as we took the train and walked toward the office. I knew that if this baby was Jack's, I was going to have to keep it. If it was Michael's...I don't know how I would feel. Jack wouldn't allow me to keep it. Why have an opinion on it when I didn't even have a choice in the matter?

We walked into a small office where a couple of other women sat. Jack signed us in and started to fill out paperwork—he knew everything about me, about my health and height and weight and even my last period. *Wait, how the hell did he know that?*

"My last period was February 23? How do you know that?" I questioned quietly as he checked off that I didn't take any medication.

Jack looked over at me with widened eyes. "That was the night of our wedding party."

My stomach dropped before he continued.

"I won't ever forget a single detail from that night, sweetheart."

His voice was low and deep. Even talking about the night that he had hurt me like *that*, the way he called me sweetheart gave me butterflies.

"Oh." I nodded, biting my lip.

"Sign here."

He held the last piece of paperwork to me; I sloppily signed my new name. *Hana Maynor*. I didn't have a lot of experience doing it and it still felt odd writing a new last name. Not even a minute later, a nurse opened the door and looked down at a clipboard.

"Hana Maynor," she called out, looking between me and the two other women.

I quickly stood and reached for Jack's hand. I let Jack lead the way as we followed the nurse down a hall and into a patient room. It looked like a typical OB-GYN room with stirrups at the end of the patient bed that had a doppler and wand attached to one side. The nurse quickly took my vitals: everything was normal. She was very straightforward and not really friendly, which only made me more nervous.

"So you're here to confirm a pregnancy, is that right?" she asked me, looking down at my paperwork.

"Yes." I nodded, wringing my hands together as I sat on the patient bed.

"Okay. The doctor will be with you shortly." She smiled quickly then left the room.

I looked over at Jack and sighed; I was shaking as I continued to wring my hands together, feeling sick to my stomach. *Great, am I going to have morning sickness? Or is this just my anxiety going through the roof?*

"It's going to be okay, sweetheart." Jack walked over to me and put his hand atop mine. His voice was so soothing and calming.

"Is it?" I asked nervously, tears forming in my eyes.

Jack flashed his dimples at me. "Yes, Hana. You're going to be a wonderful mother." He gazed at me lovingly.

How was he so confident?

"I know this because you're caring, loving, and nurturing. You take care of me, even when I'm at my worst," he went on, putting his hand to my cheek.

I started to cry. "I love you, Jack," I said through hiccuped breaths.

Jack's face turned somber before he held me in his arms, letting me cry and shake as I held onto his waist.

Someone cleared their throat. "I'm sorry to interrupt," a woman's voice said behind Jack.

Jack and I both looked over at the doctor, a middle-aged woman with kind brown eyes and graying hair, as she smiled at us.

"Sorry." I laughed, letting go of Jack and quickly wiping the tears from my eyes.

She chuckled. "No need to apologize. You're not the first woman to cry in these offices," she said lightly.

I smiled and wrapped my arm around Jack's waist; he started rubbing circles on my back.

"Nice to meet you, Hana. I'm Dr. Levin. And you are?" She looked to Jack expectantly.

"I'm Jack, Hana's husband," he answered politely.

She nodded and took a seat on a wheeled circular stool near the countertop with a sink and medical supplies that lined the wall. She began to read over my paperwork with a pen in her hand.

"Hana. You're twenty-five. Very healthy, it seems. And you suspect you're pregnant?" She looked up at me.

I nodded. "I got a positive pregnancy test. Three of them," I admitted, almost embarrassed.

"Okay." She nodded, scooting herself over to the patient bed where I sat. "Let's have a look. Any idea how far along you are?"

I looked over at Jack then back at her. "No. Maybe…six or seven weeks," I guessed.

"Hmm. Okay. If you're that early I'd recommend a transvaginal ultrasound. It's just this little wand that I'll place in your vagina that takes a better look at your uterus. Are you okay with that?" she asked, holding up the wand.

"Okay. Sure." I nodded, looking at Jack again.

He smiled warmly at me. *Ugh, if this is his kid, he better get those Maynor dimples.*

"Great." Dr. Levin smiled. "I just need you to undress on your bottom half. Go ahead and put this over you." She pulled out a little paper blanket. "I'll give you a few moments to undress."

She smiled at Jack and then exited the room.

I quietly started to take off my shoes. I knew Jack was staring at me.

"Perhaps we can manage a quickie in here after this." He smiled deviously at me.

My heart fluttered. Of course he would manage to turn me on in a doctor's office.

"You think?" I asked flirtatiously; I was desperate for any kind of distraction from our current reality.

Jack flashed his dimples at me again. "Oh yes, sweetheart. I bet I could make you come in less than sixty seconds," he teased as he pulled down my leggings.

"I bet I could do the same to you," I quipped back, quickly sitting back up on the bed.

He licked his lower lip and gazed at me longingly. "I'll take that bet," he said quietly in his tone that he knew would turn me on.

I gave him a crooked smile and placed the paper blanket over my lower half. Then there was a knock at the door and Dr. Levin appeared again.

"Let's take a look." She sat back down on her stool and set up the stirrups, guiding me through how to place my feet on them.

Jack stood next to me and firmly held my hand; I was starting to realize that he might be nervous as well.

Dr. Levin turned on a little screen, lubed up the wand, and then inserted it inside of me. I tensed up and began to squeeze Jack's hand.

"Just take a deep breath, Hana. Try to relax," she assured me.

I nodded and glanced at the screen that showed a fuzzy black and white image. It looked like all of the typical ultrasound pictures you see on pregnancy announcements. I had no idea what I was looking for. Dr. Levin moved the wand around a little more before she stopped and started to take pictures with a tap on the screen.

"So…right here," she started as she pointed to the still image of my uterus, revealing a little black circle with a tiny gray dot on the bottom of it. "*That* is the fetus. You're about six weeks along, Hana. Congratulations." She smiled, gently removing the wand.

I immediately started to cry as I stared at the tiny gray dot on the screen. *Holy shit.* There was a baby inside of me. That was my baby. *Holy shit.* Dr. Levin printed something out and handed it to Jack.

"Here you go."

"Thank you." There was a smile in his voice. "I have a quick question, doctor."

I tore my eyes from the screen to Jack and Dr. Levin. She discarded her gloves and began to wash her hands.

"Yes?" She looked to him.

Jack glanced at me and then back to the doctor. "How soon can we get a paternity test?" he asked. He sounded nervous, or was that shame?

"Oh." She dried her hands, not seeming bothered by the question at all. "Well, I would wait another week or so. You two can come in next week and we can do a blood draw on Hana, and we'll need to sample your saliva. Is there another party that needs to provide a saliva sample?"

Jack looked at me and shook his head. "No. If it's not mine, we know whose it is."

Jack

I took Hana's hand as we exited the doctor's office. I was afraid to admit how excited I was, only because we weren't 100% sure if Hana was pregnant with my baby or with Michael's. I didn't want to think about that, though. I wanted to take care of my pregnant wife, even if only for another week. I would have preferred her to have this baby, for it to be mine. I didn't know how much I actually wanted it until I saw that tiny little flicker on the screen. We would be starting a family, something I'd always wanted. I wanted to make a better life for this child of mine. I kept imagining how we would take family walks around Williamsburg, how we'd take our little one to the park, out to restaurants and show her off to our friends and strangers on the street. She would have Hana's beautiful smile, along with the Maynor dimples and lips. I hoped she would have Hana's cheekbones, her eyes, and her kindness. If it was a boy? I would make sure he was a hell of a lot better than me. Perhaps he would want to be a drummer like his dad. Or maybe he would be a writer like Hana. The possibilities were endless for this child of ours.

Hana was quiet on the way home. When I showed her the picture of our little bean in her womb, she broke down crying again. I couldn't tell if they were happy or sad tears. I didn't want to know the answer, so I didn't ask. I wouldn't be able to bear it if they were sad tears. I needed Hana to be happy. I needed to *make* her happy.

But I still had work to do. Oh, this would be so fun. Just the thought of sending Michael the sex video of me and Hana made me giddy. Bragging to him about getting Hana pregnant would be even more amazing—once we confirmed it was mine.

I kept getting hard as I edited the video, watching Hana get pounded by me and really, truly liking it. God, she was so fucking sexy. Her tits bounced on the screen while I fucked her ass—I was about to come just from watching it. I wanted to go and take her right then and there, but she was napping and I figured she needed the rest. I could give her another pounding later when she woke up. I knew I would be ready to fuck her right after I hit send on the anonymous email to Michael, as if he wouldn't know it was from me. A little mystery made it more fun.

I spliced together the final clips from both angles as the sun started to set. I saved it and then hit send. The video was almost thirty minutes long. I anxiously awaited an angry call or email back from Michael. I was about to fucking burst, so I eagerly went into our bedroom where I found Hana still sleeping peacefully on her side. Her bare ass looked perfect as I quietly stepped into the room. I stood next to the bed and unzipped my jeans. My dick had been hard for so long that I was afraid to even touch it—I knew I would come quickly. I carefully took off my jeans then my boxer briefs and lay down on the bed next to Hana. She stirred a little as I put my arm over her waist, but I waited until I could hear her breathing even out again. I couldn't help myself any longer;

my dick on her bare ass cheek threw me over the edge. I let go of her waist and took my dick in my hand after I spit into it, lubing myself up before I positioned myself perfectly next to her beautiful, warm pussy and quickly thrust myself into her. Hana woke up immediately, and my dirty little slut wife backed her hips against me, her sweet fucking moans coming out of her mouth.

"Jack," she moaned, her hands fisting her pillow.

"I'm going to make you come, sweetheart. Remember our little bet?" I reminded her, whispering into her ear.

More moans. "Yes, baby."

I pounded her harder and deeper, making her scream, before I turned her to her stomach and straddled her, still fucking her. I stuck my finger in her mouth, and she instinctively started to suck.

"You fucking whore. Always wanting to suck and get fucked," I teased then took my finger and put it in her ass.

"Oh fuck, Jack," she moaned, grinding between me and the mattress underneath her.

"Now come for me," I ordered, grabbing a fistful of her hair.

She moaned immediately, her orgasm making her pussy clench around my dick, her asshole tight, and *oh, fuck*—I was coming as well.

I slowed my hips as I emptied myself inside of Hana, her moans lingering as she continued to grind gently against the mattress.

I started to chuckle as I unclenched my fist, the mixture of her wet pussy and my seed inside of her making me horny all over again.

"I want to fuck you all night long, Mrs. Hana Maynor," I started, gently kissing her shoulder. "But I need you to suck me clean first."

Hana

I knew Jack was going to continue to edit the video and then send it to Michael. I didn't want to be around for it, so I took the opportunity to nap. I wasn't sure if it was being pregnant that was making me so exhausted, or if it was depression sinking in. Maybe it was both. Jack was being extra sweet and rubbed my shoulders before I fell asleep. His erection grew as he straddled my back, and I got wet at the thought of him getting aroused by just touching me. As "unconventional" as the start of our relationship was, I don't think it would have been so easy if I wasn't so sexually attracted to him. I knew how much he fawned over me, and knowing he went to such great lengths just for me to be "his" was…well, it was unsettling how arousing I found that. He knew all of this and he didn't hide it. I didn't even try to hide it anymore. I was, unequivocally, his forever. And he was mine.

So naturally, when he started to fuck me while I slept, that turned me on even more. I kept discovering new kinks. Would I have discovered all of this about myself if I were still with Michael? Would I have kept going back to Jack whenever we fought? Would Michael and I have lasted? Would I have been bored with our life in Chelsea, being a writer housewife that liked to be dominated? I never knew what to expect with Jack, and that was thrilling to me. Jack saw right through me the whole time; he *knew* me the whole time. But I couldn't help but feel like I was destined for a life with Michael. I wanted the opportunity to make my own decisions, my own mistakes, but that was all taken away from me. Just like the decision to have this baby or not was taken away from me. If it was Jack's, I had to keep it. If it was Michael's, I didn't get to keep it. What if I didn't want to keep it either way?

After Jack and I fucked for two more rounds, he fell asleep holding onto me, his cum dripping out of every hole in my body. His phone kept going off in the distance, so I decided to sneak out of bed and go find it. I had no idea if he had a password or not—I never dared to go through his phone. And I knew there were cameras in the living room and apparently in other places I didn't know about, but a wife being curious about her husband's phone going off multiple times didn't seem like a weird reason for me to seek it out. The buzzing was more prominent in the kitchen, and I found his phone lying on the counter when I poked my head around the corner from the hallway. I immediately recognized the number—it was Emily. I stared at the phone in confusion—why was she calling Jack? Why wasn't she calling me? I decided to answer. I was too curious not to.

"Emily?" I answered, almost in a whisper.

"Hana?" Emily replied, her tone worried on the other end.

"Why are you calling Jack?" I asked immediately; I don't know why, but I almost felt jealous.

Emily sighed. "I don't know what the fuck gets through to you on your phone. You never answer my calls. So when Michael called me, bawling and angrily threatening violence against you and Jack because of some fucking sex tape, I felt like I needed to confront *one* of you," she explained, exasperated.

Threatening violence against Jack *and* me? A lump formed in my throat. "What?"

There was silence for a moment. "Did you not fucking know that Jack sent Michael a video of you guys having sex?" Her irritation was clear in her voice.

"I…I didn't approve, *obviously*, Emily." I tried to pick my words carefully.

"Obviously you don't get to approve a lot of things going on in your new life," she snapped back.

Why was she so angry at me?

"What's going on?" Jack's tense words came from behind me.

I pulled the phone down from my ear and turned around.

"It's Emily. She was calling you. I was curious, so I answered it. Here." I handed him his phone and angrily walked off.

I was angry and hurt for so many reasons. My cousin, my best friend, who I thought was still sort of on my side, was now being so cold to me. Did Michael really think that I would purposefully do something like that to him? Did Jack make it seem like I did? Of course Michael would believe that. He believed I really had left him. So why wouldn't I do something like this too? He must have thought I really lost it.

"Leave us the fuck alone, Emily!" Jack shouted then angrily stormed down the hallway toward our room where I sat on the bed with my knees to my chest.

Jack appeared at the doorway, his eyes wild with rage.

"What the fuck did she say to you? What did you say to her?"

I was already bawling. "All she said was that she was calling you because Michael called her, fucking angry and crying and saying he wanted to hurt you," I explained.

I left out the part about him wanting to hurt me; Jack wouldn't let that slide. And I knew Michael was just hurt and angry and didn't mean it.

Jack's face suddenly went from angry to blank to...happy? He grinned widely and started to laugh.

"So he saw it." He nodded as he sat down on the bed next to me.

I looked over at him, bewildered. Of course that was his response. That's what he wanted in the first place—to hurt Michael.

"Why do you care so much about how he feels? Why keep taunting him when you clearly won this battle?"

I was genuinely curious; why did he have to bring Michael into this? Because he knew it would hurt me too?

Jack's smile faded. "I want him to hurt as much as I did when I lost you. I was fucking desperate, Hana. I *am* desperate." His voice was barely audible.

I shook my head. "You have me, Jack. You don't need to feel so hopeless anymore. You don't need to seek out revenge. I'm right here." I put my palm up to his stubbly cheek, taking in his full lips and beautiful, sweet face.

If only he was always this version of himself—the one I had fallen in love with originally. The sweet, sensitive soul that I knew he had. My hopelessly romantic, Jack, who tragically wore his heart on his sleeve.

* * *

I took a walk around our neighborhood with no destination in mind as I usually did. I needed air while Jack went into

Manhattan for meetings. All I could think about was this thing growing inside of me and how much I already resented it. How was I going to raise this child with Jack? I knew we would have beautiful children together, but why bring them into this chaotic world that Jack and I had created? If and when we had children, things needed to change with us. Our dynamic needed to change. I couldn't always be afraid of what he would do, and he needed to stop holding things over my head. Leaving him was not an option, even if I could. I don't know how the bond we created became so tight that it could never be pulled away. My love for him made no sense to the outside world, at least not to the people who knew what we really went through. As a certified people pleaser, I was surprised I didn't care more about what they thought. But the only person I really wanted to please was Jack.

I found myself on the street of Dr. Levin's office. Was Jack tracking me at this very moment? My heart began to race rapidly as I thought of an idea. I nearly ran to her office before I could change my mind.

I told the receptionist that I urgently needed to talk to Dr. Levin. I quietly whispered, "I need an abortion. Right now." I'm sure I had a wild, desperate look in my eyes.

The receptionist gave me a look of sympathy. "Honey, we need to get you an appointment. Dr. Levin isn't in the office today—we've only got nurse visits available and we're not taking walk-ins."

I turned and saw only one other person in the waiting room. I looked back to the receptionist.

"Please. Let me see the nurse then," I replied feebly.

"I'm sorry." She shook her head slowly, seemingly looking like even she was going to cry. "If you can wait till Friday, I can get you in then. First thing in the morning," she said quietly.

I started to cry. I couldn't come back here, not without Jack getting suspicious.

"I can't wait until Friday. I need it now," I whispered.

She shook her head again. "If you really need it now, there's a clinic in Fort Greene. They deal with emergencies such as yours."

"No, I—I can come Friday. I'll figure it out. Please put me down for Friday."

She nodded with a small smile. "Okay. We will see you Friday."

Jack couldn't have a say in this, not now. Having a child would make him even more controlling. We needed a plan, and, the way our life was right now, I was afraid he'd have all the say. I *knew* he would have all the say.

I would think of something. All I knew was that I was going to do whatever it took to make this happen.

Hana

My heart was trying to escape from my chest as I walked out of Dr. Levin's office. Jack would know that I went to her behind his back. He would demand to know why I had gone without him. What was I going to say to him? The need to terminate this pregnancy dominated all other needs at that moment. I didn't have an excuse already made up in my head. Maybe I could tell him I was bleeding. Maybe losing the pregnancy naturally would be easier on him than knowing I wanted to get rid of it. I just needed to get there on Friday and it would be done.

My mind buzzed as I walked, distracting me from my surroundings. When a hand tugged on my arm, my heart almost leapt out of my throat—*he caught me*. But when I turned around and saw the most beautiful man I had ever seen, I think I might have actually gasped before saying, "Oh my god." And the fact that I only felt shame, fear, and worry that Jack would somehow find out about this made my face feel hot from embarrassment.

"Hana." Michael's voice was deep and panicked, and his dark-gray eyes surveyed my face.

He was more beautiful than I remembered. His beard was longer than the last time I had seen him, even spotting some stray white hairs, and his eyes seemed even more intense, more rugged and worried. The lines on his forehead wrinkled as he held my arm, people passing by on the sidewalk and turning their heads to look at us.

"Michael," I whispered, still in shock at the sight of him.

"Please just tell me—are you pregnant? Is it mine?" His grip tightened on my arm.

Tears began to stream down my face. My heart felt like it was breaking.

"Yes. I'm pregnant, but I don't know. I don't know, Michael," I answered, my shaky voice barely audible. "I'm getting rid of it," I added, as if that somehow made anything better.

Michael's eyes widened with horror. "No you're not. You can't. If it's mine, that's all we have left," he stated, as if that thought didn't cross my mind.

"He won't let me keep it if it's yours, Michael." I put my hand to his muscled arm that felt even bigger than the last time he held me.

"Hana." Michael shook his head. "I can't let you do this."

We were talking in hushed, frantic voices, as if we were being listened in on. Maybe we were. All I wanted to do was jump in his arms and tell him to run.

"I have to," I cried out, feeling my face twist into an ugly cry.

"No." Michael shook his head again, his voice stern, and my heart sunk. "We're doing it right this time. Come on."

Michael squeezed my hand and walked me closer to the main street where a cab waited.

"What are we doing, Michael?"

He still held onto my hand tightly as he opened the cab door and pushed me inside before taking the seat next to me, hurriedly shutting the door.

"Michael!" I gasped out.

"Give me your purse. Give me your coat," he ordered, then looked up at the cab driver who worriedly looked back at us. "Go on, the address I gave you in Greenwich," Michael instructed him hastily.

The cab started moving, and my mouth gaped at Michael.

"Where are we going?" I hesitantly shrugged my coat off.

I knew what was happening. We were making a run for it. Did Michael really know that I didn't leave him, or was he just desperately trying to get me away from Jack?

He took my coat and grabbed my purse.

"Is your phone in here?" he asked as he held up my purse.

"Yes."

"Mate." Michael looked to the cab driver. "Stop here real quick."

The cab driver stopped, and Michael jumped out, throwing my purse and coat into a garbage bin on the curb. He quickly came back in, and the cab sped off again.

"Michael, please tell me what's going on," I said tearfully as I took his hand with mine.

Michael looked up at me with his intense gray eyes, and they slowly started to soften. "You're going to be mine again, Hana. Whether you want it or not."

Jack

When I realized Hana was gone, finding her coat and purse in some fucking trash bin down the street from Dr. Levin's office, I was ready to murder anyone in sight. I called Jessica and she tried to talk me down—but how could I calm down? My fucking pregnant wife was missing and I had no idea where she was. Was she with Emily? With Billie? With fucking *Michael*? There was no way she was back with Michael. She knew how much that would hurt me. She didn't want to go back to him anyway—she had the perfect fucking life with me and I knew she wouldn't deny that. She might not have liked making that sex video for Michael, but that didn't stop her from coming on camera multiple times. She was my dirty fucking wife and she loved it. Would Michael ever do anything like that? No, he was too much of a coward. I would be shocked if she was with him.

Then a thought occurred to me: What if she wasn't with him by choice? What if Emily and Michael took her the way they took her from me all those weeks ago? By surprise and by guilting her into going back to Michael, confusing her and making her believe she didn't love me.

There had to be someone I could reach out to that knew where she was. Emily, Billie...I'd even try her parents. And I knew if she had a way to contact me, she would. I refused to believe she had gone somewhere willingly without telling me. Hana just wouldn't do that to me, not now, not after all we'd been through. I wasn't going to sit idly by and wait, though—I would stop at nothing to find my wife.

I pulled out my phone and dialed 911.

Hana

We exited the city, the cab still driving toward Greenwich. I didn't know why Michael was taking me to Greenwich, but I didn't ask any questions—I was still trying to process the fact that I was in Michael's presence. I wasn't sure how I felt about it; he seemed anxious and somber. He seemed desperate. I didn't know what his plan was, but I knew the likely outcome: I would probably have no say in it.

I realized I did have a choice when it came to staying with Jack. It had been so easy to leave him behind. All I had to do was ditch my purse, phone, and coat? I could have done that a million times, yet I didn't. He had threatened me and my loved ones to get me to stay in the beginning. But I had fallen in love and he didn't need to bring any of that up anymore. He knew how madly in love I was with him. But did I still want to be with Michael?

"Michael," I whispered, pulling him out of a daze.

He turned to me and his eyes were tired, but I realized that my beautiful ex-fiancé still had the same impact on me as he did before. My heart leapt and crashed to my knees at just the sight of him. His eyes darkened as he looked down at my stomach, shaking his head.

"I can't believe you were going to get rid of it. And you

don't even know who the father is? What the *fuck*, Hana? Why would you do that?" His Irish accent sounded more pronounced than I remembered, and his scolding made heat rise to my cheeks.

"*Why* would I do that? Because it's *my* fucking body and I want some say in one aspect of my life, especially something as major as having a child!" I blurted out angrily.

Michael's eyes widened. "I don't believe a fucking thing you say anymore. You really had me going for a while, Hana," he scolded again.

My mouth dropped open. "Excuse me?"

"What? You really think I would believe you after all that you put me through? After sending me that fucking video of you and Jack having sex? God fucking damnit, Hana!" he huffed out, the angriest I had ever seen him.

"Then why am I here, Michael?" I shouted out angrily, tears streaming down my face. "Why the fuck do you want me still?"

I jumped as he shouted back. "Because you are mine, Hana! You promised to marry me. You promised to spend the rest of your life with me!"

I started bawling into my hands. I was too overwhelmed, too hurt and ashamed to face him now.

"And to top it all off, you're pregnant. Possibly with my child," he continued in a barely audible whisper.

I looked up at him through my tear-soaked eyes. Michael was weeping into his hands now. My heart ached more than it ever had, even when I was first taken away from him. *I did this to him.* Why did I keep breaking hearts like this? Why did I keep driving men to their breaking points?

I looked up at the cab driver and his eyes were still pointed at the road, no emotion on his face whatsoever.

"Can someone *please* tell me where we're going?" I asked, my voice raw and quiet.

"Why? So you can tell Jack where we are again?" Michael spit out.

Again?

"For the record, Michael, I never told him we were there. I don't know how he found us," I explained, as if it made any difference.

Michael began to laugh. It was a chuckle that turned into a frantic, manic laugh. I sat there watching him, stunned. I had never witnessed this Michael before.

"I don't fucking believe you anymore, Hana." He shrugged.

"Yet you still want me to be '*yours*,'" I quipped back with air quotes.

Michael shook his head with contempt. "You *are* mine. And I will break you, just as Jack did."

We sat in angry silence until the cab pulled up to a townhouse in Cos Cob, a little neighborhood in Greenwich not far from where I grew up. *Why are we here?* All I could think about was how much my heart ached at how I missed Jack and how I worried about his mental well-being. He had to have been going out of his mind now. Would he find me again?

Michael tipped the poor cab driver generously before taking my hand and pulling me out of the cab. We walked up to the front door, and he pulled a key from his pocket then quickly unlocked the door, looking around as if we were being watched. I mirrored him before he led me into the townhouse. The place seemed almost like a model home; it was neatly and modernly decorated. The living room was spacious and led to stairs on the left and into a beautiful kitchen and dining area to the right.

"What are we doing?" I asked for what seemed like the thirtieth time that day.

I hesitantly sat on the couch after eyeing the place for a moment. Michael crossed his arms as he surveyed me. I realized how strong his arms looked bulging from his long-sleeved cotton shirt. He wore black cuffed jeans with brown suede boots. His eyes were sullen as he shifted his weight, his arms still crossed, then made his way directly in front of me. He put his hands on his hips and looked at my hands.

"You're still wearing your sub ring. Why?" His tone was harsh and accusatory.

I looked down at my right-hand ring finger and twirled the ring around.

"Because I still love you. I've never stopped loving you, Michael," I responded quietly, unable to look up at him.

"Look at me, Hana," he snapped.

Butterflies suddenly swarmed in my belly as I looked up and our eyes met.

"And you love Jack as well," he spit out.

I nodded slowly, desperately trying not to break eye contact. He was still the intimidating, dominant boss from all those months ago.

"Take his ring off," he ordered, his eyes dark and angry.

My heart dropped.

"Why?"

What a stupid question to ask, Hana.

Michael's expression quickly went from angry to confused. "*Why*, Hana? Because you are mine, and I don't want his fucking ring on you when you're mine," he muttered, leaning down only inches from my face.

He knew how to intimidate me. It was working. But I was not the same woman I was when we met all those months ago. I wasn't going to keep my mouth shut any longer.

"I don't belong to *anyone*, Michael," I hissed, positive that my heart was going to burst out of my chest.

Michael's eyes flickered with amusement for a moment before he slowly stood. Then he raised his hand in the air and slapped me across the face. I immediately gasped and covered my raw cheek with my palm. I had felt pain far worse, but this? It truly shocked and surprised me; it broke my heart. Tears began streaming down my face before he started to speak.

"If you keep talking to me like that, Hana, you'll see just how rough I can be. But that's what you like, isn't it?" His angry gray eyes looked down at me. "I saw how much you liked getting roughed up, choked out and spat on. I can do all that and more, Hana." He paced the room, his eyes never leaving mine.

I glanced down at the bulge in his pants, his erection desperately trying to escape. He was right, because at that moment, having him scold me and hurt me...I was dripping wet.

And then a thought occurred to me.

"You *liked* watching us," I blurted out.

Michael stopped and widened his eyes at me.

I looked down at his huge erection. "Look at you. You fucking loved watching us," I continued with my heart racing, widening my eyes and opposing my body's normal urge to flight—I was fighting now.

Michael stayed silent; he almost looked ashamed with his eyes slightly widened, surveying my body.

"On your knees, Hana," he ordered, his voice deep and gravelly.

Instinctively, I did as I was told and quickly got to my knees in front of the couch. Michael unzipped his pants and slowly walked toward me.

"You know I'm the biggest you've ever had, Hana," he said quietly, stroking his cock over his boxer briefs. "Why would you fib about that, hm?"

He suddenly let his cock spring free in my face, and my pussy started throbbing with need. A gut-wrenching, terrible guilt overwhelmed me.

"I'm married now, Michael," I whispered as I looked up to him.

He narrowed his eyes down at me. "Legally, on paper, sure. But you're *mine*."

"Michael—"

He slapped my face again. I gasped and shut my eyes tightly, the sting on my cheek burning. He gripped my hair and jerked my head up, forcing me to look at him.

"I'm sir to you, Hana. You know that," he spit out.

This was not the Michael I knew. I drove this man to the edge, over the cliff and into the deep end where it swallowed him whole.

"Yes, sir." My voice quivered.

Michael let out a sinister chuckle.

"Look at you shaking and crying. And we haven't even started yet."

I hadn't even realized I was crying.

"Now open your mouth," he demanded.

I couldn't deny the fact that I was aroused, that my pussy was drenched and I ached for his cock. But I felt a profound urge to disobey, to push him and test him. I wasn't going to *not* fight this time.

"Make me," I muttered. "Sir."

Michael shook his head at me with amusement, his eyes lit up like the Fourth of July. He suddenly let go of his grip in my hair, easily picked me up, and threw me over his shoulder.

"Michael!" I screeched out, startled as he made his way up the stairs.

I knew I fucked up by not calling him sir when he slapped my ass with a heavy hand. He carried me into a bedroom and threw me down on the bed, quick to grab something from underneath it. I started to lift myself up to get off the bed when Michael popped up with rope in his hand. My heart immediately dropped. This wasn't just some ploy to get me to come back to him. This was him keeping me here.

"Michael, please. Let's just talk about this," I started, standing in front of him.

"Strike two." Michael shook his head, grabbing my hands as he pushed me back onto the bed.

He quickly and elaborately tied my wrists together. I had to do something; once my legs were bound, that was it. I waited until he reached over for more rope then I jumped up and bolted out the door. I was all too aware of how ironic this was: I was running away from the man that I had been utterly in love with for the last several months. In fact, even longer than that.

"Hana!" Michael yelled, directly behind me as I ran down the stairs.

I missed the last three steps and fell straight down on my ass on the bottom one. I tried to get up before he tugged on my hair. I screamed out, more startled than anything. Michael picked me up over his shoulder again, and I began to kick my legs, fighting for whatever kind of dignity I had left.

"Let me down! Let me go!" I cried out, now banging my fists against his back.

Michael threw me back down on the bed upstairs, face first, and quickly took my legs and started to tie them together. I couldn't help myself: I began to sob into the bed, my tied wrists on the side of my head feeling raw already.

"You're going to stay like this until you behave, Hana," he hissed, turning me over onto my back.

I don't think I had ever felt so scared before, not even with Jack. I never would have dreamed that I would be feeling this terrified with Michael, the perfect man of my dreams. I knew I broke his heart, but I had transformed this man into a different person.

I had no idea where Michael was or what he would do next. I kept my eyes closed tight as I sobbed on the bed, my tears dripping on the side of my face and trickling into my ears. My heart stung at the thought of where Jack was and how he was handling this.

"Can you please let Jack know that I'm okay? Please, sir?" I croaked out after several minutes. I didn't even know if Michael was still in the same room or not.

I blinked open my eyes and the sun was starting to set. Michael stood from an armchair I didn't even realize was there.

"You mean with the same courtesy you gave me? With a fucking email?" He sat on the bed beside me, his eyes looking ominous in the dark room.

"I told you. I didn't write that email," I snapped back; I guess I still had some fight in me.

Michael let out a soft laugh. "I'll let him know you're alright. We'll send him a special video."

I started to cry again. "Why are you both using my body to make each other jealous?" I snapped. "I'm so fucking sick of this! Let me have my body back! Let me do what I want with it!"

My chest began tightening, and I felt like I couldn't breathe. I knew what was happening: I was having a panic attack. Michael could tell; he sat me up on the bed and put my knees up to my chest.

"Come on now, Han. Breathe. Just breathe with me." He began to exaggerate his deep breaths, and I tried to follow. His voice was so soothing and calm—this was a familiar moment with Michael, and I clung to it.

I nodded as I mimicked his deep breaths until I finally calmed down. Still shaking, I looked into Michael's eyes and I knew he still cared about me. He was angry at me, but he still loved me.

"Can we please talk like normal people for a second? Please?" I whispered in between hiccuped breaths. "Sir."

"No." Michael shook his head at me. "Because we're not normal people, Hana. You're a fucking liar who shattered my heart, and I'm the man you turned into a monster."

I shook my head back at him. "Aren't you the one who said that you've gotten your heart broken before but never went and kidnapped them over it? That I can't feel responsible for how someone reacts?"

Michael smiled slowly. He gently put his hand up to my cheek then put a strand of hair behind my ear. His face grew somber again.

"That was before I knew what true despair felt like. You did this, Hana. You do this to me."

He pushed me back down on the bed and began to unzip his pants. I started to cry gently—I knew this was my fault. And the fucked-up thing was that I was still dripping wet. I wanted this.

"Come on, Hana. Don't make me be the bad guy here. You know you still want to fuck me."

He lifted my ankles and slid me to the edge of the bed where he knelt down beside it. My ankles were still bound, but that didn't stop Michael from pulling down my pants and thong. Before I knew it, he quickly stuck a finger inside of me.

Michael chuckled. I knew how wet I was for him.

"Jack was right. You like being scared, don't you?"

He easily slid another finger into me, his hard cock bulging inside his pants.

I nodded, my heart audibly beating inside my ears. I had dreamt about another reunion with Michael, but in no way was *this* ever a possibility in my mind.

"This is what you want, isn't it? You want chaos. You want fear. You want it rough and dirty," he continued, his mouth trailing kisses down the back of my thigh and one hand holding up my tied ankles.

"Yes," I breathed out, closing my eyes and trying to take my mind to its empty bliss, something I was accustomed to now.

Michael removed his fingers from me and then slapped my ass.

"I think you're doing this on purpose. Do you want to keep pushing me, Hana?" His voice was so eerily calm.

"No, sir. I'm sorry, sir." My words were on autopilot now.

"Oh come on, Hana." He slipped two fingers back inside me. "Now you're going to behave? I was starting to enjoy bratty

Hana."

There was a stillness for a moment as Michael let go of my ankles and released his fingers from me yet again. I moaned with disapproval and desire.

"Michael, please," I begged, my eyes closed.

I couldn't believe I was begging for him while literally enslaved by him; that's just what he did to my body.

"Say that again, Hana," he ordered, smacking my ass hard again.

"Please. Please, sir," I breathed out.

Michael let out a soft laugh that made me open my eyes. My heart dropped when I realized he was holding his phone above us, recording this moment. I started to cry, knowing that Jack was going to see this.

He lowered his phone to face only him now. "See how quickly she succumbed to me, mate? I've had her for only a few hours and she's already begging me—"

"No, Jack! We're in Cos Cob in Greenwich—"

I was immediately interrupted by Michael tossing his phone to the ground and grabbing my neck. He squeezed hard, his body above mine and his eyes clouded with rage. I started to get lightheaded as Michael put his other hand to my neck, squeezing tighter. I kicked my legs out, my eyes fluttering shut, before he finally let go. I gasped for air and the endorphins rushed through me, a mixture of tears and laughter and pleasure.

"You really are a sick fuck, aren't you?" Michael's eyes were nearly bulging out of his head as he stared down at me.

I nodded. "Do your worst." And then I spat at him.

Michael seemed truly shocked as he dismounted me. He grabbed his phone and took something from a drawer beside the bed then revealed the duct tape in his hand.

"For your filthy fucking mouth."

He stuck a piece to my mouth and then quickly removed my shoes. He easily tore my jeans apart before ripping off my thong. He continued by tearing open my shirt, exposing my bare tits and leaving the shreds on either side of me. I turned and saw his phone recording video on the dresser in front of the bed.

"Perfect," Michael whispered to himself. "Wait."

Suddenly, Michael removed the duct tape from my mouth and pressed his lips firmly onto mine. I couldn't help but kiss him back. Our tongues swirled together desperately before I snapped out of the trance and bit down hard on his lip.

"Fuck!" Michael yelled, hovering over me.

He quickly pressed the tape back to my mouth, and I giggled triumphantly. I eyed the blood on Michael's lip and raised my eyebrows at him. His tongue collected the red drops and then he spat down at me, the mixture of his saliva and blood on my face and tits. He pulled out his hard cock and started stroking. The tingle deep in my core and pussy made it abundantly clear that I was ready for him.

"Funny, is it?"

He grabbed my bound ankles, lifted them in the air, and then quickly thrust himself into me, making me scream out with pleasure. He pounded into me furiously and moaned loud over the sound of our bodies slapping together. The tape muffled my moans and screams. Just as I was about to come, he pulled out and quickly flipped me over onto my stomach. I moaned with disapproval until his cock started to enter my ass. My moans turned into screams when he fully plunged himself into me, deep and hard. Jack was kind enough to use lube, but Michael gave me no mercy. Tears started streaming down my face, my screams loud and muffled, when Michael pulled out and poured liquid on my ass. *Thank fuck: lube.* He rammed back inside of me, his thrusts filling me with more pleasure than pain now. I felt shame as my orgasm grew close as Michael tugged my head back with his fist in my hair.

"You better come loud, Hana. I want him to know who you belong to," he whispered in my ear right at the release of my orgasm.

I screamed out with pleasure, my mind blank, my body vibrating with the intense pulsing of my pussy, and my ass filled to the brim with his cock.

"Good girl," Michael said into my ear and then pulled out and quickly rolled me onto my back.

I figured he was going to recreate mine and Jack's cumshot, but he had more planned. He pulled something else out of the drawer and I realized it was my magic wand, the one he had gotten me at our condo. There was a sting in my chest as our old memories flooded back to me. He was so perfect. Or was that something I just made up in my head because I was so in love with him? Clearly, he was far from fucking perfect.

"I'm going to make you weep from how much you fucking come for me, baby," Michael declared as he turned on the wand.

He wasn't lying; I easily came four times in less than two minutes. Tears streamed down my face from how fierce my orgasms were. When I recovered from my last orgasm, I looked up and Michael was jerking off to me.

"Now who's the better fuck?" he said before he released his cum all over me, his warm liquid shooting all over my bare body.

I couldn't even think or move. I was depleted of all energy, mentally and physically. My eyes were closed in a state of pure bliss, so much so that I jumped when Michael quickly removed the tape from my mouth and threw it on the ground.

He left me there without cleaning me up or untying me. I let my eyes flutter shut again and realized that as much as I wanted to hate my captor, I didn't. How could I ever hate Michael? This was happening all over again and as terrified as I should have been, I wasn't. As much as Michael wanted to hurt me, to punish me, he had no idea that I was my own worst enemy…and I would hurt myself far worse than anyone else ever could.

Emily

I had to tell someone about what I saw. It couldn't be Adam—how was I supposed to explain that I was stalking my cousin? It had to be either Billie or Michael, and well…Billie didn't want to talk about Hana anymore. The last time I had mentioned her to Billie through text, telling her that everything seemed normal at our Easter brunch, she responded back: **Please give it up, Emily. The Hana we thought we knew is gone. She's Jack's problem to deal with now.**

Her words stung my chest—how could she so easily dismiss Hana? I knew she was hurt and confused about what happened, and so was I. But Hana was my fucking *cousin*, my blood. And as angry as I was about everything happening, I couldn't just give up. Whether it be getting back into her life or really uncovering what was going on, I was going to keep pushing.

And then there was Michael. Fuck, my heart ached for him. Ever since Hana left him in New Jersey, he had been an absolute mess. I knew he quit his job and sold the condo in Chelsea. He was now living in Brooklyn, where exactly I wasn't sure; he didn't offer much information—he only wanted to know about Hana. He texted me every day asking if I'd heard from her. I told him everything I knew. He finally had an online presence, at least on Instagram, to stalk Hana and bask in his own self-loathing. Any time she posted something, which wasn't often, he would call me and complain about how he didn't understand why she hadn't reached out to him. I told him it was likely that she didn't have unrestricted access to her phone—that was something she had mentioned when she told us about the horror story of hers and Jack's before. I struggled with telling him that I finally knew where she lived. Would he do something rash? He was an ally and I needed his help, so I told him anyway.

And the fucking sex tape. It was starting to concern me how angry he was—not just at Jack, but at Hana too. Michael forwarded me the video, but I refused to watch it. I knew it must have totally broken him. It would have broken me too; having to watch someone you were in love with, someone who was abruptly taken from you, have sex with someone else? That didn't seem like Michael's kink and that definitely wasn't mine. I could barely understand what he was saying as he yelled into the phone about how he was going to fucking kill both of them. I hoped it was just his anger speaking. I knew the last thing he wanted to do was hurt Hana. He wanted to hurt Jack, and I really fucking wanted him to hurt Jack too. That's why I decided to tell him.

The day after he received the video, I called Michael to tell him about seeing Hana walk into the OB-GYN office. It was too much for me to keep to myself; I needed to vent to someone who understood the pain of losing Hana. It didn't even occur to me that it would push him over the edge.

"She's fucking pregnant?" he snapped after a long silence.

"I don't know," I responded quietly. "Maybe. The place seems like it's mostly for obstetrics. Or maybe she just needed birth control or literally anything else."

I was trying to stay calm for the both of us. If Hana was pregnant and keeping it, she would be tied to Jack forever. We both knew this.

"What if it's mine?" Michael finally responded.

Wait. What? Oh shit. I totally didn't even realize it could be Michael's. Of course they had sex the night they were back together. Oh fuck, this just made things so much worse…

"I—I don't know," I hesitantly replied. "Maybe…maybe we can figure this out. I can just call Hana and ask her what's going on. Or I can just magically bump into her the next time she's out. I don't know, we'll figure this out."

I was rambling. The possibilities of what Michael would do terrified me. If he wasn't desperate before, he would definitely be desperate now.

There was another long silence. "Michael?"

"I'll take care of it."

Then he hung up.

* * *

I didn't sleep that night. Or the next night. Staying up all night was easy—I was a bartender. I was being "good" by taking my meds and not drinking; I didn't want another episode like my last to happen. I promised Adam I would do everything I could to prevent that. But Michael had me so worried that I literally couldn't sleep. How was he going to *take care* of it? I texted him afterward asking him to explain, but he didn't respond. I called the next day and got no answer. And then I got a text from him three days later at 6 p.m. that read: **Hana is back with me.**

My stomach dropped. *Oh, thank fuck.* **Is she okay? How did this happen? I need answers, please have her call me!**

I started to get angry when I didn't get a response. It was a slow night at the bar, so I checked my phone constantly. I thought about calling Jack to see if I could get anything from him, but it turned out I didn't have to. He stormed into the bar like he owned the place. His eyes darted around then landed on me. Before I knew what he was capable of, I never found his presence intimidating—but now he looked fucking terrifying.

"Emily!" he shouted over the music as he stomped over to me. "Where is she?" He planted his hands atop the bar. "Where's Hana?"

I played dumb. "I don't know. Don't you keep a leash on her?"

Jack narrowed his eyes at me. I could be brave in a room full of people, especially this crowd—my patrons loved me.

"You know where she is. Tell me," he snarled, attracting looks from my customers.

I looked around at their concerned faces and smiled, showing them I could handle this.

"Wait, I thought you had like, a tracking device implanted in her? Isn't that how you found her the last time she fled?"

I was being flippant and thoroughly enjoying myself. Now *I* had the upper hand.

Jack paused for a moment and then smiled. "Emily. You know just as well as I do that Hana didn't flee last time. You and Michael tricked my poor wife." His voice was quiet but menacing.

I snorted. "Your poor wife? Hana is not some helpless little girl. She can make her own decisions. When she's allowed to."

EMILY

I raised my eyebrow as I glared at him.

He narrowed his eyes at me again before he looked down at his phone that had begun to ring. His stupid, smug face turned into a bewildered scowl.

He put his phone up to his ear. "Where is she?" he barked out.

I watched as his face turned white before he lowered his phone and stared down at it, his eyes wide.

"What? What is it?" I was desperate for information.

Jack's jaw clenched. I strained my neck, trying to see what was on his screen, but he looked up at me and gave me the most forbidding look I'd ever seen.

"You think this is a woman who can make her own decisions right now?" He held his phone up and showed me a still of Hana on a bed with Michael fucking her, her hands and feet tied up and tape plastered across her mouth. She was naked and she looked terrified as she looked up at Michael.

"Jack, what the fuck?" I cried out. I almost thought it was something that he had saved in his phone for his own personal, perverted fantasy, but surely he'd never want to see Michael with her.

"He's taken Hana. I'm going to the police to show them that my wife has been kidnapped."

Jack

Calling the police proved useless. They had me go to the station to fill out paperwork and told me she was not a "special category" person; she wasn't a minor, she wasn't elderly, and there was no proof that she had "involuntarily disappeared." But I knew my Hana—she wouldn't have just left without a word, not again. She was obsessed with me. She adored me. She *needed* me.

I knew she had been to Dr. Levin's office without me but I didn't know why. That's another detail that was really bothering me. The tracker on my phone noted she had gone directly to Dr. Levin's office from our apartment, stayed for five minutes, and then left. Her phone and belongings were just down the street and stayed there until I found them. Was she taken from outside the office? And why the fuck was she there without me?

Going to Dr. Levin's office was also futile. The office refused to answer any questions I had about why Hana had been there. And apparently Dr. Levin was conveniently out of the office when I wanted to speak with her.

That's when I decided to go to Emily's work. The Pit, what a vile name for a bar. It was obviously not popular; the place was dead when I walked in and I immediately spotted Emily behind the bar, giving me the glaring scowl she seemed to reserve for me. My body vibrated with rage as I made my way toward her. She had to know where Hana was; she had to have somehow gotten to her again. She was constantly texting her, but my sweet wife hardly ever responded. And Hana knew better than to answer her phone calls. She knew I liked to know exactly what was going on with her at all times. She didn't know I'd be able to hear a phone conversation from the spyware on her phone, but I loved that she didn't even want to take the chance.

Emily didn't budge, just like I knew she wouldn't. She was so fucking annoying thinking she knew the truth about me and Hana, but she had no clue. She thought I kept her on a leash? No, Hana was my pet alright, but she knew straying too far would put her in danger; she didn't need a leash.

Just as I was about to leave, after getting nothing from Emily, my phone started to ring. I took it out of my pocket and realized who was calling: Michael. It was a number I had memorized from seeing his pathetic, endless calls to Hana when she first came to me.

"Where is she?" I snarled into the phone.

"I just finished fucking her, mate. Have a look."

My heart started to race. My whole face was on fire. I hesitantly removed my phone from my ear to look down at whatever message was just sent to me. And there it was: a video of Michael and Hana, Michael fucking Hana with her hands and ankles bound with rope, her mouth covered with duct tape. I couldn't hear it yet, but I knew Hana was enjoying herself by the way she looked up at him. He was fucking pounding her. I had never felt as much rage as I did watching that video. But it was also confusing. My dick hardened as I watched them. I was fuming with anger, but the sight of Hana all bound and getting fucked—I hated how much it was turning me on. And Emily wouldn't shut the fuck up. I couldn't let her see how much I enjoyed seeing this.

"You think this is a woman who can make her own decisions right now?" I held up the phone to her after I paused the video.

Emily's eyes practically flew out of her head when she looked at the still.

"Jack, what the fuck?"

Good, she looked terrified enough to believe that Hana was taken. I believed it too.

"He's taken Hana. I'm going to the police to show them that my wife has been kidnapped."

* * *

I had to go back to our apartment first to get a good look at the video. It started with Michael taking Hana's legs with his hands and quickly fucking her. Her moans, muffled behind the tape, made my dick twitch. I sat on the couch as I pulled my dick out, watching Hana get pounded. I began to stroke myself as I watched Michael turn her over and pull out, her pussy juice visibly stringing from his dick, before he mercilessly plunged himself into her ass. Fucking ruthless; he better not have hurt her. I watched as Michael pulled out, put some lube on his dick and her ass, and then thrust back into her. Hana came easily. She loved being fucked in the ass from behind. He made her come with a wand too, her nipples perking and her moans like screams underneath the tape. I fucking lost it when I watched him come all over her—what the fuck was wrong with me? I came so hard into my hand, watching my wife get fucked by another man. Not just any other man, *Michael*. Perhaps I just loved seeing Hana get fucked, being the dirty fucking whore she was. And watching her enjoy it was even better.

But I still couldn't let Michael have her all to himself.

I cleaned myself up and went to the same police station where I had filed the missing person's report. I demanded to see the same officer I had spoken with before. He led me into an office and sat me down, and I didn't even wait until he sat in front of me to show him the video.

"My wife is fucking terrified and was taken by her ex-fiancé. A clearly jealous ex that will stop at nothing to have her. And now he's showing off," I said as the officer watched the video.

Could he tell that Hana was enjoying herself, or was that something only I could tell?

The stone-faced officer looked up at me and then back down at the video. He sighed and nodded. "Do you know where they could be?" He handed me my phone back.

"No." I shook my head. "That's not any place I've ever seen before. Can't you track where they are by this video he's sent?"

"We can find out where the last ping was from this phone number. It can give us a general idea and we can go from there. I'll need his name and cell phone number and I'll have our IT guy look at your phone and get that video off there."

I eyed the officer suspiciously. I didn't want anyone else to see Hana getting fucked. But I had to cooperate. I needed to get my wife back.

"Whatever I can do to help, officer."

Emily

I had someone cover the rest of my shift at the bar. I don't know how many times I called Michael, but I did it over and over until I almost arrived home. Adam had no idea what was going on, but I needed to tell him now that the police were getting involved. I'm sure Jack would start playing the part of worried husband too, and he'd tell everyone he was close to that Hana had been taken from him.

I finally sent a text to Michael before I walked into my apartment building: **Jack called the police and showed them that video. What the fuck is going on, Michael? Please tell me that Hana is there willingly.**

I started walking toward the stairs when my phone began to vibrate in my hand. I answered immediately. "Michael! What the fuck is going on?"

"Jack went to the police?" Michael hissed into the phone. "Real fucking rich of him."

"Let me talk to Hana," I insisted. "You're not giving me any fucking answers, and I'm fucking done."

There was a pause.

"Fine. But she's fine, Emily. However Jack made that scene out to look, it's not what you think. You know how mine and Hana's sex life is," he said lightly.

I rolled my eyes. I wish I didn't.

"Put her on the phone, Michael," I ordered.

There was a long pause before I finally heard Hana's voice.

"Em, hey," she croaked out; it sounded like she had been crying all day.

"Hana, please tell me you're okay. Please tell me you're there on your own volition."

Hana let out a little laugh. "Emily, I have no idea anymore."

"What the fuck does that mean?" I shouted angrily into the phone—I had had enough of this go-around with them.

"Tell Jack we're in Cos Cob in a white townhouse by the school—"

The phone cut off.

Holy fucking shit. Hana *was* fucking taken against her will? And she wanted me to tell Jack where they were? Had she been with Jack willingly this whole fucking time? My mind was officially blown, but I didn't have time to overthink things. I immediately dialed Jack as I stood in the stairwell of my apartment building. He answered after one ring.

"I just talked to Hana. She wanted me to tell you she's in a white townhouse in Cos Cob by the school. That's in Greenwich, near her parent's house. The call ended before she could finish talking," I blurted into the phone quickly.

Jack sighed. "Fuck! Anything else?"

I shook my head, as if he could see. "No. That's all I got."

"Okay. Thanks, Em." Calling me by my nickname? Did he trust me now? Did I trust him?

"Let me go with you," I asserted. "I know the area. I could help you find it."

"No," he replied quickly. "I have to do this myself. If he's dangerous, I don't want anyone else in his cross hairs."

I never imagined Michael being violent before, but I was starting to see him in a whole new light and it was terrifying. And now Jack was the knight in shining armor? I felt like I was in the twilight zone.

"At least tell the police. Tell them you have some hint of where they are," I pleaded.

"No. I can handle this, Emily. I'll let you know what's going on when I've gotten to Hana. Thanks for your help," he said then hung up.

I looked down at my phone and began to sob. Everything I thought I knew was crumbling beneath me. Maybe Hana had been with Jack willingly this whole time. Maybe she was not in any danger with him. What about before, when she told me and Michael that Jack had drugged her and took her to his loft and threatened all of us? Was that true—was it still true? I had so many questions that I wasn't sure would ever be answered. All I knew was that my cousin was in danger, yet again, and it was completely out of my hands.

Hana

Michael grabbed the phone from my hand and hung up, throwing it down on the ground before he took my arms and pinned them above my head. He had cleaned me up and untied me earlier, but he stayed in the bedroom with me, holding me in his arms as he rested his back against the bed frame. I didn't want to think about how he had violated me, how he hurt me and then made me enjoy it. I was still in shock at how he was treating me, how he was behaving toward me. He was so angry, yet he didn't want to let me go. And I didn't want to think about Jack and how much I missed him, how I literally ached for him. I wanted nothing more than to be in *his* arms right now. Except…feeling Michael's strong arms wrapped around me was familiar and calming as well. In that moment, I felt guilt and shame all over again. It was supposed to be me and Michael all along. But somewhere along the lines, this twisted, fucked-up love life of mine started tearing my heart in two.

"Hana," Michael said gently into my ear.

I turned my head to acknowledge him.

"I still love you. I don't know what's happened, I don't know what the truth is, but I'm still utterly in fucking love with you," he whispered before gently putting his lips to my shoulder.

I nodded. I knew that already, but it didn't stop the sting in my chest. I still loved him too. But I also loved Jack. And clearly, I was never going to have a choice on who I was with.

"I don't know what's gotten into me, Hana. I've become obsessed. I've become someone entirely different. The anger I felt when I saw you walking out of that office…" He gulped. "I'm a changed man, Hana. You may not love the man that I am now. I'm sorry."

Fuck. My eyes started welling with tears. I shook my head as I squeezed onto his hold of me.

"I will love you forever, no matter what, Michael," I whispered as I looked down at his hands.

"Even if that child isn't mine?"

He turned me around so I could face him. His brows were pulled together, his gray eyes boring into mine. His beautiful fucking face—he looked so utterly heartbroken. I didn't blame him for anything he had done to me. In fact, I could completely understand. *Classic Hana.*

"Tell me how you felt when I was gone. How did you feel when you got that video?"

I didn't want to answer his question. I wanted to see the lust and anger in his eyes again. I wanted to know that he really did get turned on watching me and Jack, that my theory was right. I guess I was a fucking masochist after all.

His eye twitched with irritation "Why do you want me to bring those feelings up again?"

"Because I want to know how much you love me."

Michael shook his head at me. I could see I was starting to provoke him again.

I was desperate to let Jack know where I was. I was desperate to get these two men in the same space and give them my all—

the truth, the hurt I felt, the desire I felt for both of them. Not just desire, but unwavering love and devotion to each of them.

Michael pinned my arms down, straddling me and pressing his hips into mine, and I pushed him further.

"You're obsessed. Show me," I challenged, no longer resisting his hold on me.

Michael held me down tighter, his eyes ablaze. "Haven't I shown you, Hana? Isn't it fucking clear?" he spit out.

I had a plan for what I was going to say next.

"Call Jack." I narrowed my eyes at him. "Tell him where we are. Show me what you'll do to him."

Michael hesitated before furrowing his brows at me. "You really think I'll tell him where we are? When he's gotten the fucking police involved?"

"Threaten him. Threaten my life," I answered back confidently. "He won't risk it. I'm betting he's already on his way to Greenwich, all by himself."

Would Michael take the bait?

He shook his head at me, like he disapproved. Then he jumped off me and grabbed his phone, tapping the screen a few times before putting it to his ear.

"I'm sending you the address of where we are. If you bring the police, I swear to god I'll kill her." His voice was so sinister and deep, his Irish accent making it somehow more frightening.

Michael lowered his phone from his ear and began typing—I assumed our current address.

"Why here, Michael?" I asked, still lying on the bed, sick to my stomach with fear.

He stopped typing to look up from his phone and glare at me.

"Just because I told you I love you doesn't give you the right to call me by my name. Do you want to try that again, Hana?"

I rolled my eyes. I used his name just a few minutes ago and he didn't even flinch. But I suddenly realized what a grave mistake I had made when Michael gently set down his phone and walked over to me, eyeing the rope that still lay on the desk beside the bed.

"I'm sorry. Sir," I corrected myself.

If my plan was going to work, I needed to be his good girl.

"Oh, how I've dreamed of all the ways I could punish you, Hana." Michael smiled down at me.

My heart began to race with a mixture of fear and desire.

"Please, sir. Can you wait to punish me until Jack gets here?"

Something glimmered quickly in his eye.

"Why do you *really* want him here, Hana? You're in love with him…so why would you want me to hurt him?" He hovered over me, his muscular arms on either side of me and a vein popping out of his temple.

I put my hand to Michael's face before I whispered, "Whoever wins this fight gets to keep me."

Hana

Does he buy it?

Michael tilted his head to the side, eyeing me suspiciously. "You want us to fight each other?" he asked, still hovering over me.

"Yes." I nodded, purposefully biting my lip.

Does that still work on him?

"Have you really gone mad, Hana?"

He finally stood, backing away from me and then crossing his arms. I sat up on the bed and watched as he surveyed me; he still seemed amused by me. And he was still aroused—I could tell from his hard dick underneath his jeans.

"Think about it, Michael—sir. This is the only way I have the power to decide *how* my fate will end up. You two just need to fight it out."

I was making this up as I went. What I really needed was just one minute alone and my plan would work.

Michael still eyed me, putting his hand up to his beard and scratching it; I knew that was a nervous tick of his. I was getting to him.

"And what if the person who wins this fight isn't the father of your child?" he finally asked, his eyes all of a sudden nervous.

I panicked for a moment. "Then we can make another one,"

I offered.

A quick flicker of a grin washed over his face before he tried to hide it.

"So you have all the answers then, hm?"

"I try my best, sir."

Michael narrowed his eyes at me before he finally gave me a grin.

Were we all of a sudden getting playful with each other? It felt like old times, me being the subtle little brat that I was, and him trying his hardest not to show how much I amused him.

"Okay, if this is how you want to play, Hana." He slowly walked toward me. "Then you do as I say before he gets here. A last little soirée before I bludgeon him with my bare hands."

My heart raced, and my chest began rising and falling quickly. Fuck, he could be so intimidating and scary.

"Yes, sir," I responded, tears flowing down my cheeks.

Michael put his hand to my face as he looked down at me, tracing his thumb over my lip.

"When he gets here, I want you to be choking on my dick. I want that to be the first thing he sees when he walks through that door."

As spiteful as it was, I couldn't help but get wet at his words, at his voice, at his dominance. I knew it would destroy Jack seeing us like that, but it got me one step closer to my plan.

"Yes, sir," I breathed out.

Michael held my hand as he took me downstairs; I was still completely naked and almost felt self-conscious being this way with Michael. He sat me down on the couch that sat directly adjacent to the front door. He went into the kitchen and started going through drawers. I eyed every inch of the living room to see if there was anything I could use to my advantage for my little plan. Well, my big plan. Only seconds later, Michael came out of the kitchen holding a butcher knife, a smile plastered on his face.

"An incentive if he, or you, tries anything funny," he explained as he walked to the couch where I sat. "Stand up," he ordered.

I quickly stood and waited for my next command. Michael took my seat and motioned to the floor.

"On your knees. Take my dick out and worship it."

Fuck. His words caused an ache deep in my core that shot straight to my pussy.

I licked my lips and slowly got to my knees in front of him. I had longed for this moment for so long, to be his submissive, to give in to him. I reached my shaky hands to his zipper and pulled down his boxer briefs, his huge, hard cock springing free. I looked up at him for approval, and he nodded as he watched me take him in my hand. I noticed he had put the butcher knife on the end table beside him, his hands now pushing my hair out of my face and putting it behind my head.

"Take me all in, baby. Best as you can," he said, his deep, velvety voice and erection making my mouth water.

I licked my lips, teasing him with my tongue first. Then I placed my mouth on his cock and tried to inch down further. His hands shoved my head down so I was literally choking on his dick, my gagging making my spit fall down to his jeans and my chin.

"Oh baby, how I've missed your pretty mouth around my cock," he moaned.

I moaned as well, hoping the vibration would satisfy him even more. I did it louder as he pushed his hips up so he could get further down my throat and fuck my face.

"Touch your pussy, Hana. Make yourself come with my dick in your mouth," he demanded, knowing I would be dripping for him.

I put my hand between my thighs and started to rub my clit, my pussy already slippery and eager for release. The tension and pleasure build, and I moaned loud as Michael fucked my face before I heard him say, "Come *now*, Hana."

My orgasm released with fury, my pussy clenching around my fingers and my moan now practically a muffled scream around Michael's dick.

"Perfect timing, baby. He's here."

Michael's cock slipped from my mouth as I looked over at the headlights approaching the house then Michael gave my face another hard slap.

"I didn't tell you to stop, Hana. Keep your mouth on my dick," he ordered angrily.

I hesitantly put my mouth around his hard cock, bobbing up and down as I heard a car door shut.

"Hana!" Jack yelled from the other side of the door, his footsteps approaching.

I was able to poke my head up as the front door slammed open, Jack appearing in the door frame. His eyes were wide as he took in the scene.

"Get away from him, Hana," he growled, his eyes seething with rage.

I started to stand, but Michael took my wrist in his hand and dragged me down onto his lap.

"No, mate. She's going to stay right here until I tell you the plan," Michael responded. Then he lifted me up quickly and sat me down perfectly on his cock, sliding into me as I faced

Jack.

I gasped, and Michael tugged my hands behind my back, keeping them there and forcing himself deep into me. Jack's face turned into boiling outrage.

"Jack," I moaned, unable to lift myself off Michael as he forced me to look at Jack while he fucked me.

"Don't you fucking move, Jack. Or I'll take this knife and slit her throat as I fuck her," Michael spit out, the knife already in his hand as his other held my wrists.

Jack's eyes were wide as he stared at us, and I had to squeeze my eyes shut—seeing him like this, having *him* see *me* like this was too much to bear.

"Get her the fuck off you before I fucking rip you to pieces," he spit out.

"What's wrong, mate? Can't stand to see your wife get fucked better by another man?" Michael jested and then released his hand from my wrists, freeing them before wrapping his arm around my belly and my arms to keep me from getting up. My eyes already back open, I looked up at Jack.

"Fuck, she's so fucking wet. So fucking tight," Michael moaned, and I was finally able to see Jack's erection growing under his jeans.

Oh my god, maybe this would be easier than I thought.

Jack was stunned still, anger and confusion clear on his face. He liked watching too. These two men, who absolutely hated each other, loved watching me get fucked.

"Jack," I moaned. "Jack, please...I'm gonna come." I didn't know what I was pleading for, but my pussy throbbed as my climax edged nearer.

"Jack, put your dick in my mouth. Please," I begged.

Michael didn't say anything as he continued to pump his

hips up and down, going deep inside of me as his breaths hitched. Jack slowly walked toward us like he was approaching wild animals.

Michael finally spoke quickly as he set down the knife. "Come on then, mate. Give your wife what she wants."

Jack was already pulling out his cock as he stopped in front of me, and Michael let go of me, gripping my hips with both of his hands as he continued to fuck me. I grabbed Jack's erection and quickly took him in my mouth as his fists gripped my hair. He began to fuck my face, grunting and enjoying himself. The two men that I loved were inside of me. As I realized this, I finally came, my moans loud and my orgasm so intense that it rolled into two, and my head feeling dazed. I suddenly felt Jack's warm release shoot into my mouth, and then Michael dug his nails into my hips, both of them moaning and grunting loudly.

It was quiet except for the sound of all three of us catching our breath. I looked up at Jack, and his eyes were closed as his head pointed upward; I turned my head and saw Michael eyeing me, desire still clear in his eyes. *This is your chance—do it now, Hana.*

I quickly grabbed the knife from the end table and bolted for the other side of the room. I turned around to face them and held the knife to my neck. Michael's and Jack's faces seemed angry and terrified.

"Don't either of you fucking move," I yelled, my voice strong and loud. "You both listen to *me* now, or else I'll take this knife and slit my throat before you two even blink."

Jack and Michael stood still in the living room, their faces stunned as they watched me. I had their attention; they were listening to me.

"This is what I want from both of you."

"If you're going through hell, keep going." — Winston Churchill

Hana

I knew I was never going to get a chance to choose who I wanted to be with. Not anymore. I was stuck in this twisted fairy tale, torn between two men, both of them disturbingly obsessed with me. If I were being honest with myself, I felt the same about them. I knew it was fucked up for me to still be in love with these men after what they'd done to me, but, in a warped way, I loved that they were both so madly in love with me that they would do absolutely anything to be with me. So while I knew giving *them* no choice but to share me was an absolutely absurd idea, they wouldn't say no. And if they didn't cooperate, I knew what I had to do. I wasn't afraid to do it. I couldn't live my life being torn between them anymore.

"Hana, please put the knife down. Let's just talk about this," Jack said calmly, his arms held out in front of him.

"Please, Han. We don't want you to hurt yourself. We will listen, just put that down," Michael continued just as calmly, mimicking Jack's stance.

I shook my head quickly, the huge knife only an inch from my throat.

"No. Listen to me," I shouted, my adrenaline coursing through my whole body. "I've seen the way both of you enjoy watching me with the other. I like it too. That's why you'll both get me. If you want me, you're gonna have to share me," I demanded confidently.

Michael's face soured with disgust. "Hana, no. You said we were going to fight—"

"What? Fight?" Jack interrupted with a laugh, looking over at Michael. "Oh, you fucking know I'd tear you apart, you knob."

"Shut the fuck up!" I yelled.

They whipped their heads back at me.

"Michael, I said you were going to fight as a ruse to get Jack here," I explained, looking between the two. "You're not going to fight. If you two touch each other, to hurt each other, I swear to God I will end my life."

"So you're just going to hold that knife to your neck for the foreseeable future?" Michael asked with amusement.

"Of course not. That's my little *incentive* for both of you. And if either of you tries to take me away from the other again, it will happen. I will make sure of it," I spit out angrily.

I could see both of their minds working quickly as they stood there silently, breathing heavily. They were considering it. This was a good start.

"How would that work, Hana? Like a joint custody thing?" Jack asked with raised eyebrows.

"No. We'll all live together. We'll all learn to get along with each other," I muttered out, not really knowing what my plan was beyond this point.

Michael rolled his eyes. "Fucking hell, Hana," he sighed.

"What about the baby?" Jack asked quietly, almost morosely.

I shook my head. "I'm not having it. This is not what I wanted." I motioned to my stomach.

Both of their eyes widened in terror.

I continued gently. "We can have kids later, but not this way."

Jack shook his head bitterly.

"I know you fucked with my appointment to get my shot, Jack. I know you did. That's not fair. I have to have a say in this, otherwise I will always resent you," I argued.

They were both quiet again, their faces sullen.

"I promise I will give both of you children. We need to figure this shit out first," I went on, knowing they were both heartbroken.

Michael shook his head, his eyes ablaze with anger. "I can't share you, Hana. I can't. Especially not with him," he gestured his thumb at Jack.

Jack was quick to respond. "Oh, fuck you—"

"Shut the fuck up!" I yelled again. "You're gonna have to. Otherwise you won't get me at all."

I stood there shaking, the knife still to my throat, and my weak, naked body bouncing between each foot.

Jack looked up at me, defeated. "If this is how I prevent you from fucking kill yourself, Hana, then I'll do it," he said softly.

Michael scoffed, still angry, as he put his hand to his beard. "Fuck!"

I could tell I had won.

"Fuck this. Fine! Fine, Hana. God damnit," he spit out, his jaw clenched.

My heart dropped to my knees. *Holy fucking shit, this worked. Now what?*

"Okay." I nodded. "Okay. Jack, give me your shirt. Let's sit down and talk."

* * *

We sat at the dining table, Jack to my left and Michael in front of me. I didn't trust them yet, so I left the butcher knife on my lap, ready for action if I needed it. I couldn't believe I was sitting with Jack *and* Michael about to have a civil conversation about how they were going to share me. They were both quiet as they watched me carefully, still looking like they were going to have to catch a wild animal.

"Michael, first I have to ask—where the fuck are we?" I raised my eyebrows at him, waiting.

He clenched his jaw; he was not used to me talking to him this way, and I reveled in it.

"I bought this house shortly before you were *taken* from me." He glanced at Jack with narrowed eyes. "So we'd have a little place to stay close to your parent's house. I was going to surprise you with it," he explained to me.

My heart melted. There was my sweet Michael.

I nodded and smiled. "That's sweet. Thank you."

I reached my hand out to his on the table. Michael smiled faintly at me as he put his hand atop mine, interlocking our fingers. I glanced over at Jack to see if the jealousy had kicked in yet. His tongue darted out before he bit down on his lip, watching our hands. His toned arms distracted me while his elbows sat on the table, his strong chest bare.

I reached my other hand out for Jack, and he took it quickly, squeezing gently. I felt Michael tense.

I was holding both of their hands; it felt like a dream. I let go and clasped my hands together on the table.

I sighed heavily before I spoke. "I don't know how to do this. I want us all under one roof. Maybe we can stay here for a while as we get the hang of things," I suggested, looking between the two of them.

Jack nodded as he glanced over at Michael.

Michael sighed and raised his eyebrows. "Alright." He shrugged.

"What about…how are we going about…getting rid of…" Jack hesitated, tears welling in his eyes.

Fuck. I hated breaking his heart but I had to do this.

I tried to be gentle as I spoke. "I'll figure it out tomorrow."

Jack nodded again, staring down at the table.

"I'm okay with both of you tracking me," I started, the statement absurd to me as I said it aloud. "But I need my phone. I need my laptop. I need *freedom*," I continued.

Michael looked to Jack with contempt. "You weren't giving her freedom?" he asked with disdain.

I quickly interjected. "*He* was. *You* weren't," I quipped back.

Michael shook his head. "That was only going to be temporary, Hana," he clarified softly.

I shrugged. "Whatever. I just need to not feel like I'm being shut out from the world." I looked to both of them.

They nodded slowly.

"You two cannot fight. Physically or verbally. I won't have it," I declared.

Jack quickly glanced up at Michael then back at me. "As you wish, love." He smiled, his perfect dimples emerging.

I looked at Michael. "Deal?"

He was sulking, but nodded hesitantly. "Deal," he agreed.

"And no fucking with my birth control anymore." I narrowed my eyes at Jack with annoyance. "We'll talk about having a baby when the time comes."

Jack gave a devious smile and shrugged. "Deal, sweetheart." I could tell he was being brave in front of Michael, but I knew how much this was hurting him.

I looked down at the table as my mind raced.

"We'll figure out more tomorrow. I'm fucking exhausted." I looked to the two of them. "I want you both sleeping with me."

It felt amazing having this power all of a sudden. Michael looked at Jack then to me and rolled his eyes. I knew Jack was the more willing participant in this situation and Michael would need more time.

Jack smiled at me as he stood and put his hand out for me. "You lead the way, darling."

I stood and took his hand and then turned to Michael. I put the butcher knife that lay across my lap back on the seat and raised my eyebrows at him.

"I won't need that anymore, will I?" I asked, sounding like I was lecturing a child.

Michael sighed and stood. "No," he answered slowly, walking over to me and putting his hand to my face.

I figured they were going to try to show off. And when Michael gently put his lips to mine, our kiss passionate and slow, Jack released my hand and put his strong hand to my pussy, slowly slipping a finger inside me. I moaned, and Michael pulled away from me to look down at what was happening. I looked to Jack who was now pressing his lips against my shoulder, making his way up to my neck. Michael quickly pressed his lips to mine again as I reached down and put my hand to his hard erection through his jeans. I struggled to pull down his zipper, so he reached down and quickly unzipped his jeans, letting them fall to the floor as I rubbed his erection through his boxer briefs. I was breathing heavily as I reached for Jack's, surprised that it was already out and fully erect. I pulled back from Michael and quickly got to my knees between both of them as they stared down at me with desire. I eagerly reached for Michael's cock before he slapped my hand away and took it out himself.

"If you want this cock, Hana, you're gonna have to beg for it." He smirked down at me.

I licked my lips, my pussy clenching and already needing release. I looked at Jack and he nodded, holding himself with one hand and the back of my hair with the other.

"Please, sir. Please let me suck your cock," I breathed out. I turned to Jack. "Please, Jack. I need your cock too. I need them both in my mouth, right now." I looked up at him with wide eyes.

Jack licked his lips and then smiled down at me, teasing me by putting his cock right up to my face and rubbing it on my cheek.

"You want both of us inside you, you little fucking whore?" Jack looked down at me.

"Yes, please," I moaned and looked at Michael. "Please, sir."

"One at a time, take us both in all the way," Michael instructed before putting his cock to my mouth and shoving it down my throat in one quick motion.

I gagged before he pulled out of my mouth, and then Jack had his cock in my face.

"Open wide, sweetheart," he said before he rammed his cock into my mouth, unable to shove it as far down because of his width.

They started to take turns doing this, using my mouth to fuck quickly, their pre-cum already salty on my tongue. I started to put my hand to my clit before Michael quickly slapped my cheek and pulled away from me.

"You won't come until I tell you to. Put those hands on your lap," he ordered.

My pussy was fucking drenched.

"Please," I moaned. "I need you both inside of me," I pleaded.

Jack smiled and then looked at Michael. "Let's fill her up," he said excitedly.

Michael looked to Jack and then back down at me. "Is that what you want, baby? You want us both inside of you? Filling you up like the fucking whore that you are?" It was clear his desire to fuck me overtook any apprehension about sharing me with Jack.

"Yes, please, sir!"

Michael suddenly put his hand to the back of my hair and lifted me up, and they both moved me to the couch. Michael had already fucked me earlier, and the thought of having Jack now made my pussy throb with desire. Jack sat down and took my hips, guiding me to sit on top of him as I faced him. I slowly sat on his dick, his width making me moan with pleasure and pain as I took in his full length, goosebumps dotting my whole body. He began to thrust his hips up and down, putting one hand to my hip and the other to my face.

"You're gonna come so hard for us, aren't you, love? You're gonna scream so fucking loud while we use your holes in whatever ways we please," he spit out, grabbing my face to look at him.

"Yes," I breathed out, already feeling like I was going to come.

"Hold still," Michael said from behind me.

Jack and I both stilled as I glanced back and saw Michael slathering lube over his cock.

"God, I can't fucking wait to feel you so full," Jack whispered in my ear.

I winced as Michael started putting the head of his cock into my ass. He chuckled as he went in deeper, and I quickly shut my eyes tight as I grabbed a hold of the back of the couch.

"Oh, fuck," I moaned, my body taking over of my mind, and my hands now grabbing my ass cheeks to spread them for him.

"So fucking eager as always," Michael said before fully plunging into my ass, making me scream.

Both of them started to move in a rhythm, thrusting their dicks into me hard as I whimpered with pleasure that I didn't even know existed. Michael grabbing my hips hard and Jack pulling my hair as he bit down on my shoulder had me close to coming.

"Please," I whined. "Please, I'm gonna come," I cried, asking for their permission.

"Fuck yes, baby. Come hard for us," Michael moaned between grunts.

The release of my orgasm hit hard as I screamed, my pussy clenching around Jack's dick. I moved my hips slowly, riding out the most intense release I had ever felt. Michael didn't slow as he dug his nails harder into my hips, making me come again as tears streamed down my face.

"Oh my God," I moaned when Jack began to thrust his hips quick and hard again, giving me my third orgasm in just a minute.

"What do you say, mate? Inside her or all over her?" Michael asked Jack.

So now they were coordinating where they would come on me? *Holy fuck.*

"Let's give her a proper cum shower," Jack responded with a smile in his voice.

They suddenly pulled out and had me on my knees, both of

them hovering over me and stroking themselves.

"Fuck, please give me your cum, sir," I moaned to Michael and then looked to Jack. "Jack, baby. I need your cum, please."

They both watched me intently, their faces clearly revealing they were about to come.

"Open your mouth," Jack moaned before his load shot straight at me, my mouth wide open and taking in every drop I could get.

"Look at me," Michael ordered, his cum shooting all over my face, tits, and stomach.

I smiled as I moaned with the pleasure of having the best sex I ever had with the two men that I loved more than anything in this world. *Is this gonna be way easier than I thought? We got the sex part down, but how are they going to do when they have to share me out in the real world?*

"Leave that cum all over you, my fucking whore," Jack said finally, lowering his hand to me.

I grabbed his hand and stood, looking at Michael who had sat down and let his body fall back onto the cushion.

"Sir. Will you please join us?" I held my other hand out to him.

My heart dropped to the floor when he smiled at me. He stood as he took my hand, and we all went upstairs together.

Jack

I never knew I would enjoy watching Hana with someone else so much. And fucking her at the same time as someone else? Holy fuck, even better. I had had my share of threesomes in the past, but none with a woman I was utterly in love with. When she brought up the idea of Michael and I "sharing" her, I was fucking furious. Share her with that twat? But she gave us no choice. If anything ever happened to Hana, I wouldn't want to live anymore. So I had to do what she said.

How exactly would sharing Hana work? When we fucked her on the couch, that was the best orgasm I had ever had. But sex, privately or together or what the hell ever it was, was different than everyday life.

And then there was the life growing inside Hana. She was getting rid of it. I was all for pro-choice and equal rights and shit, but not with Hana. But, again, she was giving us no choice. And we would never know who the father was. Not that it mattered anymore.

Hana looked so fucking beautiful covered in our cum as she slept. I couldn't take my eyes off her naked body cast in a soft glow from the moonlight. Her arm and leg were draped over my body, holding onto me as if I would flee. *Never.* I looked over at Michael who seemed to be asleep as well. His arm was underneath her pillow, his back flat on the bed. I knew he was a good-looking man—it was just a fact. His body was fucking killer, which was one of the main reasons I got so buff. I wanted to be just as hot for Hana as Michael was. I thought I was pretty close now, if not better.

My mind raced as I thought of the day that had gone by. Hana woke up as my wife, all mine…and now she was sleeping naked next to me and Michael. It wasn't exactly the Wednesday I had imagined.

"Baby," Hana whispered, startling me.

I looked down at her; her wide green eyes scanned over my face before she smiled.

"I love you. Please get some sleep."

I smiled and nodded at her. "I love you, sweetheart," I whispered back before I gave her a kiss on the forehead.

She closed her eyes and lowered her head against my chest. My heart stung at how much I loved this woman. And I knew she was still all mine. She was still my wife. I was never going to let her take that away from me.

Michael

I couldn't believe Hana was making us share. *Forcing* us to share. As hot as it was fucking her with Jack, I wasn't sure if I could just go about my day pretending everything was normal. I fucking hated Jack with every fiber of my being. The way he looked at her with the same lust in his eyes made my skin scrawl. How were we going to live our lives this way? I knew Hana was serious about killing herself—I had never seen her look so desperate and afraid. But there had to be another way.

Learning about her decision to get an abortion devastated me. While I wanted her to have bodily autonomy, that was still potentially my child. And when she woke up the next morning declaring she wanted to go get it done right away, that very next hour, it broke my heart even more. Had she given thought to this, or was this just another rash decision of hers?

We had some clothes delivered to the house for her to wear when we went out. I preferred her to be naked inside. Jack and I drove her, but she was adamant about going into the clinic by herself and doing this on her own, so we sat and waited in the parking lot.

"How did you find Hana? Did she go with you willingly?" Jack started to interrogate me right away as he sat in the driver's seat; he had apparently gotten his driver's license weeks ago, but I never had any use for one.

I shook my head as I stared ahead, watching traffic go by. "This isn't the time for us to reveal all of our secrets. And honestly, I don't want to chat with you at all." I looked over at him with contempt.

Jack scoffed and shook his head back at me. "You don't get to decide if we chat or not. Hana has made it clear that we need to start getting along," he said with equal contempt.

I looked ahead again, the traffic getting lighter now. "Since when did she get all the power?" I asked, more to myself.

"Oh, she's always had the power, my friend. She just hadn't used it," he responded.

I scoffed a little as I continued to stare at the cars passing by. He was right. Hana was so empathetic, so willing to give to others. She never knew what kind of power she could have over each of us…not until now. She always had some power in our relationship before; she willingly gave herself to me, gave me the opportunity to make her decisions, to decide her punishments. Then she went and left me and hung me up to dry.

"Did *you* take Hana?" I blurted out, needing to know the truth. I wasn't sure if I would hate Jack more knowing he took her from me, or if it would make it easier somehow.

Jack was quiet. I turned to look at him, and he was staring at the street as I was, seemingly lost in his thoughts.

"I like to think I just gave her a little push to be with me," he said quietly.

"What does that mean?" I shook my head at him, annoyed at his vagueness.

He looked over at me, his eyes full of tears. "I did. I took her. I was desperate. And then she fucking fell in love with me," he admitted, his eyes wide and almost confused.

I didn't know why I wasn't more angry with him. Perhaps because I knew his despair and desperation. Perhaps I had let all of my anger out in the days and nights of drinking excessively to the point I'd black out and wake up next to a stranger. Or worse.

"She was always in love with you, mate. Don't flatter yourself." I broke our eye contact to look back at the road.

"And with you. That's how we're here now," Jack sighed.

I sighed heavily. "What about in New Jersey? Did you force her then as well?"

I couldn't believe I was getting all the answers I thought I'd never get.

"I didn't force her. She just didn't want you to die."

"That's still coercion," I explained, turning to him.

He quickly responded. "And *you* haven't forced yourself onto Hana ever?"

His eyebrows were raised at me knowingly. I easily led her into that cab—it seemed like she *wanted* to go with me. And she was such a fucking brat when we finally got to the house. She was trying to be loyal to her "husband," but I knew she wanted me; she was fucking drenched for me. And when I tied her up, I was punishing her. She knew why I was doing it. But did she *not* want it? I didn't think of that possibility. She knew her safe word. But…she was also unable to speak with her mouth duct taped. *Fuck.* I put my hand up to my beard and scratched it, growing nervous. What she must think of me.

"Let's talk about something else."

"No need." Jack looked beside us at the clinic. "She's coming back."

Hana

No one had ever told me that all you had to do was take a couple of pills and that was that. It was simple and it was done. I would bleed for a bit, but that was fine. It meant I had my body back.

Michael and Jack were silent on the ride back to the house. It was starting to sink in that I would no longer be pregnant, and I felt an ache in my chest. I was allowed to not want it, but I was also allowed to be sad about it ending. I didn't think Michael nor Jack would ever comprehend that, so I wouldn't tell them how I felt about it.

It felt odd walking back into the house with Michael *and* Jack behind me. Would I ever get used to them both being in my presence and being civil?

"Let's talk some more," I announced as I set down my purse; luckily Jack had brought it back to me the night before.

I turned around, and they both stared at the ground, looking uneasy.

"What?" I looked between the two of them.

"Don't you want to talk about how you're feeling? About what just happened?" Jack asked me carefully.

Michael had the same concerned look on his face.

"No. I don't want to talk about it. I'm glad it's been dealt with," I answered, tears welling up in my eyes.

Jack shook his head and walked to me slowly, wrapping his arms around me tightly. I couldn't help it—I started to bawl. I felt Michael's hand on my back, rubbing circles. I felt Jack crying too, his chest heaving up and down. My poor, sweet, sensitive Jack.

"I love you, Hana," he said into my ear.

"I love you too, Jack," I responded into his shoulder.

I let go of him and turned around to face Michael. His face was sullen, his dark-gray eyes wide and mournful. I took his hand and sighed.

"Let's figure everything else out," I finally said quietly.

We needed to lay down some ground rules. We needed to figure out how this would work. I let go of Michael and sat on the couch, putting my knees up to my chest. Jack sat down first and Michael followed.

"I want alone time with each of you. You both get me alone, at least once a day. For an hour," I muttered; I was making shit up as I went.

"An hour? That's it?!" Jack exclaimed.

"I mean, yeah. *At least* are the key words here. We can negotiate." I looked between the two of them.

Michael didn't say anything; Jack pouted next to me.

"Do we have to all sleep together in the same bed every night? Or do we get to take turns or what?" Michael asked, already exasperated.

I knew he was having a hard time with this. They both were. I put my hand atop his and gave him a small, crooked smile; I knew he loved that smile.

"We can take turns. I do like sleeping with both of you, though. I feel safe," I explained.

I felt *safe*? Sleeping between two men who kidnapped me, fucked me, threatened violence against me, and had me scared for my life? How fucked up in the head was I? Speaking of my fucked-up head...

"And I get to manage my own medication. I have no idea when I last took my meds." I looked at Jack, eyeing him warily.

He put his hands up with a devilish smile.

"So we're staying here till when? And then what, where will we live?" Michael pressed on, removing his hand from mine to stand. "We each get date nights? What about holidays? We're all going to show up at your parents' house as a big happy family?"

He was pacing now.

"We'll figure that out, Michael," I answered calmly. Michael's eyes darted to me. "Sir."

"And she always has to call you fucking 'sir'? Or else what? You get to go punish her, just the two of you?" Jack stood now too. They were both spiraling.

"Hey!" I shouted.

Their eyes darted to me.

"All that matters is that you *both* get me. You're either all in, or nothing." I looked between the two of them, standing between their angry glares.

I felt ridiculous telling them they needed to calm the fuck down because I was their shiny little prize.

"I need my hour. Right now," Michael responded, taking my hand.

He started to lead me up the stairs as I looked back at Jack; he was obviously upset as he frowned up at us.

"One hour, Jack," I called out to him before Michael took me into the bedroom and slammed the door shut behind us.

Michael threw me down on the bed and hovered over me.

"Hana. This is fucking crazy. I can't share you with Jack," he spit out, his eyes clouded with rage as he held down both of my wrists.

My heart started to race. Would this not work after all? He was so against it…but we had to make it work. I got a taste of getting them both and now I needed it.

"Yes, you can. You *have* been," I responded quickly.

"The logistics of this working in the long run just don't make sense. Everyone would have to know we're…" he trailed off, seemingly looking for the right words.

"All fucking?" I offered.

Michael suddenly smiled. "Yes, to put it eloquently, Hana. We're all fucking."

It was so nice to see him smile. I couldn't help but smile too, and then my smile turned into a laugh.

"Fuck, Hana." He let go of my wrists and sat on the bed. "I love seeing you laugh and smile like that."

I sat up beside him. "And you will see that much more often if you decide to stay with us."

I was giving him a choice to leave right then and there. I didn't want to force him to be with me in this situation. I didn't want to force anyone to do anything, not like they had with me. I didn't count my threatening to kill myself "forcing" them to do anything; it was merely me getting myself out of a situation I couldn't get out of otherwise. I was giving them choices. And it worked.

I could tell Michael's mind was working as he surveyed my face.

"I don't want to lose you again, Hana. That would kill me. Literally this time." His voice was quiet and sullen, matching his face.

I nodded. "I don't want to lose you either, baby. You have no idea how happy it makes me knowing you're both here with me. Safe, right next to me."

I stood and straddled his lap, draping my arms around his shoulders. I bit my lip as I tried to hide my smile. He wasn't arguing with me anymore.

"Fuck, Hana," he sighed, putting his hands to my hips. "I can't believe I'm doing this. I'm fucking crazy for you, do you know that?"

He was getting hard underneath me.

Suddenly, a painful cramp shot through my abdomen.

I quickly stood and sat on the bed next to him. "Fuck. Michael. I think it's happening."

He knew what I meant.

For the rest of the day, the two of them tended to me like I was a queen. I mostly stayed in bed, watching Netflix or reading, cuddling both of them by request. By night time, I demanded they both stay in bed with me. I fell asleep with Jack spooning me and my head on Michael's chest, a satisfied smile on my face.

Hana

I felt much better over the next few days; it was done and there was tremendous weight off my shoulders. I knew I would have a mixture of emotions, but it was an overall feeling of relief. Michael and Jack were supportive and loving and tended to whatever I asked for. I was surprised at how civil they were being with each other. I didn't even hear them argue once—maybe they left it for when I wasn't around.

I had to show them that I appreciated their efforts in a way I knew they would enjoy.

Jack had a music business meeting via Zoom in the guest room, and Michael and I sat on the couch in the living room, his hand on my thigh while we both read. It was only our first week together, in whatever our relationship was, and it somehow felt normal.

"Baby." I turned my head to him as I put my hand atop his. Lowering my voice to sound sultry, I said, "I would really love to show my appreciation for you."

Michael's eyes lit up, flickering up the stairs then back to me. "Just us two?" he asked eagerly.

I bit my lip and nodded. We hadn't had real "alone time" since Jack had come to the house. We hadn't had any semblance of normal at all since we had been reunited. He had gone fucking haywire on me and now he seemed like the usual, perfect Michael, if not a little reserved. I wanted us to have our connection back—I also wanted to talk about what had happened, but I wasn't ready yet. I just wanted to show him how much I loved him in the only way I really knew how: physical touch.

Michael closed the book on his lap and put his arm atop the couch behind me.

"And how do you think you could show your appreciation?" His voice was deep and seductive.

I licked my lips before I slid down onto my knees on the floor and turned to face him. "May I please, sir, suck your cock?"

Fire blazed in his eyes, an eager smile flickering across his lips. The erection under his jeans was already evident and ready to spring free.

"My lovely Hana." He put a strand of hair behind my ear. "I should be pleasing *you*."

My mouth flew open, shocked. "I'm open to that, sir." I smiled as I bit my lip.

Michael leaned down and put his hand behind my head and pressed his lips against mine. He was gentle and passionate, but I grew feral with need. I broke our kiss to stand and straddle him, taking off my shirt in one quick motion. I fervently pressed my lips against his, putting my hands to his face and grinding my hips over his erection.

"I need you, sir. I need you inside me," I moaned, grabbing his hair with my hands and kissing his neck.

Michael suddenly lifted me up and set me down on the couch, quickly taking off my underwear and throwing them to the ground. He grabbed my thighs and pulled me to the edge of the couch, lifting my legs over his shoulders. I watched as he put his face to my pussy then gasped when he shoved his tongue inside of me, lapping my wetness like he was starving for me. I moaned as I grabbed his hair with my hands, the feeling of his tongue inside me and the roughness of his facial hair against my clit overwhelming me with ecstasy.

"I'm gonna come, sir. Please let me come," I moaned loudly, lifting my hips up and down in an attempt to chase my orgasm.

He moaned into my pussy, swirling his tongue on my clit before looking up at me with a smile. "Now, Hana," he said quickly then put his face back to my wetness.

I came onto his mouth, dazed in my pleasure as he continued, pulling me even closer to him.

"Fuck, Michael. Sir—" I came again, the intensity of his mouth and tongue overwhelming me.

He quickly pulled away from me and grabbed my hands as he laid his back on the floor and tugged me on top of him, my pussy perfectly lined up to his face.

"Fuck my face, Hana. Smother me. I want you to keep coming until you can't stand it anymore," he said before pulling down my hips so I could ride his face.

It was something I had never done with Michael; he was usually the one with the power, dominating me with his body, ordering me around and tying me up. I felt self-conscious all of a sudden, hesitating as I looked down. His eyes were eager with desire, and I realized he was still in control. And he wanted me. All I had to do was move my hips and he could do the rest.

I let my hands fall down to the floor above Michael's head and began to grind on his face, his tongue swirling around and his hands holding down my thighs. The pleasure was overpowering; I instantly came, unable to stop my hips from moving, one orgasm turning into two then three. I could only recover for a few seconds before I felt the pressure of another orgasm building, and I lost count after five. Michael chuckled underneath me as I ran out of breath, my eyes shut tight as my thighs trembled.

"I...can't...anymore," I breathed out as I sat up and onto Michael's chest.

He smiled triumphantly. "I think eight is a record."

"Eight?!" I exclaimed. "Fuck."

"Let's keep it going," Jack said from afar.

I turned around and he was smiling at the end of the stairs, his arms crossed and an erection clear underneath his jeans.

I instinctively looked down at Michael for approval. *Hana, you don't need his approval anymore.*

"I want one of you inside me and the other in my mouth." I looked between the two of them, my heart pounding.

I was learning to make my own decisions after months of having almost no say whatsoever and it was terrifying.

I stood and waited for some type of negative reaction from Michael, but it never came. I sat on the couch as I watched them eagerly undress, taking their cocks in their hands and stroking themselves as they slowly walked toward me.

"I'm fucking that sweet pussy of yours that I can taste all over my mouth," Michael asserted, quickly pulling me up and turning me around so I could bend over.

Jack stood beside me and hungrily put his hand to my mouth, parting my lips with his thumb. "I'm fucking your mouth first. Then I need your pussy clenching around my cock."

I looked to Michael then to Jack. "I don't want you two to be gentle with me. Fuck me how I like it."

Michael and Jack glanced at each other then looked back down at me.

"Then watch that dirty fucking mouth of yours and take my cock like the little slut that you are," Jack said before shoving himself into my mouth with no mercy.

Michael grabbed my hips and slammed himself into me, pounding hard and quick. Jack took his hands to my head and forced my mouth further down onto him, making me gag and gasp for air. My hands were suddenly clasped together behind me, Michael keeping them there snugly on my back as he vigorously pumped himself in and out of me. With my moans muffled around Jack's cock, I could feel my orgasm approaching, but I was suddenly lifted as Michael turned me around and threw me on my back. He was back inside me instantly, and Jack was already putting his hands to my tits then making his way up to my neck.

"Look at her pretty face. Let's make her scream," Jack mused, tightening his grip around my throat, stroking himself as he watched Michael fuck me.

I started to get lightheaded before Jack let go and positioned himself beside me and over me, shoving his cock back into my mouth. I suddenly felt a hand on my clit, flicking it rapidly and making me come instantly, my screams muffled by Jack gagging me.

"Oh, fuck yes," Jack moaned. "Tap me in, mate. I need to fuck her."

They quickly switched positions, and Jack suddenly thrust inside me, putting both hands to my neck.

"You filthy fucking whore. You like being used as a fuck toy by two cocks?" he asked, his eyes wild.

"Fuck yes," I moaned as he loosened his grip around my

neck.

Michael stroked himself beside us before he leaned down and kissed me urgently, his hand also gripping my neck.

"Fuck, Hana. You really are so good at taking two cocks," he muttered before shoving his cock into my mouth.

"Oh fuck, Hana…this perfect fucking pussy. I'm gonna fill you up—" Jack grunted loudly, still pounding me as he spilled his cum inside me.

I was moaning loudly, my body completely overwhelmed and exhausted, but somehow wanting more.

"My turn," Michael growled as Jack pulled out of me and stood beside me, putting his hand to my clit.

Michael looked down at me as he quickly thrust inside me, the same wild look in his eyes as Jack. With Jack circling my clit and Michael pounding me in the perfect spot, I came instantly.

"God damn, Hana," Jack said into my ear before he pressed his lips against mine, gripping my neck firmly.

My eyes started to flutter shut as I got lightheaded, and I could hear Michael grunting loudly. Jack put his hand to my clit again, his other hand still gripping my throat. I came just as Jack let go and I caught my breath. Tears were streaming down my face, my breath hiccuping as the intense orgasm washed over my entire body.

"You fucking went too far. Look at her," Michael said.

"She likes it, you knob. We always do that shit," Jack retorted.

My eyes flickered open, and I saw Michael on his knees beside me, stroking my hair above my forehead. His concerned gray eyes scanned my face.

"Baby, are you okay? Was that too much?" he whispered to me.

Jack was standing on the other side of me. "Oh don't fucking act like I'm a monster. You know you're a fucking monster too. You came when you saw that shit."

"No." I shook my head, clearing my throat. "No. It was all perfect," I confirmed, nodding to Michael.

"See. I know her better than you do," Jack declared, pulling on his boxer briefs.

"Please, stop." I lifted myself up with my elbows, my voice strong again. "It was fucking perfect, no need to dig further into this. I need both of you to trust me."

Michael and Jack were glaring at each other. *Fuck.*

"I need my alone time now, Hana." Jack took my hand and lifted me up.

"No wait," I interjected. "You two can't just declare your alone time when we're all disagreeing."

They were both silently pouting like fucking teenage boys.

"You both know me in different ways. And you'll get to know me in different ways too. Please…let's not get petty right now." I turned to Jack.

I could still see the anger on his face. I turned to Michael who continued to glare at Jack, seemingly not hearing a word I had said.

"You two just fucked me. *Together.* Did you ever think you'd be able to do that…to *share* me? You both are more open-minded than you think." My hands were on my hips, and I felt like I was giving a lecture.

"No, we're both just fucking obsessed with you," Jack muttered, finally looking at me with his famous blue doe eyes.

"To a fucking fault." I raised my eyebrows at them, unable to contain my smile at how ironic this all was.

Jack flashed his dimples at me. I turned to Michael, and his eyes were soft again. I had put out this fire for now.

"I'm gonna shower. *Alone.* I need Hana time too." I eyed them as I slowly walked upstairs, almost afraid to leave them alone.

I took my time in the hot shower, trying to gather my thoughts as best as I could. We needed more ground rules because it seemed like they could easily fly off the rails. Hell, *they* needed their own safe word. And what the fuck was I even doing? Was this really going to work out long term if they still hated each other? Michael's questions got to me: How are we going to go about in the real world? Where would we live, since I demanded they both stay under the same roof with me? I had to make this work, otherwise someone would get hurt…not only emotionally, but physically.

I threw on some leggings and a T-shirt and had my hair wrapped in a towel when Jack barged into the bedroom. He handed me his phone with a concerned look on his face. I looked down at his phone and it was a text from Emily: **Fucking call me or I'm filing a missing persons report on you too!!!!**

"We need to tell her everything is fine," Jack said sternly.

I looked up at him with confusion. "Everything *is* fine." I nodded my head at him.

"Is it? I haven't gotten any alone time with you, Hana. How the fuck are we going to do this? I can't fucking lose you. I don't want to live without you." His eyes were wide and afraid.

I shook my head and put my hands to his face. "I'm not going anywhere, Jack. You have me. I'm your wife. Till the day we die."

He shook his head, and his eyes started to well with tears. "I feel like I'm going to lose you again. Michael always seems to get his way with you. I'm fucking scared, Hana. That's why I kept you to myself before. That's why I did what I did. I've always feared you leaving me."

I bit my lip and started to cry as well. My sweet Jack was returning more and more. "I promise I'm not going anywhere. The past doesn't matter anymore. All that matters is that I'm in love with you. I'm so fucking in love with you. How many times have I forgiven you for such terrible shit? It's because I love you so goddamn much that I don't want to live without you either."

Jack's tears fell down his cheeks as he grabbed me and kissed me, luring me onto the bed and starting to take off my leggings.

"Wait. Wait," I breathed out. "Emily."

Jack looked at me like I had grown two heads.

"The text," I reminded him. "I need to call her."

Emily

It had been almost two days since I had heard anything from anyone. Michael wasn't answering his phone, nor was Jack. Hell, I even tried Hana, but that went straight to voicemail. I finally sent an urgent text to Jack: **Fucking call me or I'm filing a missing persons report on you too!!!!**

I had sort of looped Adam into what was going on—he just thought Hana was being Hana again, unable to choose between Jack and Michael. I didn't want him to know that his best friend had potentially just put himself in grave danger. He didn't even bat an eyelid when I shot up while we ate brunch at home, telling him I had to take Hana's call; I almost had a heart attack when I saw that it was actually Hana's number calling.

"Hana!" I answered, out of breath while I stood in our tiny bathroom.

"Em," she breathed out.

The relief of finally hearing her voice made me sob. I fully believed that they were all dead in some fucking townhouse in Cos Cob.

"Where the fuck are you? Are you okay?" I asked between my tears.

"Yes, Em. I'm okay. I'm with Jack right now. And Michael,"

she explained calmly.

My heart dropped again. "Both of them?"

Hana laughed. "Yeah. Both of them. Things are…they're good now, Em," she said with a smile in her voice.

I was rendered speechless. *"What?"*

She fucking laughed *again*.

"No seriously, Hana. *What?* And they're both alive?" My brain just couldn't comprehend what was going on.

"Yeah. You wanna FaceTime?" she asked casually.

I almost burst into tears again. We hadn't FaceTimed in months.

"Please," I choked out.

The FaceTime tone rang, and I immediately answered. Hana popped up on the screen, fresh faced, wet hair, and a big smile.

"I'm so fucking happy to see you, banana. You have no idea," I said, letting tears stream down my face.

Hana gave me a frown. "Oh, I'm sorry, Em. I didn't mean to make you cry."

"Oh, shush, Han. Tell me what the fuck is going on right now. Everything!" I demanded as I wiped away my tears.

Hana let out big sigh. "Well, basically…me and Michael and Jack are together now. We're like…you know, *together*." She gave me her classic crooked smile before finally looking at me.

"Hana Anne Miller or Maynor or what the fuck ever. You're fucking with me."

I still couldn't comprehend. Jack went over there ready to kill Michael, and now they're all magically fucking?

Hana let out another laugh before she spoke. "No, I'm not fucking with you. It's…a lot to explain, but I'm happy right now, Em. I'm very, very happy."

EMILY

I could see my eyes widen in the video preview at the bottom right of the screen.

"But like…what? How?" I needed to know how this came about.

"I gave them no other choice. I didn't want them to keep fighting over me. I couldn't choose. So it was either this or nothing," she explained nonchalantly.

"And…so…*you* decided this?"

Hana nodded.

"Han, I'm happy for you but I'm also thoroughly confused. I can't imagine either of them being okay with this," I told her, my mind still blown.

Hana shrugged. "Like I said. I gave them no other choice: share me or leave. They're happy to have me in any way they can get me."

I smiled; I was liking this confident, bold, self-aware Hana.

"Okay. If things are going so well, then let's hang out," I suggested then held my breath.

Hana looked up from her phone; were the guys in the room with her? She smiled and looked back down at the phone.

"Sure. Why don't you come out here to the house? We can have some alone time to chat."

I tried to contain my excitement. "I'd love to. Text me the address."

Hana

"Emily knows about us?" Michael's eyes widened with worry as he sat in the living room with a book on his lap.

I nodded. Jack was in the shower, so I was all alone with Michael for only the second time since this all happened. My insides twisted at the thought of being alone with him and talking to him without asking permission for…well, anything.

"Fucking hell. I can't believe you're letting her come here. We're still trying to figure all of this out, Hana." He stood and sighed, placing his book on the end table beside the couch. He was lecturing me like always, and my barriers were beginning to fall.

"I need her in my life, Michael. She's been worried sick, and I haven't seen her much. Jack has been…reluctant to let me see her," I admitted, wringing my hands together.

Michael gazed at me while he slowly walked closer, putting his hand to the side of my neck. Goosebumps raised over my entire body, and my nipples harden. His touch distracted me so easily; did he even hear a word I said?

"Michael," I whispered, leaning into his hand.

His hand suddenly gripped my hair, pulling my head back.

"Sir," I corrected myself, instantly knowing my mistake.

He licked his lips and smiled. "Hana," he whispered, before

bringing his lips to the other side of my neck.

"Please, sir…we need to get ready for Emily to get here," I said quietly, my eyes already closed as I basked in his gentle touch.

He ignored me and continued to graze his lips on my neck. My knees felt like they would buckle at any moment, and my pussy was already soaking. He knew as well as I did how easily he could seduce me.

"I'm going to make you come just by kissing your neck and pressing your body against mine," he declared quietly into my ear, moving his hand from the back of my head down to my ass.

"Yes please, sir," I moaned, pressing myself against him harder.

Feeling his erection against my stomach sent me into a frenzy as I quickly put my hands to his hair and tried to press into him, searching for any friction I could get.

Michael chuckled as he took my hands and put them behind me, easily locking them there with his grip. He shook his head at me. "So greedy, my sweet Hana. You need to learn patience."

He put his lips to my neck again, his other hand slowly making its way up my shirt to graze my tits. I moaned as he pulled on my nipple, tugging hard before releasing it and letting his hand fall down to my ass again. He quickly slipped his fingers into my leggings, grabbing my ass cheek and squeezing hard. My pussy was drenched and desperately needing release.

"Please, sir. I need to come," I whimpered as I quickly put my leg up and around him.

"You may grind against me here. But you're not getting my cock right now. You need to earn it, Hana," he ordered, holding onto my leg.

I felt like a horny teenager, desperate to get off in any way possible. Michael's touch, his strong body against mine, and his words always seemed to get to me. I started to move my hips against him, almost feeling embarrassed at how much I needed to find release. Was this a new kink I was figuring out? Because as embarrassed as I felt, I was immensely turned on.

"That's right, baby. Come just by fucking touching me," he demanded eagerly, still grasping onto my leg.

I tried not to think about how ridiculous I must have looked dry humping Michael; all I could focus on was chasing my orgasm. I kept pushing my hips against him, grinding up and down and moaning loudly as my climax approached.

"May I please come, sir?" I cried out, just on the edge of release.

"Yes, baby. Come for me," he growled out eagerly.

Just like that, the friction of my pussy against Michael's body made me come, my pussy pressing against his jeans, desperately searching for more.

"What a good girl," he said into my ear with a smile.

"Have I earned your cock, sir?" I asked desperately, needing to be filled.

Michael removed his lips from my neck and smiled down at me triumphantly. He finally released his hold of my hands and let my leg fall back down to the ground.

"Yes, baby. But you need to wait. I want you aching for my cock all day."

Fuck. I had no idea how I was going to be able to make it through the day without having him inside me. But then I remembered who was showering upstairs. I smiled to myself as I looked up at the stairs, trying to decipher if this was a bad idea or not.

Michael somehow read my mind. "You're staying down here. His cock wouldn't satisfy you anyway, not like mine," he huffed.

I squinted at him with welcomed irritation. He was already ordering me around, and I was letting him. This little teasing game was one I enjoyed, so I let him have it.

"Are you sure you're gonna be able to go all day without coming inside me?" I cocked my head to the side, a smile creeping up my lips. "Teasing can go both ways, you know."

Without thinking, I pulled off my shirt and pushed my leggings and thong to the floor. I sat on the couch and put my legs up and my feet to the edge, slowly moving my hands around my tits and my thighs. Michael narrowed his eyes at me, and I could see him breathing heavily. He slowly sat down on the arm chair beside the couch, watching me intently. I smiled at him before putting my hand to my pussy and feeling around at my wetness. Then I lifted my fingers to show him the juice drenching them. I was surprised that he was letting me go this far. I bit my lip as I put my hand back to my pussy, teasing around my clit, knowing I was close to an orgasm already. I couldn't keep my eyes off Michael as he watched me, his eyes hardened and aroused.

"I know how much you like watching, sir. You know you're a fucking pervert," I moaned, wanting to rile him up.

"Watch your fucking mouth," Michael ordered as he started to unzip his pants, letting his cock spring free and quickly stroking it.

"See, you can't even watch me without touching yourself. And you don't want that nice big cock of yours inside me?" I huffed, trying to hold off my orgasm.

From the corner of my eye, I spotted Jack walking down the stairs.

"Having a masturbating party, are we?" he mused, stopping at the end of the steps.

"Fuck off," Michael responded instantly, not breaking his eye contact with me.

I smiled as I looked over to Jack. "Let's play a game. Whoever comes first just by watching me gets to fuck me first tonight."

I never knew this kind of confidence before having two gorgeous men lusting over me. The fact that they both wanted me so much made me feel like a goddess.

My eyes darted back to Michael's, and I could see anger seething through as he stroked his cock. I loved getting him riled up and being a brat. He wasn't used to this Hana, and I was thoroughly enjoying it.

Jack walked into the middle of the room and chuckled. "That's fucking easy, sweetheart." He took out his hard cock and started to stroke, his eyes intent on my pussy.

With their eyes on me, I suddenly felt my orgasm approaching quickly and without hesitation. I moaned as I watched Jack. My pussy clenched against my fingers, my hips rolling up and down quickly and my eyes fluttering shut. I caught my breath after a moment and looked at Michael who was still furiously stroking himself.

"Do I need to come again for you two?" I looked back at Jack and started rubbing my clit again.

"Look at me, Hana," Michael ordered. My eyes locked with his, and he started grunting as his cum shot up and over his hand.

"Fuck!" I instantly came at the sight of Michael coming for

me.

"Hana," Jack moaned, then quickly came all over the floor, his cum shooting out in spurts, making my second orgasm roll into the third.

I let my head fall back to the cushion behind me as I caught my breath, my eyes closed.

"Lick this cum off the floor, my dirty fucking whore," Jack's gravelly voice ordered.

I opened my eyes and raised my eyebrows. As disgusting as that sounded, I wanted to please him. I wanted to show him that I wanted his cum so much I'd lick it off the dirty floor in front of me.

"Don't fucking make her do that," Michael growled, zipping up his pants as he stood.

"Don't fucking make decisions for her," Jack spit back, putting his cock away as well.

I watched as they both huffed their chests and slowly started to approach each other.

"No? That's your job, hm?" Michael started to get in Jack's face, and that's when I shot up and wiggled my way in between them.

"Hey!" I yelled. "New rule? Let's not contradict each other while fucking unless I say so. You both know I have a safe word, right? I'm not gonna do anything I don't want to do. At least, not anymore." I eyed them both with contempt. "And while we're at it, let's give each of you a safe word too."

They both looked at me with confusion.

"If something is happening that you just absolutely cannot do, use your safe word. Michael?" I turned to him.

He glared at Jack. "Puerile."

I rolled my eyes. Of course Michael would use some random,

uncommon insult. I turned to Jack, and he glared right back at Michael.

"Plonker."

I sighed. This was pointless. "Okay, we're using the universal 'red' for everyone's safe word."

A knock on the door interrupted us. Surely that couldn't be Emily yet. It had only been an hour or so. Maybe she was just *really* eager to get here. I looked down at the cum on the floor and on Michael's jeans.

"You two clean up your own messes. I'm getting dressed and answering the door," I instructed, quickly grabbing my clothes. "One sec!" I called toward the door.

Jack disappeared into the kitchen, and Michael jogged upstairs. I knew they were both nervous about seeing Emily. Jack reappeared with paper towels and a cleaning solution.

"For the record"—I eyed him as I shrugged on my shirt—"I would lick your cum off anything."

I gave him a crooked smile as he looked up at me with widened, hungry eyes.

"Fuck, I love you, Hana Maynor," he sighed as he cleaned up his mess.

I waited until he went back into the kitchen to answer the door. There was my beautiful cousin, her dark-blonde hair long and wavy, flashing me her dimples. The air was starting to warm with the sun shining down brightly, and a lump formed in my throat as I looked at Emily. As much as I loved Jack and Michael, Emily felt like home.

"Emily." I quickly wrapped my arms around her and began to weep onto her shoulder.

"Hana," Emily responded, squeezing me tight.

It took a while for me to stop crying. I felt some sort of

cathartic relief crying in her arms. I felt like I was truly, finally free.

"I'm sorry. Everything is okay. I just missed you," I said as I let go of her, wiping the tears from my eyes. "Come in."

I guided her in just as Michael walked down the stairs; Jack was nowhere to be seen.

"Emily," Michael greeted her stiffly as he walked into the kitchen.

Emily shook her head at him with confusion. "Michael." She looked to me and frowned. "What's up with him?"

I closed the door behind us. "We had sort of a disagreement before you got here," I explained, taking a seat at the armchair.

Emily laughed as she sat on the couch. "Trouble in paradise already?"

I sighed heavily and gave her a small smile. I wanted to talk candidly without worrying about the guys overhearing me.

"Actually, let's go take a walk. It's so nice out." I stood. "Boys! We're taking a walk! Don't kill each other while I'm gone!" I called as I slid on my Nikes.

Michael rushed out of the kitchen, and Jack stood at the top of the stairs.

"Hana. Take your phone, please," Jack instructed, being polite in front of our company.

I frowned at him; I knew he wanted to know where I was, and my phone could easily tell him that. I knew they both weren't 100% certain that I wouldn't leave. I decided to humor them and grabbed my phone off the kitchen table.

I eyed the both of them as Emily and I walked out the front door. "Don't worry. I'm coming back."

Jack

My anger began boiling over the moment Hana walked out the door with Emily. It wasn't directed at her, though; it was at Michael. He acted as if he knew her better than me. Now we were finally alone without Hana stopping us from saying or doing whatever the fuck we wanted to each other.

I stealthily followed Michael into the kitchen, hoping he wouldn't notice me behind him. I didn't have a plan, I just wanted him to know that I wasn't fucking around, that Hana was mine and I was so happily obliging only because I loved her so much.

"You're cooking," I observed. "What can't the amazing and perfect Michael do?"

He slowly turned to look at me. I leaned against the opposite counter, my arms crossed as I glared at him.

He grinned before looking back at whatever he was stirring. "I can't convince the love of my life to leave the fucking psychotic twit she married," he responded sharply.

I let out a fake laugh. The nerve of this fucker. "You're never going to convince her of that, my friend. She would rather die than live without me."

"Yeah, because you've brainwashed her. She was going to marry me and then you fucking stole her from me. If this were a game, that'd be considered cheating." He ignored his food as he pointed a wooden spoon at me.

"It *is* a game, and I've won." I grinned at him, waiting for him to try something.

I bet he didn't even know how to fight, the fucking pretentious arsehole. I wanted him to try me.

"You fucking *kidnapped* her. That's not winning," he spit out, inching closer to me.

I still had the grin plastered on my face. It was fun prodding him on. I shrugged like I didn't know what he was talking about; I really wouldn't consider it kidnapping if she fell in love with me.

"And she still stayed. Then begged for me to come find and rescue her from her demented Prince Charming." I had my hands in a fist on my sides, ready to take him.

Michael was finally right in front of me, obviously fuming with anger.

"What, you want to fight me?" I raised my eyebrows at him.

"That wouldn't be a fair fight. I could easily kill you."

I chuckled then quickly raised my left fist and punched him right in the eye at full force. He lost his footing and bumped into the counter behind him.

"That's for when you stole her from me the first time," I spat out, adrenaline coursing through my veins.

Something flickered in his eyes, a darkness I hadn't seen before. Maybe he did have it in him after all. He suddenly barged forward and tackled me into the cabinets behind me, glass shattering to the floor as his fists pounded into my ribs. I was able to get away, ducking underneath his arm. I spun around and took my arm to his neck, putting him in a chokehold.

"Listen to me, Michael," I growled out into his ear. "You have no idea what I'm capable of. You think you're so fucking tough? Just try insulting me again, and I'll show you what I can do."

I let go, and Michael gasped for air, reaching for the counter.

"Hana is *mine*. I'm only sharing her because if I don't, she will end her life. Don't you fucking believe for one second that I'm weaker than you because I'm compliant. If anything, it's because I care about her more than you do," I spat out.

Michael didn't look back at me. He gripped the counter, his head hung low. Then the fucking psychopath started laughing.

"What's so fucking funny, you nimwit?" I asked with annoyance.

"You think Hana is yours because you forced her to marry you? Because you're fucking *compliant*? No." He turned around, glaring at me. "No, Jack. Hana is not yours and she never has been. She's been mine this whole time and you wanna know how I know?"

I narrowed my eyes at him. I wanted to hear what this delusional fuck really thought.

"She fucking salivates when she looks at me. She hangs onto my every word as if I were a fucking god. I know for a fact she doesn't look at you the same way." He smiled smugly, his right eye starting to swell and hints of blood on his lip.

I chuckled. "If that's what you need to tell yourself, mate. Might wanna clean yourself up a bit before the girls get back." I waved him off as I walked out of the kitchen.

I barged up the stairs into the room that we all three somehow ended up sharing and punched my already raw fist into the wall. He somehow knew how to get under my skin, figuring out my biggest insecurity: the fear that I wasn't as good as him. Hana could tell me she loved me all she wanted, but Michael was right. Hana practically had stars in her eyes while looking at him. I needed to figure out how to show her he wasn't perfect. I needed to find his biggest weakness and tear him down with it.

Emily

Hana sighed heavily as we walked down the tree-lined street through the neighborhood. The sun shone down on us brightly, and I noticed our feet walking lazily in sync. The late April afternoon was perfect, sixty-three degrees with no clouds in sight. The birds were chirping overhead, and I realized how different our hometown was from the city. There were no assholes bumping into us on the sidewalk and you could walk down the street without having to step around trash. I looked over at Hana as she smiled down at the sidewalk in front of us; I hadn't seen her so carefree in such a long time. Her long, blonde, wavy hair was drying in the sunshine as she flipped it over her shoulder to look at me.

"I have a lot to tell you," she said, a hint of a smile on her face.

I let out a laugh. "Um, no shit," I scoffed. "First, I need to know: Were you really with Jack this whole time? And what the fuck did Michael do to you, because I swear to God I will fight him."

Hana laughed and shook her head. I couldn't believe how nonchalant she was being about this.

"Um...Jack and I...it's complicated. Everything I told you before, at that hotel in Jersey, was true. But...he's so different now. And I am...*obsessed* with him." She stopped walking as she spoke, her hands in her zip-up hoodie pockets.

My heart sunk to the concrete under my shoes. "Hana," I scolded, shaking my head at her. "He *took* you. He...did some unimaginable things to you. Why in the hell are you *obsessed* with him?" I couldn't understand how she could go from terrified of him to absolutely in love with him.

She shook her head back at me, chewing the sides of her cheek. "I don't expect you to understand, Em. I just really want you back in my life, and if you want answers, I'm gonna give them to you whether you like them or not."

I started to tear up. I didn't know if I could ignore their past. "And what about Michael? Did *he* fucking kidnap you too?"

Hana sighed heavily. "Yes. He was desperate. And then I became desperate too," she started, averting her eyes.

"Please explain, Hana," I begged.

"Remember, Em. Don't ask questions you don't want to know the answers to." She eyed me, her eyes full of hesitation.

I nodded, bracing myself for all of the horrifying details I'd surely be hearing.

"And please know...I know none of this makes sense. I know how this all sounds. If I were in your shoes, I'd be just as concerned as you are. I *know* that. But listen to all of this knowing that *I* know all of this, and yet I can't walk away from these two. Even if I could, I would never leave either of them."

Her words came out so quickly that they could barely sink in before she spoke again. Her hands were shaking as she spoke.

"Michael brought me here with the intention of keeping me here. And then I got the chance to talk to you and Jack, and I knew what I had to do. Neither of them would ever let me make my own decisions if I didn't threaten them with this," she started.

I shook my head at her again, and my brows pulled together. "Threaten them with what?"

She surveyed my face before answering. "I threatened to take my life. That's the only way I was going to get out of any of this. And then I realized that they were capable of sharing me. I guess I didn't even get to that part." She laughed, shaking her head. "Before I threatened them, I had sex with them. At the same time. And it was fucking *incredible*, Emily. I knew that I needed both of them. So I told them: You either share me, or you don't get me at all."

I was speechless. Was this another one of her ploys to convince me that everything was okay, but things really weren't?

"This is the truth, Emily. I'm not gonna lie to you anymore," she explained, somehow reading my mind.

A huge, involuntary smile washed over my face. "Hana. This is fucking nuts." My immediate thought shot out of my mouth before I could stop it.

Hana frowned and started to walk away. "I know that, Emily. I told you it didn't make any sense. But this is my life now." She shrugged, eyeing me from over her shoulder as I struggled to catch up with her.

"Hey, Han." I grabbed her arm to stop her from walking.

She turned to me with tears in her eyes. "My life is an absolute mess, Emily. It's fucking chaotic, but I'm somehow happier than I've been in a long time," she explained, talking with her hands.

I nodded, taking her hand. I didn't understand any of this; I didn't understand why she wanted to be with these men that dominated her, that took away her free will, that threatened her life. I was afraid to question it any more, though, because I didn't want another fight. I didn't want to hear anymore but I didn't want to lose her again.

"I'm your family, Hana. I won't judge you. I just need to know that you'll be okay."

She nodded, squeezing my hand with hers. "As okay as I'll ever be."

Michael

Jack knew what he was doing when he picked a fight with me. He knew how to fight, I'd give him that. I had to stop myself from lunging toward him again and beating him senseless. I could've killed him, but that meant risking Hana's life, so I had to be smart. I could tear him down in other ways. For example, stating the obvious: Hana was mine. Her body couldn't resist me, even if she wanted to. She didn't look at Jack the same way she looked at me. Granted, I hated the way she looked at him with that lust in her eyes, but it wasn't nearly as much lust as she looked at me with. She wanted me so badly she fucking came just by pressing her pussy against me. She could be a brat all she wanted, but at the end of the day, she was fucking crazy about me.

I spent the last seven weeks of my life doubting myself. Any confidence I had was crumbling beneath me. Hell, I lost most of it the day she first left all those months ago. And I spent so much time hating Hana, wanting her to hurt as much as I did. That's when something in me changed. I became obsessive. I teetered between loving her and hating her, my feelings for her changing daily. And of course, I began stalking her.

It started when I began watching her and Jack at his loft. I would sit for hours on the street in the Lower East Side, waiting for a glimpse of her. I watched as they went apartment hunting in Brooklyn. That's why I got the apartment I have now—it's right across the street from where Hana and Jack live. I would sit on the benches by the waterfront for hours, watching Hana come and go, sometimes with Jack, sometimes without. I didn't have any plan; I just wanted to watch her, see where she went, see how she lived her life without me. I got on Instagram, following her from a fake profile. I watched every story she posted. She often shared views from her apartment, which I didn't think was very smart. If someone wanted to find her, they easily could. Sometimes I wondered if she did that for me, as if she knew I was quietly watching her. Was she waiting for me to come capture her?

And that's when I got the video of Hana and Jack having sex. I might have jerked off while watching it—several times—but I figured it was because I was seeing Hana be demeaned in a way I wanted to do with her. It stirred up so many feelings inside of me, but I mostly felt hate. I took to my best friend, Jack Daniels, and watched the video over and over. I might have even called Emily, drunkenly telling her how I felt, but that might have also been a dream. I knew I needed to do something, but I couldn't figure out what.

I saw Emily following Hana and Jack to the OB-GYN office. She was not a very good stalker; she kept too close and she didn't even see me. It didn't occur to me to look up what building they were in, but when Emily called me and told me, I finally knew what I had to do: I had to take Hana.

She might have been carrying my child. It was a long shot, but it was a possibility. And on the day I took her, so easily guiding her into the cab that waited for us, I realized I loved her more than anything. How could I possibly hate this beautiful creature, especially if she was going to bear my child? I had spent the last several weeks watching her from a distance, hating her. But when I was finally face to face with her, I was so fucking in love again. That's what she did to me. And she was so fucking compliant. I think that's what startled me when she began to resist me at the Greenwich house. I was so used to getting my way with her and then it was as if a whole new aspect of her personality had taken over. I enjoyed the brattiness on occasion, but I knew it was because she wanted to get punished. Ever since finding out she liked to be slapped, I knew I had to use it on her. When she kept resisting me, not even willing to fuck me? *That's* what threw me over the edge.

I didn't want to think about what happened after that. Anger had taken over me. It had been a long time since that anger had consumed me. I had warned her, a long time ago, that my anger could control me. I was out of control, even I knew that. It had happened before. But I waited and waited for the safe word. It never came. It didn't even occur to me that she couldn't let out her safe word until Jack talked about me forcing myself upon her. What did she think of me now?

My thoughts returned to the present. How was I ever going to be happy sharing Hana, the woman who was perfect just for me? I started fantasizing about hiring someone to kill Jack, some sort of random mugging in his sketchy LES neighborhood that he still frequented. I would plan it all perfectly: I would be with Hana so that she could be my alibi. She would be heartbroken but she'd have me to take care of her. *Only* me.

Hana

Emily was silent on the walk back to the house. Maybe I shouldn't have told her the truth about what Jack and Michael did to me. It wasn't her burden to carry. It just felt imperative to reveal what led me to this, what had made me so desperate. I began to question if any of this was worth it. Michael kept pushing back against the entire situation. I knew it was unfair. I understood why he was so unwilling. He was so much more stubborn than Jack. Jack would die for me; I wasn't sure if Michael would. Was that how I measured their love? It was twisted and toxic and wildly unhealthy, and isn't that what led me to this entire situation? I was so far beyond having Stockholm Syndrome—I was fanatical. I drank the punch and jumped over the cliff with both of them.

When we walked into the house, Michael was sweeping up glass in the kitchen. The cabinet glass was shattered, and kitchenware was strewn everywhere.

"Where's Jack?" I asked frantically.

As I walked closer to Michael, I realized he was sporting a swollen right eye. He looked up at me through his lashes, as if he were disappointed in me.

"He's upstairs, probably icing the knuckles he used to punch me with." His tone was understandably irritated and short.

I raised my eyebrows at him in shock. *"He* did all of this?" I pointed to the mess around us.

Michael set the broom aside and crossed his arms. "In part. Are you surprised? Aren't you going to ask if I'm okay? Don't you see this fucking bruised eye that I can barely see out of?"

I shook my head as I walked closer to him. I put my hand to his face and observed his swollen eye; even with the bruise he was still beautiful. "I'm sorry," I whispered.

Emily cleared her throat. "I'll give you guys some space."

I turned as she walked out of the kitchen. Michael took my hand and kissed the top of my fingers, pulling me back into his gaze.

"Are you okay? What happened?"

He shook his head, disgust clear on his face. "He walked in here just to pick a fight with me. He sure does talk a lot of shit. I can see why he has such an extensive criminal history." He twirled my hair casually as if we were talking about what we were making for dinner.

I scoffed. Would this be a common occurrence? Would I have to worry whenever I'm not in their presence? I told them not to touch each other if they were going to hurt each other; Jack had broken the rules.

"Well, what did he say?" I prodded.

Michael sighed. "Nothing you don't already know."

I sighed heavily as I shook my head. "I need to go talk to him." I turned on my heels before Michael could respond, but I heard him muttering angrily under his breath.

I walked into our room to find Jack sitting on the bed, looking down at his phone. There was a hole in the wall next to the bathroom door—had he done that?

"Jack," I said quietly as I shut the door behind me.

"I'm sorry, Hana. I'm sorry I hit him. I couldn't help myself." Jack looked up at me, his jaw clenched and his wide blue eyes full of regret. "Please don't hurt yourself."

He stood and wrapped his arms around me snugly, his chest heaving up and down as he started to cry. Fuck, this was taking a toll on everyone. Probably on Jack the most.

"I won't, baby. I won't," I assured him, rubbing his back as I held him.

"I just need you, Hana. I need you, please don't leave." He sobbed.

I continued to calm him down, reassuring him that I forgave him and that I wouldn't leave him. Of course I would never leave him; I already knew that he would die without me. If I took my own life, so would he. And I think it was the same for me.

We softly pressed our lips together just before there was a knock at the door. I sighed as we parted and opened the door. Emily looked concerned as she eyed both of us.

"Is everything okay?" she pried, clearly eyeing the hole in the wall.

I nodded. "Yeah. I think Michael is making dinner. Should we all go downstairs?" I glanced at Jack. His eyes hardened at Emily; he was probably upset at her interrupting us.

"Yes, let's." Jack suddenly smiled. Of course it wasn't his real smile, it was a vicious smile he had saved for people he didn't like. Emily gave him the very same one.

I grabbed Jack's hand, and we all headed downstairs, the smell of something delicious filling the air. Michael had the table set, and the kitchen was now sparkly clean apart from the busted cabinets without glass in them. Emily sat at the table and pulled her phone out as Jack and I walked into the kitchen.

"Ah, there's my love. And fucking Jack the ripper." Michael glared at Jack as he held out a plate for me.

I cleared my throat. "Jack's sorry he hit you. Right, babe?" I turned to Jack.

This felt so juvenile but it needed to be done.

Jack glared right back at Michael. "I sure am." He smiled half-heartedly.

You could cut the tension in the room with a knife. Ironically, I could see the butcher's knife sitting on the counter near the fridge.

Michael clenched his jaw and turned to me. "Let's eat."

Dinner was awkward. Emily and I chatted, trying to drag Michael and Jack into the conversation, but they were quiet. Jack kept playing with his phone, and Michael finished eating quickly then went into the kitchen to start dishes.

Jack looked over at me and smiled once he was gone. "Do I get my hour soon?" he asked almost mockingly.

Emily turned and looked at me.

"Yes." I nodded.

"I'm sure I don't want to know." She laughed to herself.

Jack kept his eyes on me then winked. My heart dropped to my knees. I was so in love with him. I was starting to wonder—but trying my best not to think of it—what if I loved him more than Michael?

* * *

Emily and I took another walk after dinner while the sun was setting. Jack went to turn in the rental car that he drove to Greenwich, so I wasn't worried about them being alone again.

HANA

I hugged myself as the air started to get crisp and looked down at the cement as we passed houses on the same route we took before.

"So," Emily started. She seemed hesitant to speak. "You really think this is going to work out?"

I bit my lip as we continued to walk. I didn't want to look at her—I wasn't so certain anymore. How could they ever *not* hate each other? There was so much history, so much resentment. I was also scared of what Michael could do to Jack. Seeing Michael's angry side frightened me, and I could tell he was holding back a lot of his enmity while we were all together. Would he snap? Would Jack? Jack was so passionate and impulsive—what if he threw another punch?

I sighed before I answered. "I don't know. I'm hopeful, though." I shrugged as I looked at her.

Emily eyed me warily. She looked terrified, like she wanted to tell me to run. She was holding back her true emotions as well, something she didn't usually do.

"Well, you already know this is all fucking crazy," she started. *Ah, there she is.* "But I want you to make your own decisions, Han. And please just…please be careful." Her face was worried and torn.

I nodded. I knew what she meant. "Are you sure you don't want to stay? We can all go back in the morning." I was trying to change the subject.

Emily laughed. "Yeah. It's too fucking awkward being in that house. No offense." She put her hand to my shoulder.

"As an outsider…I'm sure it is."

We continued our walk until the stars were twinkling above us. We reminisced about our wild teenage years, roaming the streets of Greenwich, throwing crazy house parties that our parents somehow never found out about. I was laughing and starting to feel more like *me* again. And for the first time in a long time, I was starting to like myself.

Hana

Our Uber arrived the next day, and we all three squeezed into the backseat of the SUV.

"One of you can sit up here if you'd like," the kind Uber driver suggested as he glanced back at us.

"No," Jack and Michael answered in unison.

I rolled my eyes to myself. We were off to a good start.

"So…we're going to mine and Jack's apartment. And then what?" I asked, as if they were the ones still making decisions.

"We can stay at my apartment. There's three bedrooms. One for each of us," Michael answered as he put his hand on my bare thigh, slyly pulling up my dress an inch. It sent an electric jolt throughout my entire body; my desire for him seemed to double ever since he so kindly and forcefully reunited us.

I nodded and put my hand on top of his. I reached for Jack's thigh and squeezed it, glancing over at him with a smile. I knew he needed constant reassurance with this arrangement.

"Where's your apartment?" I asked curiously.

Michael sighed a little and put his hand to his beard. "It's… it's across the street from yours."

My eyes bulged. I shouldn't have been shocked, but I was.

Jack started chuckling to himself. "Why do you attract so many men that stalk you, Hana?" he jested.

I ignored Jack. "So...you knew where we lived this whole time?" I asked Michael quietly.

He nodded and bit his lip as if he were ashamed.

My mind started to race. *Why didn't he ever approach me? Why didn't he try to take me earlier?*

"I was waiting for the right opportunity to approach you. I guess the video sort of pushed me into action," he responded ominously.

All I could do was nod; I really had pushed Michael to the edge.

"What about the Chelsea condo?"

He shook his head. "It's sold. I didn't want to live there alone." His voice was quiet and somber.

I put my head on his shoulder after a moment, my heart breaking all over again. I wondered how our life would look if Jack had never taken me. We would have been getting married soon; maybe I would have had a bachelorette party. Would I have still thought about Jack? Would I have kept wondering what my life would have been like with him? And what if I did choose Jack over Michael before—what would our lives look like then?

Jack didn't give my thoughts any more time to continue spiraling; his hand began to caress my thigh, his strong grip squeezing my flesh. My nipples hardened as I looked over at him with a devious smile, wanting him to know how much I wanted him. He stared at me, his eyes wide with lust, as he slowly continued to make his way up higher on my leg, digging his hand between my thighs. I quickly gasped as he moved my thong to the side and stuck his middle finger inside of me, the slickness of my pussy guiding him easily. Michael tugged my head back with his hand, forcing me to look at him. He had the same eager, lustful look in his eyes as Jack. I quickly pressed my lips to his; the urgency forced a quiet moan from my throat as we passionately made out, his tongue swirling around mine, and his teeth biting softly onto my lip. Jack continued to move his finger inside of me, slipping another finger in, his palm causing friction against my clit. I was wholly aware that there was an Uber driver in the front seat of the car and that somehow made what they were doing even hotter.

"Come on, sweetheart. Come on my fingers and clench that perfect pussy around them," Jack whispered in my ear, gently grazing his lips against my earlobe.

I had to part my lips from Michael's—I was about to come and I needed to bite my lip to muffle the inevitable moan I would let out. I looked down at Jack's hand discreetly under my dress and bit my lip as I gently grinded against him, my orgasm close. Suddenly, Michael had his hand up my dress, grabbing my bare breast and using his fingers to tease my nipple.

"Fuck," I whispered, then released a quick gasp as I grinded against Jack's hand, my orgasm exploding onto his fingers as my pussy clenched around them.

"Good girl, my dirty fucking wife," Jack whispered in my ear. He released his fingers from me and brought them up to his mouth, gently tasting my wetness.

"Come on then. Our turn, baby," Michael said into my ear.

I looked down and realized his hard cock was popping out of his pants.

Jack chuckled. "I like the way he thinks," he said quietly as he pulled his hard cock out as well and started to stroke himself.

I looked up at the Uber driver, and he seemed completely

unaware—unless he was hiding it well. I glanced down at Michael's cock then Jack's as I spit into my hands and took them both in each hand. Feeling their warm, hard cocks in my hands somehow made me feel powerful and in control. I did this to them, and I knew I could make them come just like that. I began to stroke each of them slowly, working my way to a steady rhythm, my pussy dripping wet again. It was rare that I had their cocks in my hand; usually they were either shoved down my throat or inside of me, so this felt new and painfully sexy.

"Come on, baby. Come in my hand so I can lick it clean," I whispered in Michael's ear.

I turned to Jack and grazed my lips against his ear. "I know you love watching these cocks in my hands, Jack. You fucking pervert. Come for me so I can taste how badly you want me."

Suddenly, Jack pumped his hips quickly up and down and let out a small grunt, his load shooting around my hand as I continued to stroke, wanting every last drop of it on me. I felt Michael doing the same and looked down at his cock as he covered his load with his hand, most of his cum shooting out and dropping back onto his cock. I smiled as I brought each of my hands to my mouth, licking their cum off my fingers and turning to each of them as I did so.

"There's more here, baby. Wipe me clean," Michael whispered, putting his palm to my mouth.

I tasted his warm, salty cum and smiled.

"That's my good girl," he grinned at me.

"I love any way you make me come, sweetheart. But I need to be inside of you the second we walk into the apartment," Jack whispered in my ear.

I bit my lip to refrain the huge grin that would give away

just how badly I wanted the same.

"I'm gonna pound my good girl so hard, baby," Michael continued in my ear.

I grinded against the seat beneath me, their words turning me on even more, and I wondered how the hell any of us were going to get anything done. All we wanted to do was fuck. Was that even a problem? Maybe the more we all had sex, the closer Michael and Jack would get. Or would that cause even more competition, more arguments? There had to be a way for them to unite…I just needed to figure out how.

* * *

It almost felt eerie that Michael was walking into our apartment with us. I never imagined he would be in this apartment, yet all this time he was directly across the street. I wondered how many times he saw me walking out of the building alone, wandering around Williamsburg with no real destination. I wonder what he felt when he saw Jack and I exit, hand in hand. Did he see us the night that Jack pushed me against the building as we made out? Did he watch me when I watched the sunset from the waterfront, hugging myself in the cold? Or all the times Jack and I watched it together, Jack holding me from behind and pressing his lips to my neck?

I turned to look at Michael as we walked down the hallway and into the kitchen and living room area.

"Um…make yourself comfortable. I'm just gonna pack some clothes and the necessities for now." I took his hand and smiled, waiting for a reaction from him.

His eyes were emotionless as he scanned the living room, stopping at a framed picture of me and Jack from the day we got married. He let go of my hand and walked up to grab it, examining it like it were a piece of art.

"Why would you want to display this when you were coerced into marrying him?" he asked me sullenly.

I quickly looked to see if Jack was around; he had gone into our room, I assume to look for suitcases.

"It was coercion at first, Michael. But it turned into something real," I answered, knowing how crazy that sounded.

Michael snorted and set down the picture.

"Does he still have the gun?" he asked me quietly as he looked across my shoulder, as if to watch for Jack.

I knew he did. It was in the safe, locked away from me. I nodded as I looked down to the floor.

"Don't let him bring that. He could shoot me in my sleep," he hissed with indignation.

I feared that would be true. "Wait here," I instructed before walking down the hallway and into our bedroom. I found Jack with the safe open, two suitcases on the bed with his clothes thrown in and his laptop beside it. I walked closer to the safe to see if anything was still in there. There wasn't.

"Jack," I started gently. "Please don't bring the gun."

He stopped at his dresser and eyed me. "I'm bringing it for protection, Hana. I won't use it unprompted."

I sighed heavily. "Jack," I started to argue.

Jack grabbed my arm and turned me toward him; my heart dropped as he glared at me, anger clear in his eyes.

"Hana, you're lucky we're doing this at all. I'm not going there unless I feel we're safe," he hissed.

Tears started welling in my eyes. "If you take it, you have to tell me where you keep it," I argued, courage taking ahold of me. "And you better fucking remember *why* you're doing this."

Jack's eyes went from angry to confused and then bolted right back to angry again. He took my face with his hand then quickly grazed it down to my throat.

"Don't abuse your power, love. You better fucking remember who you're talking to." He squeezed hard before he let me go, and I gasped for air.

It took everything inside me not to fight back. He had no idea how much I had changed in the last week. I was not his property anymore; in fact, if anything, he was mine.

I stormed back into the living room where Michael sat on the couch with his phone in his hand. He eyed me as I walked into the kitchen to grab a glass of wine to calm down.

"Hana." Michael approached me from behind.

My hands shook as I poured my Merlot, adrenaline still coursing through me. Michael put his hands to my shoulders, seemingly trying to soothe me.

"Hana, you know this isn't a good idea. Drinking can—"

"Please, stop. I drink all the time." I shook my head as I set down the bottle and put the glass to my lips.

He sighed behind me. "*All* the time, Hana?"

I rolled my eyes before I turned around to face him. "Not *all* the time. Sometimes. What does it matter anyway? Clearly I've been doing something right." I shrugged, ready for an argument.

The concern was clear on Michael's face. My heart dropped at the way he was looking at me, the way he used to—the way he did when all he wanted was to protect me.

"Hana," he whispered, putting his hand to my cheek. "I love you. I'm going to take care of you now. I'm not going to let Jack continue to be a bad influence on you."

Jack *was* a bad influence on me. He poured me glasses of wine at night as we talked until the sun came up. He didn't care if I took my meds or went to therapy. He didn't notice when I wouldn't eat all day while reading a whole book in one sitting. He did, however, let me make all those decisions myself, whether they were unhealthy or not.

Michael watched me closely. He took my hand and kissed the top of my knuckles softly, pulling me closer to him.

"Let him pack. Come back to my place with me."

Before I could answer, Jack startled us by throwing down his suitcase on the hardwood floor in the living room.

"She's not going anywhere without me," he huffed.

I turned and saw the fire in Jack's eyes. There I was standing with my "perfect" Michael and my "scary" Jack. Oh, how they could so easily change between their personalities.

"Yeah, maybe it's better we all go together," I suggested. "I think we still need to establish some trust."

Michael snorted. "That's an understatement."

I sighed heavily as I looked between the two of them. "Michael, if you're not welcoming *both* of us into your apartment, we're not going. We definitely haven't started on the right foot," I said with my head held high.

I needed to at least pretend I had some confidence and faith in this relationship we were all building.

"Come on then, sweetheart. Let's continue to pack your bag," Jack said sweetly, holding his hand out for me.

I tensed as I took Jack's hand and let him lead me to our bedroom. I glanced back to look at Michael, his glare burning holes through Jack's head. I looked away, realizing deep down in my heart that this was never going to work.

Hana

Michael's apartment was insanely gorgeous. We all three walked in, and I gasped when I saw his two-story, floor-to-ceiling windows displaying a perfect view of Manhattan, the city lights twinkling under the night sky. Walking in further, I noticed the beautiful kitchen to my right, its white marble countertops sparkling clean, and the built-in appliances looking untouched. An electric fireplace stood in front of the living room couch that was adjacent to the kitchen, and behind that were stairs. The living room and kitchen looked like a model home the way the Greenwich house did.

"Upstairs are three rooms. There's a lovely patio out there as well. I would love to have a drink with you up there." Michael eyed me with a smile.

A drink, after he just lectured me? I didn't care; I smiled with a nod as he took my hand and led me up the stairs. I looked at Jack as he walked toward the windows, admiring the beautiful view.

"Sure, I'll just make myself comfortable," he called sarcastically.

I frowned down at Jack while Michael ignored him and guided me carefully up the modern wooden stairs.

At the top of the stairs, there was a hallway that split; one side led to a glass door to the patio and the other side led to all of the rooms. Michael gave me a brief tour of the rooms before hauling me out to the patio. The weather was starting to get warmer, but the nighttime still held a chill. I stared wide-eyed at the Manhattan skyline, the view not much different than the one from mine and Jack's place. Michael stood behind me and wrapped his arms around me, breathing in my hair.

"What I really want is to bend you over and make you scream for all of our neighbors to hear," he said quietly into my ear, his voice deep and smooth.

I giggled to myself. He could so easily make me feel like a teenage girl with her first crush. "I would love that, sir," I breathed out.

Suddenly, Michael's hands were to my waist, pulling my dress up before he quickly pushed down my underwear and slipped his finger inside of me. I gasped as his strong hand gripped my pussy, and he quickly pulled away.

"You're dripping wet for me, baby. Let's see how many times I can make you come," he said into my ear. Then I felt his thick, long cock thrust inside of me, forcing me to moan loudly.

I was desperate to be filled after only having hands inside of me earlier; I backed my ass toward Michael's hips, pushing myself onto him. His hand gripped my hair and pulled hard.

"So fucking greedy as usual, Hana," he scolded me, pounding me harder.

I let out a scream as he furiously pumped in and out of me, his length feeling like it would split me in half. Michael's hand reached for my clit and began to tease it as he pumped hard and quick. I closed my eyes as my body melted and released its much needed orgasm.

"Oh my fucking God," I screamed loudly, chasing another

orgasm as he continued his speed, his finger slipping around my wetness.

"That's right. I'm your fucking God," Michael growled.

I came again as I clenched the glass patio wall, almost afraid it would break with the way Michael continued to pound me.

Michael grunted as he let go of my hair and slammed into me, spilling his cum inside of me. It dripped down my thighs as he started to slow and took my face, turning it toward him.

"You're mine, Hana," he said before pressing his lips to mine, an eager kiss that almost felt like a plea.

"Yes," I whispered back.

Michael smirked. "Come on. Let's go christen the shower."

* * *

After mine and Michael's shower, I found Jack working and sulking in the room that he had claimed as his. He watched as I untied my robe and dropped it to the floor. I had come so many times already, but I needed Jack inside of me. I longed for his touch, for the look he gave me as he pounded me senseless.

"Are you trying to seduce me?" he asked from his bed, setting his laptop aside.

I nodded and smiled, slowly walking toward him. His eyes were wide as he stared me up and down, eagerly unzipping his jeans and moving to sit on the edge of the bed. I straddled him, his hard cock underneath me and his boxer briefs the only thing between us. I began to move my hips and run my hands through his hair, unable to take my eyes off him. I stared at his pouty lips and pressed mine against them, gently biting down. He moaned as he ran his hands around my ass, helping me move my hips.

He parted our lips. "Hana," he breathed out in his deep, sexy voice.

"Jack," I moaned.

"I love you so fucking much. I need you." He quickly pulled his boxer briefs down and shoved himself inside me, the slickness easily guiding his thrusts.

"I love you, Jack," I cried out. "I need to come all over your cock." My eyes fluttered shut as I let my head hang backward.

Jack chuckled before he put his finger to my mouth. Instinctively, I wrapped my lips around it and began to suck. He quickly released his finger and lowered his hand to my ass, sticking his finger inside and driving it in and out. The movement of Jack's cock pumping in and out of me with the added pleasure of his finger inside my ass instantly made my pussy pulse with pleasure, my orgasms coming one after the other.

"Oh fuck, baby," I gasped. "Your cock is so fucking perfect."

I knew praising him would send him over the edge—with Michael now in the picture, he needed perpetual reassurance.

"Fuck, Hana." He grunted as he came inside me, our bodies sweaty and clinging to each other.

We caught our breath as he slowed his hips, never once parting his eyes from mine.

"You are my life, sweetheart. I will never get enough of you." He gently caressed his fingertips across my lips. "Please sleep with me tonight. Just me," he begged, his lustful eyes turning desperate in a panicked plea.

Fuck. My sweet Jack. He was showing his vulnerable, gentle side constantly now. I think his self-doubt had doubled now that Michael was in our lives.

With him still inside of me, I nodded and took his face with my hands.

"Okay, baby. I will." I nodded, my tone almost sympathetic.

He began to move his hips again, and I could feel him get harder inside of me. He grinned deviously and threw me onto my back, never once parting from me as he hovered over me.

"Since I have you all night, I plan to fuck you until you can't walk straight," he teased, his sultry, low voice sending a tingle throughout my body.

I nodded, my breath quickening as he took my arms with his hands and held them down onto the bed.

"My sweet, dirty, slutty wife." He grinned. "Time to fuck you like the whore you are."

Jack

I was starting to lose it. I could feel the desperation butting its head in again, the urge to steal Hana away and make her all mine once more so overwhelming. How was I going to do this without her hurting herself? That was what was tearing me apart. I needed her to be all mine, but she wouldn't allow it anymore. And there was no way I couldn't *not* have her. I needed to get Michael out of the picture for good. I needed him to do something so terrible, so unimaginable, that she would never forgive him.

My trusty sister, Jessica, was good at investigating. She was my own personal Sherlock Holmes. I knew she would be able to dig into Michael's past and find something I could use against him. I called her that night while Hana slept in her room. Of course, she demanded that both Michael and I sleep with her, but I just couldn't get my eyes to stay closed. It was getting harder and harder to be in the same room as him.

"Brother," Jessica answered, sounding surprised.

"Jess. I need you to do some investigating," I whispered as I stood in "my" room, the guest room that held my suitcase.

"It's so nice to hear from you too, my sweet brother. Oh, I'm so glad you're asking how I've been doing and telling me how much you miss me!" Jessica retorted, sarcasm dripping in her tone.

I sighed. "I don't have time for that, Jess. This is urgent."

"Why? What's wrong? Is Hana okay?" Jess perked up; she loved Hana and they had miraculously gotten close during the last several weeks.

"Yes. I can't explain, though. I need you to find out some shit about Michael. I don't care what it is, just find out everything you can. I want to tear him apart," I hissed, my anger already boiling over.

Jessica sighed. "Right. I'll do this. It's for Hana's benefit, right? I don't want to wrong her anymore, Jack."

I rolled my eyes. "Yes, Jessica. Trust me."

She was quiet for a moment. "Okay. I'll do it. I'll get back to you tomorrow."

* * *

I didn't sleep at all that night. I was too wired and angry to sleep. I held Hana close to me as we lay in bed; she tossed and turned, and I kept adjusting my hold.

As the sun rose and Hana started to stir awake, I put my hand to her face and kissed her shoulder gently. She smiled as she blinked open her eyes; she had the most beautiful face I had ever seen with her gorgeous cheek bones and that fucking mouth of hers. My favorite thing about her was her eyes. I had memorized the way she looked up at me while my cock was in her mouth. I suddenly had the epiphany that I should paint it. I was starting to get hard as I grazed my fingers across her smooth skin, over her collar bone, and down to her breasts. Thank God she slept naked. I couldn't help but put my mouth to her nipple, licking my way around it as it perked up beneath my tongue.

She began to moan, and Michael started to stir awake too. *Fuck, I almost forgot he was here.* I ignored him as I trailed my fingers down to Hana's pussy, not hesitating to put a finger inside her wet, warm slit.

"Fuck yes, baby," she whispered, her eyes closed as I stared up at her, my mouth still grazing her nipple.

She ran her hands through my hair as I slid another finger inside of her, then another, prepping her for the way I was going to slam inside of her.

Michael's hand reached to Hana's other breast as he mirrored me, flicking Hana's nipple with his tongue. His hand slid down to her pussy too, rubbing her clit above my fingers and enticing another loud moan from her.

"Fuck, I'm gonna come," she breathed out before she let out a whimper and her pussy clenched around my fingers. She rolled her hips up and down slowly.

"Again," I ordered as I bit her nipple softly then dug my teeth into her.

"Ow! Fuck!" she moaned, and I felt her pussy clench again. I let out a soft chuckle; she loved pain and I loved giving it to her.

"Wait, wait—" she breathed out, sitting up and putting her hand to both mine and Michael's faces. "I want you two to be together."

I froze. "What?" I immediately questioned. *What the fuck?* There's no way she was asking for what I thought she was asking.

She smiled and looked between us. "I had a dream that you two fucked each other while you fucked me. It was amazing," she explained, dead serious.

"No, Hana," Michael hissed. "No fucking way."

"For once, I agree with this fucker," I chimed in.

Hana frowned. "Okay. It's just…that's my biggest fantasy. You know that, Jack," she explained as she looked to me.

I vaguely remembered asking her what she wanted that she had never gotten. She told me double penetration, which we gave her. She also said a threesome with another man or woman. I had always pictured a woman in that situation. Besides, we had given her a threesome plenty of times already.

"You never said you wanted to see me with another man," I argued.

"Well, that's what I meant." She furrowed her brows, getting upset that Michael and I wouldn't fuck each other. Maybe she actually *was* crazy after all.

"Never mind. That was stupid to ask for. I'm just…I'm *so* horny," she breathed out as she leaned over to stroke my cock then reached for Michael.

I might have been horny as fuck for her too, but I don't think I could ever let Michael touch me in that way, or vice versa. I didn't have anything against two men fucking; I had some bi exploration in my twenties. It was Michael that I was against.

"Let me fuck you hard then, sweetheart. I can satisfy you in *many* ways," I murmured before returning my hand to her pussy.

My dirty wife easily spread her legs, willing to do whatever I wanted.

"I want both of you inside me again." She took Michael's face with her hands and they began to make out.

With that, I pushed Hana's legs further apart and quickly thrust myself inside of her. She let out a quick scream as she let go of Michael and locked eyes with me.

"Oh my God, baby. Yes," she moaned as I quickly pounded her, unleashing all of my anger with my cock.

I quickly put my hand to her neck and began to squeeze, taking her perky tit in my other hand. Michael got up and started stroking himself, watching us. *That's right, she's mine.* When Hana's eyes began to flutter, I let go of her neck but didn't let my pounding slow. She gasped for air and then turned to Michael, reaching a hand out for him.

"Please, sir. Fuck my ass," she pleaded.

I pulled out and started positioning Hana at the edge of the bed to make it easier for us both to be inside her.

"Wait." She sat up. *Fuck, not again.* "I want to suck your cocks first."

She slid down the side of the bed and reached for Michael's cock then mine. She had both of our cocks in her hands and looked so fucking beautiful as she smiled up at us. She licked her lips then put her mouth around me first. Her warm mouth wrapped around the head of my cock, my sweet girl trying to go down further. Her mouth was suddenly off me, and she turned to Michael, quickly putting his cock in her mouth as she stroked me. *Christ, this woman will be the death of me.* When she took her mouth off Michael, she looked up at us. "Get closer together. I want to suck you both easier."

This woman was testing me. I didn't care; I stood closer to Michael and let her pull my cock closer to his. I don't know what Michael was thinking, but he didn't protest.

"Fuck, you two are so hot." She observed our cocks before putting her mouth over my head then his, moving back and forth quickly. I knew what she was doing; there was no way she'd be able to put both of our cocks in her mouth at the same time. She was just trying to have us close, to potentially touch each other.

"Enough," I huffed. "I need to be inside of you."

Hana smiled and stood, locking eyes with me as she grabbed my cock and started to stroke.

"I want you in my ass."

I loved when she asked for anal. My size made her scream, but she fucking loved it. Michael sat on the bed, pulling Hana over to sit on his cock, a little too aggressively for my liking. I stroked myself as I watched him hold her weight up and pound into her. Her arms clung to his shoulders as she let out her beautiful moans. I grabbed lube from the bedside drawer and continued to stroke myself as I watched them. Fucking hell, why did I enjoy this so much? I grabbed Hana's waist and stilled them before slowly pressing my cock into her ass. Her eyes shut tightly as she turned toward me, her whimpers making my cock even harder.

"Just fucking slam into her," Michael ordered impatiently.

I ignored him. I wasn't going to listen to that fucker. With him in her pussy, her ass would need to be stretched slowly, especially without preparation. He wouldn't know that, not with his size. Not unless he just fucking slammed into her all the time without caring about what she needed?

"Take a big breath, baby. I'm going to stretch you out," I whispered in her ear.

She nodded as I slowly went in and out of her, going deeper each time. I finally pushed myself all the way in and started to pound her, taking her hair with my fist and lifting her up to my chest. I put my mouth to her neck and watched as her tits bounced, her nipples needing my touch. I grabbed her tits then inched down to her pussy, feeling her slick clit under my fingers. I felt Michael inside of her and that almost sent me over the edge; she was taking two cocks, feeling so fucking tight, and loving every second of it.

"Oh my God. I'm coming," she moaned, throwing her body against Michael's and whimpering as neither of us slowed.

"I'm gonna fucking come in your tight asshole," I grunted then spilled myself into her, grabbing onto her hips as I let out every single drop.

Michael started grunting shortly after; he grabbed her face and kissed her eagerly, and I almost passed out from how amazing she felt all filled up.

We all caught our breaths before I pulled out and took Hana's hand, aggressively taking her from Michael.

"Come on, love. Let me clean up my dirty whore."

After Hana and I showered in the bathroom I had claimed, she gleefully got dressed and headed into the kitchen, wanting to prepare a brunch for us. I checked my phone and saw that I had a missed call from Jessica. I made sure Hana was out of ear shot before I listened to her voicemail.

"Jack, it's Jessica. Call me. I have some...interesting things to tell you about Michael."

I immediately called her back.

"What did you find out?" I asked urgently after she answered.

"Michael has an ex-girlfriend named Jackie. She was willing to discuss him in great detail," she explained.

"And?"

"Well, apparently he tells everyone that *she* was the one that went crazy on him. In reality, Michael became very possessive of her. She was basically at his beck and call and she wasn't a very willing participant. He told her he'd pay for anything she wanted if she obeyed him. When she tried to call things off, he tied her up and *carved his name* into her skin."

Jessica barely took a breath as she spoke. My eyes were wide open and a slow smile stretched my lips. Michael was fucking crazy after all.

"He said he wanted to mark her body so no man would ever want her. He told her he'd ruin her life if she ever told anyone."

I laughed. "Fucking hell, Jess."

She scoffed. "Why are you laughing? That's fucking terrible, Jack!" she scolded me.

"I'm not laughing at that, Jessica. I'm laughing because I've got something I can use against him."

She sighed. "Well, that's not all."

I perked up again.

"She saw him after Hana left him. She said he drunkenly called her and begged her to go to him. He fucking did it to her *again*, all while he carved Hana's name onto himself."

Holy shit. This was good. Now I just needed to confirm if this was true; I needed to find Michael's scars and then present it all to Hana.

The question was, would Hana think this was too disturbing to still love him? Or would she forgive him, as she always forgave me? It was my favorite quality about Hana, how she was so empathetic and kind. It worked in my favor many times. But now Hana's kindness may get in the way—it may even work against me.

Hana

I don't know what came over me when I asked Jack and Michael to have sex with each other. It was absurd to even think about; I knew there was no way in hell they would do it. I was getting greedy. But having them both at the same time was exhilarating, and I wanted more.

Having either of them, at *any* time, was exhilarating lately. It almost felt like we were sneaking around when Jack and I would take a hot shower together, or when Michael and I would have a quick fuck against the giant glass window in his room.

Only five days into living at Michael's apartment together and I almost thought we were all going to get along just perfectly. Jack had a lot of meetings during the day, leaving Michael and I alone together, and Jack and I would stay up until the wee hours of the morning while Michael slept. It seemed like everything was going to work out just fine, until I woke up to yelling in the living room. It was dark outside, so it must have been early morning—*why would they both be up without me at this time?*

I crept my way into the hall and heard scuffling and murmured voices downstairs. As I poked my head around the corner, I saw Jack holding Michael's arm behind his back and

Michael trying to shove Jack off him. They were *trying* to be quiet as they shifted their weights, Jack's grip loosening from Michael's arm, until they both backed into the fridge behind them.

"What the fuck is going on?" I yelled.

They suddenly broke free from each other, shock spreading across their faces. I quickly stepped down the stairs.

"Jack?" I turned to him expectantly, waiting for an answer.

"He's fucking crazy, Hana. He's made up some ridiculous story," Michael started, out of breath.

"It's not ridiculous, Hana. Look at his skin to see what I'm talking about," Jack chimed in.

My eyes were bulging out of my head. "What the fuck do you mean?" I asked Jack, walking closer to them to prevent another fight.

"Look—look right there on his bicep. On his left arm." Jack pointed.

Michael crossed his arms, looking at Jack with narrowed eyes and a scowl on his face. "You're fucking out of your mind," Michael hissed at Jack.

Now my curiosity was piqued.

"Why not just show me your arm, Michael?" I asked gently as I walked closer to him.

Michael watched me with hesitant eyes. He *was* hiding something. He had never given me that look before. I waited as he scratched his beard and looked to the floor.

"Before he tells you this ridiculous story, Han, I'll tell you what really happened," he explained, his voice quiet as he looked up at me.

Jack snorted. "Yeah, let's hear your version."

I whipped my head to look at Jack. "Please. Let him talk,

Jack," I snapped and then turned back to Michael.

My stomach dropped as Michael lifted his left arm and revealed scars that started from his elbow and ended almost to his armpit. I walked closer and realized those scars spelled something...*my name*. I looked up at him with wide eyes.

"I told you I went mad while you were gone, Hana." His eyes were sullen and almost black in the faint kitchen light.

I ran my fingers over my name on his arm. How had I not noticed before? They were slightly raised and pale red, almost white.

"How did you know about this, Jack?" My voice was barely audible as I removed my fingers from Michael. I looked over at Jack when he didn't respond.

He crossed his arms before he spoke. "Jessica spoke to his ex-girlfriend, Jackie."

My heart dropped.

"Why does *she* know about it, Michael?" I turned to him.

Michael clenched his jaw. "You and I weren't together anymore, Hana. I made some bad decisions. I'm not proud of myself," he answered defensively.

As much as he was right, I still felt a pang of jealousy. But what right did I have? Here I was asking for both of them.

Jack cleared his throat. "Do you want to continue with that story, Michael? About what you did to poor Jackie?"

I could tell he was having a good time patronizing him. Tears started pooling in my eyes. Whatever it was, I knew I wasn't going to like it. My heart started to bang in my ribcage as I stared at Michael expectantly.

Michael sighed and shook his head. "This is where you're wrong, Jack," he started then turned to me. "She told Jessica that I tied her up and cut my name into her. That's absolutely not true. I told you how she got when we were dating, Hana."

"Nope," Jack butted in. "No, Hana darling. The truth about *that*—well, Michael was pretty awful to Jackie. Weren't you?" He turned to Michael then back to me, not letting him answer. "He made her comply whether she wanted to or not. She tried to break things off and that's when he tied her up and carved his name onto her the *first* time. Poor thing. He said he wanted to ruin her for any other man. He also threatened to ruin her life if she ever told anyone."

I was speechless. I shook my head at Michael as a tear fell down my cheek.

"Hana, you know that's not true." He shook his head at me, disgust apparent in his face. "Are you going to believe someone who fucking *kidnapped* you?"

Jack immediately chimed in. "You're going to believe someone who fucking put a knife to your throat and threatened to kill you *as* he fucked you? Hana, that's fucking heinous and you know that!"

My head spun as I tried to process everything. "Shut up, both of you!" My breathing was heavy and shaky.

They both looked at me with wide, angry eyes. I didn't know who to believe. Was I really going to believe Jackie's word against Michael's? But what if Jackie was telling the truth? He admitted to cutting my name into himself. He likes to tie up his subs. If he had gone "mad," what was to stop him from doing all of those things?

"I need to talk to each of you alone. Michael." I took his hand and guided us toward his room.

"Remember everything he's been doing to you lately, Hana," Jack called as we went up the stairs.

I closed the door behind us, and Michael started pacing

around the room.

"Please just tell me the truth, Michael. I will try to understand if you tell me something I don't want to hear," I said quietly as I sat on his bed.

He stopped pacing and put his hand to his beard quickly. "I don't know what I did, Hana. Honestly, I drank so much that I blacked out. But you need to believe me, Hana. I wouldn't do something like that," he explained with tears in his eyes. He got on his knees in front of me, holding onto my waist for dear life. "Please, Hana. I can't let you leave me again. You can't believe what they're saying." He started sobbing into my stomach, clenching my shirt with his fists.

"Okay, baby," I whispered, crying along with him; my heart hurt so badly at the sight of him like this. I looked down and took his face in my hands, looking at the despair in his eyes. Did I believe him? What if he really did do those horrible things? Was this his guilt seeping through? But who was I to judge when I fell in love with someone who kidnapped me? But…these horrible things weren't happening to me. I could forgive the things that were done to me. But what if this poor Jackie wasn't "crazy" after all?

I took Michael's hand and led him onto the bed. I wasn't in any mood for sex; I wanted genuine cuddling and connection time with him. And when he continued to sob into my chest as we lay in bed, I started to believe that everything he was saying was true.

* * *

I didn't sleep much after that. Jack moved around the apartment loudly; I had left him hanging, but I felt like Michael needed me more at that moment. When Michael finally let go of me during his sleep, I rolled out of bed and went to search the apartment for Jack. I found him in his room, hovering over a canvas with a paintbrush in his hand.

"Jack," I greeted him quietly.

He looked up at me quickly, his face void of emotion, then looked right back down at his painting.

I walked closer and sat down next to the canvas; I realized it was an outline of my face, my eyes looking right back at me.

"You're painting me?" I smiled, already flattered. He had never painted me before, and I didn't know why it never crossed my mind.

He pointed at a sketch next to the canvas and it finally dawned on me what he was painting: It was me giving a blowjob, with great detail, right down to the highlights of each strand of my hair. I immediately rolled my eyes; *should I still be flattered?* I didn't say anything as I stood and wrapped my arms around his shoulders, just wanting him to talk to me.

"Baby," I whispered.

"No, Hana. I don't want 'baby' right now. I'm fucking livid," he spit out, shaking me off his shoulders.

"Livid?" I questioned. "Why? Because I spent a couple of hours with Michael?"

Jack threw down his paintbrush, red splattering all over the canvas. He turned around to face me, his eyes filled with resentment as he stared down at me. "No, Hana. Because my own wife doesn't believe me when I tell her that the other dick she's sucking is actually a *huge* fucking psychopath."

I shook my head and crossed my arms. "I don't know what to believe, Jack. I don't think Jackie is a very reliable source," I bit back.

Jack let out a forced laugh. "You're delusional if you believe for a second that he wouldn't actually do that." He narrowed his eyes at me angrily.

My face twisted into an ugly cry, a panic attack on the horizon. "What if I do believe it?" I whispered, throwing my hands into the air. "We all do terrible shit, Jack. You should know that."

His eyes popped wide open, and his jaw went slack.

"Hana." He shook his head, putting his hands to the sides of my arms. "What if he was going to do that with you? What if I had never come? What would your fucking excuse be then?"

I felt sick to my stomach. Jack always told me the truth, whether it was something I wanted to hear or not. Jack could scare me, he could hit me, he could even fucking force me to marry him so everyone I loved didn't die. But he always admitted when he was wrong. He admitted to all the horrible shit he did. He didn't pretend to be a good person. I knew he was trying to tear Michael and I apart; I feared that it was working.

"I don't know, Jack. I don't know. I need some sort of evidence. It's his word against hers," I finally choked out as I sat on his bed, my whole body shaking.

"God damnit, Hana!" Jack yelled, putting his hands up to his head. "You need evidence? I'll get your fucking evidence."

I continued to sob as Jack lifted his shirt off and unbuttoned his jeans. I knew he was getting worked up, and I wanted him to fuck me hard. I scooted back on the bed, wanting him to rip off my clothes. I didn't want to think anymore, I just wanted to feel good.

"That's right, my fucking whore. You like seeing me angry? You like getting me all riled up?" he spit out as he tugged down my leggings and underwear in the same motion.

"Yes," I moaned. "I want you to hurt me."

"Now that your body is all yours again, it's *mine*. You want me to hurt you like I did the night of our wedding party?" He hovered over me, his arms on either side of me.

I started to laugh, a surprise even to myself. "Since when does Jack Maynor ask permission for anything?"

The anger in his eyes dissipated instantly and was replaced with a heart wrenching somber stare. "You're right. I'm just as bad as he is. If not worse." His eyes widened as he looked from my eyes to his hand beside me.

"No." I shook my head. "I love you. I love you, Jack. I didn't mean it like that." I sat up as he rolled over and lay on his back.

Jack scoffed and eyed me intently. "Then how did you mean it?"

I shook my head again. "I know you've done terrible things, Jack. But you own up to them. And I still love you," I explained, gently circling his chest with the tips of my fingers.

Jack was quiet for a while. "Do you love me more than you love him?" he finally asked, hesitantly waiting for an answer.

My heart ached. Staring at my doe-eyed Jack, I knew what my answer was.

Michael

Jack's snooping was starting to tear Hana and I apart, I could feel it. That's why I begged her, begging someone for the first time in my entire life, to believe me…more importantly, to not to leave me.

It was true that I didn't remember exactly what happened the night Jackie came to my apartment. I was fucking drunk. I did know that I cut myself, desperate to feel something, and Hana's name started writing itself into my flesh. I remember Jackie coming to my apartment, but I don't remember why or how she got there. I also know that I tied her up—that memory had been burned into my head since that night. I didn't want to see her in my mind anymore, it was a waste of time. She was a weak, clingy narcissist and would do anything to drag me down with her.

And of course I did those things when she tried to leave me. I couldn't have anyone touch what was mine. I might not have liked her, but she was still mine. I knew my name on her skin would garner too many questions and she would be too ashamed to answer them. I knew she would never tell anyone; she was obsessed with me, and despite my cruelty to her, she was in love with me. But I never loved her. I never loved anyone until Hana. That's why I could never tell her the truth about me and Jackie.

I was more afraid of Hana leaving me than her finding out. If she could forgive Jack for everything he had done, clearly she could forgive me. However, I still needed to get Jackie and Jack out of the picture. Matching names for two despicable people. I knew how I could get rid of Jackie—I could simply tell her to kill herself and she would do it for me. She was obsessed with me and it was fucking exasperating, but I kept stringing her along in case I needed something from her. But I needed to give it some time before I killed Jack—doing it too soon would only make Hana suspicious. I was even going to give her what she wanted from me and Jack. I wanted to appear more compliant so she wouldn't have any doubts about me or my love for her. My pride got in the way when she first asked, and I immediately shot down her idea. However, if she asked anything of me again, I would do it.

I woke up to an empty bed, as usual. Jack made Hana stay up with him until the sun came up and then they would pass out in his room. I needed to change that, but that was just another thing for me to figure out.

I did my daily morning jog on my treadmill in the apartment's gym. I lifted weights to get some anger out; it always relieved it just a little bit to the point where I wouldn't break. I went back to the apartment to shower, trying to figure out how I could meet with Jackie without raising any suspicion from Jack or Hana. I wouldn't call her, that would leave too much of a paper trail. Maybe I could show up at her place, pretend I finally realized that I was madly in love with her, and then have her do the deed.

When I got out of the shower, I found Hana lying naked and splayed across my bed, her beautiful ass on display as she read a book. She looked up at me and smiled, giving me that lip bite that drove me crazy.

"Come here," I ordered as I loosened the towel that covered my lower half, letting it drop to the floor.

It was amazing how quickly I could get hard for Hana. She licked her bottom lip as she slithered off the bed, slowly crawled to me, and got onto her knees in front of me. God, I fucking loved her willingness and eagerness to submit to me.

I started stroking myself, watching her waiting impatiently to touch me.

"Do you think you've earned my cock, sweet girl?" I looked down at her.

"Yes, sir," she breathed out, her green eyes locking with mine.

"Let's see. Turn around, on your hands and knees."

I couldn't wait to tease her, to keep her on the edge of climax and deny her of it. She would need to work harder for my cock.

I walked over to my drawer of toys I had just for her, grabbing the wand that she loved. I took out her collar and leash. It had been too long since I used them with her. I got even harder as I buckled the collar on her and she moaned, already so greedy for my cock. I pulled on the leash as I turned on her wand and began to rub it against her pussy and her clit. She backed into it like the slut that she was. I tugged on the leash, making her whimper, before I removed the wand from her.

"Fuck!" she shouted with aggravation.

I slapped her ass hard. "Don't fucking speak unless I tell you to. Do you understand?"

"Yes, sir."

Fuck, those words out of her mouth made me want to come

all over her pretty ass. I grazed my hand over the mark I just gave her ass then gently rubbed my cock on her, slowly on her ass at first before teasing her vulva with it. My cock slid through her folds easily with how wet she was already. She moaned quietly as she tried to back against me, but I removed my cock and slapped her ass again.

"Greedy girl, Hana." I smiled. I loved teasing her.

"Yes, sir," she breathed out.

I turned on the wand again, going straight for her clit, rubbing her furiously for only a few seconds before turning it off and throwing it on the ground.

She let out an angry grunt. "Please, sir. I need to come," she pleaded.

I slapped her ass hard on the other cheek. "Quiet."

I grabbed her leash and tugged back quickly, making her stand as I did. I guided her over to the bed and pushed her down, exposing her ass and pussy as she lay on the edge. I got on my knees and opened her up, noticing her wetness dripping out of her. I couldn't help myself—I hungrily put my mouth to her warm pussy and began to lick, devouring her and lapping around with my tongue. She let out muffled moans; she was covering her mouth with the back of her hand. I moaned into her as I put my hand to her clit and began to rub swiftly, knowing this was a sure way to make her come. She almost began clenching around my tongue before I removed my mouth and hand from her, chuckling to myself. This was so fucking fun.

"God damnit!" she cried, moving her hips as she tried to chase her orgasm against the bed.

I pulled on her leash and stood her up, turning her around to face me as I grabbed her neck above her collar. Her green eyes widened, almost with fear.

"Safe word, Hana. What is it?"

"Red," she pressed out.

I pushed her down on the bed and parted her legs, lifting them up as I began to rub my cock over her drenched pussy.

"Oh, my fucking sweet girl. So wet for me. Do you want my cock, Hana?" I smiled down at her; I was fucking edging myself at this point too.

"Yes, please, sir," she moaned, her brows pulled together in frustration, never once breaking eye contact with me.

I quickly thrust myself inside her, pounding her hard as I held onto her legs and pulled her against me. I could tell she was once again about to come; I could so easily turn her on and make her come and it was fucking incredible. I pulled out just as quickly and slapped her pussy with my cock, laughing as she groaned out in frustration.

"Please, sir. I will do anything you want. Please let me come, sir," she cried, desperation in her eyes.

"So polite. I will let you come once." I thrust inside her again, rubbing her clit with my thumb, knowing this would make her come instantly.

I was right—she moaned with pleasure, her pussy clenching around my cock as her eyes clamped shut as she grabbed onto the sheets around her. I was surprised when liquid started gushing out of her around my cock; I was making her squirt. I smiled as I removed my cock from her, getting down on my knees and furiously rubbing her clit again.

"One more time, baby. I want you to come all over me," I demanded, wanting to taste her.

And there she went again; she screamed as she squirted, lifting up her hips and releasing all of her sweet juice onto me. My face was fucking drenched. I pressed my mouth to her pussy, trying to suck on her clit, needing more of it. I felt fucking feral as I pressed my face against her, her warm pussy so wet I could almost drink it.

"I'm the only one who gets you so fucking wet like this. Isn't that right, baby?" I hovered over her, needing to be inside of her again.

"Yes, sir," she moaned as I rubbed my cock against her.

"Good girl," I muttered before thrusting myself into her, taking her leash and wrapping it around my hand, tugging on it swiftly.

"You think I can make you squirt again, baby?" I breathed out over her moans as I pounded into her.

"Yes, sir. Please," she responded urgently.

I quickly pulled out of her, turned her over, and pressed my cock to the tip of her ass, trying to squeeze my way in; her pussy left my cock drenched, perfectly lubing me up. She started screaming as I pushed myself into her quickly and my balls slapped against her wet pussy.

"Oh my God. Oww fuck. Harder," she moaned.

Fuck. I love this woman. I pounded harder and then wrapped my arm around her, pressing my palm to her clit as my fingers slipped inside her. I put my other hand to her head, pushing her down onto the bed. She began to clench around my fingers as she screamed, my pounding never ceasing and liquid shooting out of her again as I frantically rubbed her clit.

The bedroom door flew open just as I began to come, draining myself into Hana's ass, the orgasm so intense I couldn't even open my eyes as I grunted with pleasure. I knew it was Jack who opened the door and I wanted him to see how fucking wild we could be, how feral I could make Hana.

"Hana," Jack shouted. "Are you okay?"

"Yes," she cried. "Yes," she continued, her pussy still pulsing around my fingers.

"I heard screaming," he said less urgently.

"Screams of pleasure, mate," I finally breathed out, quivering from the aftershocks of my orgasm.

"May I join you, Hana?" Jack walked slowly up to the bed, looking at the scene in front of him: me still inside Hana's ass, Hana naked and leashed, my little pet on display.

"Please," she breathed out, turning her head to look at Jack. "Sir?" she asked me, seeking my approval.

Now was my time to show her my cooperation. "Yes, baby." I finally released myself from her ass, and she whimpered, still catching her breath as she lay over the bed on her belly. I quickly picked her up from her hips and turned her over on her back.

"Why don't we give you that threesome you wanted?" I suggested. This was the last thing I wanted, but I needed to show Hana how willing I was to please her.

Hana's eyes widened as she smiled at me and then at Jack.

"Jack?" she asked him with her hopeful, wide eyes.

Jack was clenching his jaw. He knew he had to do it too, that fucker.

"Okay, baby." He finally smiled at her then pulled his cock out from his boxer briefs and began to stroke himself. "You two can suck my cock first."

Hana

I couldn't believe what was happening. I watched as Jack stroked himself and looked at Michael, almost smugly, then back at me.

"Fine," Michael huffed, sitting on the bed next to me and putting his hand on my thigh, squeezing hard.

What fucking world had I stumbled into? Did I come so hard that I died and now I'm in heaven? Michael was going to do this with me?

"Have…either of you done this before?" I looked up at Jack and then to Michael.

Jack shrugged. "Yeah. Just a few times," he responded nonchalantly.

I almost expected that answer from him. He seemed so much more open-minded than Michael.

"I have not," Michael admitted as he shook his head, his eyes narrowing as he looked at me hesitantly.

"Baby…you don't have to do this. I don't want to force you," I said quietly, placing my hand on his thigh.

Michael clenched his jaw and shook his head. "I want to make you happy, Hana."

I hesitantly smiled. I wasn't sure if I could make them do this; it almost seemed too bizarre.

I stood and made my decision. "We're not going to do this yet. You two aren't ready. Maybe when…you hate each other a little less," I suggested, putting my hands to my hips as I eyed both of them.

"Okay," Jack quickly responded. "I still need you to suck my cock."

I chuckled a little bit and then turned to Michael who still sat on the bed, his erection in full force again. "Sir? Would you like to fuck me while I suck his cock?"

He nodded and then stood, heading for the bathroom. "Let me clean up first."

"Come on, love," Jack perked up, pulling my gaze away from Michael's ass. "I need to fuck your face."

I couldn't believe I still had energy left, but I sank down to my knees and eagerly took Jack in my hand.

"Let me do the work, baby." I smiled up at him.

His eyes widened eagerly.

I put my mouth around him and began to stroke him gently with both hands, twisting my hands to add to the pleasure. I couldn't keep my eyes off Jack—he stared down at me with his lips slightly parted, watching me like I was a fucking goddess.

"You make me feel so fucking good, Hana," he breathed out. "Come on. Come out in the hallway. I don't want to come in his room."

I stopped and took him out of my mouth. "He's coming back out, though," I argued in a hushed tone.

"He'll figure it out." He shrugged and took my hand, lifting me up and guiding me out of Michael's room.

I could understand why Jack didn't want to be in there. I also didn't want to upset Michael. But then I remembered how fucking hard he just edged me and I wanted to rebel against him in some way.

Jack leaned against the wall right outside of Michael's room and pushed me down to my knees.

"As you were, love." He gave me a devious grin as he rubbed his cock around my lips.

I instantly took him in my hands again and wrapped my lips around his head, giving a moan to vibrate onto his cock.

"You know just how to please me, don't you, sweetheart?" He panted as he stared down at me.

I began to move my hands and mouth quickly as Jack held my hair back to keep it out of my face. His breathing hitched as I continued to moan, staring up at him with a smile.

"You want me to come for you, don't you? You want me to come all over your beautiful face?"

I nodded with him still in my mouth, my pussy slick for him and needing release again.

He grinned and then pulled his cock off my mouth. "I've changed my mind. Let's go back in his room."

He pulled me up and guided me back into Michael's room. I could hear the shower still running in his bathroom.

"Lay on the bed. Put your head right on the edge here so I can fuck your mouth and taste your warm pussy at the same time."

The ache in my core shot a tingle right down to my wetness. I did as he said and lay on the bed, putting my head perfectly in line with his cock. Jack hovered over me and softly grazed his fingers against my belly, making his way down to where I so desperately needed his touch. I gasped when he finally started to gently rub my clit before dipping his rough finger into me. It was then that I grabbed his cock and put it in my mouth, waiting for him to fuck it. His hips began to move slowly, his cock trying to force its way into my throat. Pleasure built as he continued to rub my clit; it sent me over the edge when his hot mouth pressed against my pussy, his tongue sliding into me as he continued to stimulate my clit. His hips moved in a quick rhythm as I started gagging, and then the pleasure exploded. I lifted my hips to keep chasing my orgasm as he continued, not once removing his face or fingers. I continued to gag on his cock until he pulled out of my mouth and quickly demanded me on my knees in front of him. I looked up at his lustful eyes as he stroked his cock, my mouth opening to wait for him to come on me.

It was when Michael's bathroom door opened that Jack's load shot straight at my mouth and face, dripping onto my body; he groaned so loud that I wondered if he was putting on a show.

I smiled as I let Jack's warm cum slide down my throat. He grinned down at me and placed his thumb on my cum-covered face, hooking his finger into my mouth. I could see Michael from my peripheral view, watching us with a towel around his hips. I looked over at him and saw his hard cock begging to be released.

Michael smiled. "I'm ready for round two when you guys are."

I turned back to Jack. He rolled his eyes slightly at Michael then looked back down at me. I don't think his plan for making Michael jealous had worked, unless he was really good at hiding it.

"I can fuck Hana all day. Are you ready for more, sweetheart?"

I sat down on my knees and leaned back against the bed. "I need a bath and a nap. You two are welcome to join me."

I saw them both glance at each other. They were definitely competing now.

Jack quickly held his hand out for me. "I'll run that bath for you, love."

Emily

I was still processing everything that was happening with Hana. She told me they were back in the city at Michael's apartment, right across the street from where her and Jack had been living. I was starting to have more and more doubts about Michael, especially after learning he knew way more about Hana than he let on. He had stalked her the whole time they were apart. I guess he checked off all the things on Hana's list, just as Jack did. Stalk her? Check. Kidnap her? Check. Tie her up and make her stay with him whether she wanted it or not? Check. *Fucking swoon.*

I didn't even know what to tell Adam about their whole situation. He seemed to be happily unaware of what was going on in his best friend's personal life. I loved that Adam was so chill, so easygoing and sweet—but now was not the time for being those things. Maybe actually telling him would stir something up. Maybe he would be able to learn more from Jack.

I walked into our apartment after a horrible night at the bar, finding Adam strumming on his guitar. "Hey, babe."

"Hey, Em." He smiled, setting down his guitar next to the couch to stand and give me a kiss.

I loved his big brown eyes and his messy brown hair, his

EMILY

facial hair growing wildly around his jaw. *I shouldn't tell him. No, I should.*

I chewed on the side of my cheek, unsure of how to start the conversation.

"What's wrong?" Adam tilted his head at me, his face suddenly distressed.

I wrung my hands together and shook my head as I slumped onto the couch. Adam sat next to me, his eyes widened and looking at me like I was about to deliver the worst news of his life. I took a big, shaky breath before speaking

"It's not about us, babe." I smiled, taking his hand with mine. "It's uh…about Jack and Hana. Did he…tell you what's going on?"

They had been in meetings with each other and got together to work on some music. I had no idea what the hell they ever talked about; they probably only focused on their music.

I took another deep breath when Adam shook his head and looked at me like he had no idea what I was talking about.

"They're like…they…I guess Michael is like, in their relationship now? They're like, poly or something," I tried to explain.

Adam looked over at the window as he pulled his eyebrows together. "Okay." He nodded as he looked back to me.

I widened my eyes. "Okay? That's your response?"

Adam laughed. "What the hell is my response supposed to be? I don't care what the fuck Jack does in his sex life." He shrugged.

Ugh, if only I could explain how complicated this all was. I knew I would sound crazy if I even attempted to explain their whole deal from the beginning.

"I guess you don't need to care. It's just…"

Just tell him. I began telling him their whole story, pacing around the living room as I did so. I knew it sounded crazy but I didn't care—I had to get it all off my chest.

"Em." Adam put his hands to his hair then back down to his lap. "Have you been taking your meds?"

I almost started crying when I realized he was serious. It probably sounded like my manic ramble before my suicide attempt.

"Yes, Adam, I've been taking my meds," I answered with irritation.

Adam just sighed and shook his head. He shrugged and almost seemed speechless. "I just…I can't believe it, Em. Does she actually love them? Or is she like…what's it called—"

"Delusional?" I offered.

Adam eyed me with a frown. It was rare that my sometimes ill-timed humor didn't make him laugh.

"Stockholm Syndrome? But like…way worse?" he suggested.

I threw my hands up as I shrugged. "Do you get why this is fucking crazy now?"

Adam nodded, his expression unreadable. "Yes. This is… fucked up." He stood and walked to the window, observing the spring rain trickling down from the sky. "I feel like I don't even know who my best friend is."

I almost regretted telling him. I walked over to him and put my arm around his waist.

"It's been a fucking rollercoaster the last few months," I admitted quietly.

"You didn't have to go through that alone, Emily," he responded, holding me closer to him.

I scoffed. "Then you guys wouldn't have made a hit record,"

I joked.

Adam eyed me, apparently still not in a joking mood. "I'm serious, Em. I love you. You matter more than any of that." He held onto me tighter.

I finally let myself cry. The last few months were the most devastating I'd ever had to go through, mostly because I was going through them alone. Even when my mom died, Hana was right by my side. Now I didn't know whether or not Hana would be on my team anymore. Things were so chaotic with her, so touch and go, that I wondered if the suffering was worth it. And then I remembered she was my blood; she had always been there for me in the hardest of times for my entire life. I knew I had to stick around, whether I agreed with her decisions or not. The tough part would be whether or not she'd let me in…or shut me out all over again.

Jack

I sat at a bougie coffee shop in Chelsea, far from anywhere I would usually hang out. I watched as she walked into the shop with Jessica, our "middle man." My sister smiled as she spotted me and eagerly walked over, Jackie in tow.

Jackie seemed like a Brooklyn hipster as much as Hana did. Her hair was blonde, perhaps not naturally, with blue tips. She had light eyes, also like Hana. Michael obviously had a type. However, Hana was far superior; Jackie was cute, but Hana was a goddess. And it seemed Jackie was more easily manipulated. She seemed eager. I could see the appeal to her.

Once she found out that I had close contact with Michael, she was very interested in meeting with me, and Jessica set the whole thing up so we could talk right away.

"Hello, brother." Jessica smiled, outstretching her arms for me as I sat comfortably in my seat. She waited as I begrudgingly stood and gave her a quick hug. Then she turned her attention toward Jackie, putting her hand on her shoulder as if they were great friends. In fact, I didn't doubt they were friends—Jessica could make friends with a toaster oven.

"Hello." Jackie smiled at me, almost flirtatiously.

I narrowed my eyes at her as I sat, both of them quickly following.

JACK

"So I'm sure my sister has told you why I agreed to meet. You and I both have a problem with someone we know," I started, setting my folded hands on the table.

Her smile faded quickly. "That's right. How exactly is he a problem in your life?" She eyed me curiously.

"You don't need to know that. All I need to know is that you're telling the truth. May I see, please?" I cut straight to the point, not wanting to waste my time.

She quickly glanced over at Jessica, who only smiled stiffly and nodded.

Jackie looked hesitantly back at me. "Well I can't exactly show you *all* of it, unless you want me to pull down my pants and expose myself," she responded angrily.

"No, but perhaps you can show me *some* proof so I know you're not a fucking liar." I glared at her, leaning against the table.

"Jack!" Jessica scolded me, but Jackie put her hand up as if to stop her.

She sighed heavily before taking off her cardigan. She put her right hand on the table. Multiple scars covered her arm, some newer than others, and I could easily read what had been carved into her skin: *Michael* on her forearm and *slut* on her upper arm. It was so fucking hideous that even I had a hard time looking at it.

"It's on my stomach and legs too," she stated, almost emotionless, as she put her cardigan back on.

"Why haven't you reported him to the police?" I questioned suspiciously.

She shook her head and looked down at the table. "Because I love him."

I knew how ironic this conversation was.

"You do know that he's back in a relationship with Hana, yes?" I asked, testing her.

She looked up at me with wide eyes. She shook her head as she mouthed "no." Tears filled her eyes, and I could tell she really was in love with him. I couldn't judge; Hana loved me, and *him*, despite all we had done to her.

"Listen, Jackie," I said quietly, trying to appear as sympathetic as possible.

She listened intently.

"You must go to Hana with this information. Give her all the details. She will undoubtedly leave Michael, thus, giving him back to you." I shifted in my seat. "But I swear to fucking God, if you lay one finger on her, I *will* kill you."

Jessica gasped as if she were surprised by my behavior. I quickly glanced at her, seeing her dumbfounded expression, and rolled my eyes. She knew I fucking took Hana and forced her to marry me—did she not realize what I was capable of?

"I won't, I swear," Jackie responded keenly, her eyes wide again.

"Good. My band has a show at the Bowery next Friday. Hana will be there, perhaps even Michael. Coordinate with Jess on the details." I stood, grabbed my coffee, and then walked away, not waiting for her response.

I couldn't wait for the look of surprise and disgust on Hana's face. She couldn't forgive Michael for this—it was too heinous, too diabolical. It even surprised me, and I was obviously no saint. I just had to make sure she was safe from him in the meantime. I knew she wanted to keep both of us, but she kept hinting that she loved me more, that she was mine. It scared her how much she was sure of it. It only fueled the fire more for me. I was going to ruin Michael.

Hana

We were beginning to figure out how to navigate our lives in the outside world. Jack was scheduled to start interviews and shows with Adam for their album and he asked me to go with him. It was only in Manhattan, but it was as if Jack still didn't trust me alone with Michael. Was he trying to protect me...or keep me away? Michael stayed at the apartment, informing us that he was starting a new business deal with some former college mates and needed to work, although he seemed hesitant about me and Jack going somewhere alone.

On the train ride to a recording studio in midtown, Jack kept glancing at his phone, seeming distressed.

"What's wrong, babe?" I asked, wrapping my arms around him as he sighed, holding onto the overhead railing for support.

"Adam is being fucking weird. Do you think Emily told him something?" he asked as he looked down at me.

I wouldn't be surprised if she did. I told her we would be open about our relationship, but I'm sure she didn't leave out any dirty details. I bit my lip as I looked down at my phone.

"I don't know. Why don't you ask him?" I suggested, putting my phone back in my pocket.

Jack sighed heavily, anger clear on his face. "I knew you

shouldn't have told her the truth. She's going to fucking ruin everything," he hissed, not looking at me.

I let go of him and crossed my arms. "I'm not lying to her anymore, Jack," I huffed.

"Yeah well, let's see what fucking good that does."

The subway stopped and the doors pinged open; Jack quickly stormed out, but not before grabbing my hand to pull me along with him.

I kept up with Jack as he quickly walked toward the studio, the warm, late April weather finally feeling like spring. We walked into a tall building and headed to the seventh floor. I stood on the opposite side of Jack in the elevator with my arms crossed and, I'm sure, a scowl on my face.

"I'm sorry for snapping, love," he started quietly. "I just don't want this to affect the relationship I have with Adam. I need to know if Emily gave him all the horrid details or not."

I couldn't be mad at him. It was probably a really bad idea for my well-meaning, but very loquacious, cousin to have this sort of information.

"It's okay, babe." I shrugged, still trying to shake off my bad mood as I glanced up at him.

The warm weather prompted him to wear a plain white T-shirt that showed off his strong, muscular arms. His tattoos poked out from under his sleeve.

"Fancy having a fuck in here?" Jack quipped, slyly showing me his dimples as the elevator doors pinged open.

I wasn't able to contain my smile; I wanted him, and he knew it.

"After you, Mrs. Maynor." He motioned his hand toward the elevator doors, waiting for me to move.

I turned on my heel, and we walked into a sleek music

studio with neon signs, art work, and gold albums of famous musicians lining the wall. An older man who already knew Jack greeted us excitedly. I assumed he had been here before and was well-liked judging by the treatment he was receiving.

"This is my wife, Hana." Jack introduced us, and my heart swelled at those words: my wife. It had turned from a feeling of impending doom to loving, welcomed words.

"I'm Sal, the owner here. Great to meet you. Your husband is a rock star!" Sal widened his eyes for effect, patting Jack on the back. "Go on to room three. They're all set up in there."

Jack grinned down at me as he took my hand. I sensed he was nervous. Maybe he really only wanted me here for moral support and not just some way to keep me in check.

We walked into a huge acoustic room with several people already walking around, professional cameras and lights pointed at Jack's drums and Adam's guitar. I noticed a few couches lining the walls and realized Emily was sitting there, looking at her phone and oblivious to our presence. I gasped with excitement then quickly realized that Jack might not have been so excited. I turned to him, and he eyed me hesitantly but nodded anyway.

"Go on, love. Enjoy the show with your cousin." He winked at me before giving me a passionate, slow kiss. If he was trying to turn me on, it had worked very well.

I stood there for a moment watching Jack walk away, gathering my wits as my nipples hardened underneath my thin black T-shirt.

"Han!" Emily exclaimed from behind me.

I turned, and she stood. Her face was lit up like *I* was the rockstar in this room.

"Em." I smiled back at her before I wrapped her in my arms.

"It's so good to see you. Can you believe our boys are going to be fucking *famous*?" She laughed then turned to look at Adam who had just approached Jack.

They stood close together, talking alone, and Jack laughed loudly. He shook his head and turned to look at me. Adam followed his gaze, clearly confused. He turned to look back at Jack and quickly put his hand to his shoulder, smiling uneasily.

"I told him," Emily blurted.

I turned to her with a frown. "You did?"

Her eyes were full of uncertainty. "You didn't ask me *not* to," she defended.

I nodded as I sighed. "It's fine, Em. Let's sit." I motioned to the couch behind her. "Did you tell him…everything?" I asked curiously as I sat down and crossed my legs toward her.

She mirrored me as she nodded. "Yeah. He's…he's really surprised. I mean, I told him *everything*. As I told him, it sounded so insane, but like…you've lived it. I can't believe your strength, Hana." She shook her head at me.

My face turned hot as I stared at her. I wasn't sure how I felt about her last statement. I decided to ignore it.

"So…what, he's accepted all of this?" I inquired quietly.

I looked over at the front of the room and realized Jack and Adam were starting to set up.

"I don't know. He didn't really talk about how he felt. That's just…the way he is," Emily answered.

I sighed and watched Jack warming up on the drums, doing a mic check as Adam played with buttons on his extensive guitar pedal. Adam looked uneasy; I wasn't sure if it was nerves or if being close to Jack made him feel that way after what he'd learned. Jack looked content as he rested his hand on his thigh and then looked over at me. I went into full on groupie mode again when he winked at me and smiled.

"Are you doing okay? Are they treating you well?" Emily asked quietly, leaning into me.

I nodded. I knew she was concerned about me but I didn't want to be looked at like I was some helpless victim. I used to be, but now I was in control.

"Like I said, Emily. I'm finally happy."

That's when the person maneuvering the camera yelled, "Quiet on set!"

The room went quiet. Emily and I looked at each other with wide eyes before we both turned back.

"Camera rolling. When you're ready," the camera person said to the guys.

I could see Jack's chest moving up and down quickly before he nodded to Adam; Jack began banging on the drums perfectly in sync when Adam started stroking his guitar. Jack kept his eyes on his drums before he turned his head to his mic and began singing. This was the dark song Emily had told me about; I knew it as Jack began singing about heartache, betrayal, taking what's his. He continued with the chorus, singing about how he was a fool, bloody hands, broken promises. Emily looked over at me, probably wanting to see my response to Jack's words. All of these songs were written when I chose Michael, and it was clear how broken he felt about it. The song ended with Jack banging on his drums passionately. Jack looked over at me, out of breath, his eyes someplace else…in his dark, scary place that made my heart drop and my cheeks red hot.

Someone appeared out of nowhere with a mic in his hand and began asking Jack and Adam questions like where they were playing in NYC, when the album was coming out, and what inspired them to write the song they just played. Adam glanced over at Jack expectantly, raising his eyebrows at him.

Jack put the mic up to his mouth. "I wrote it when I was in a really dark place in my life. I was heartbroken and depressed and angry. The whole album is basically based around that." He smiled shyly.

He looked so nervous as he spoke, but they finished the interview quickly. The next song they played was the one about the monster and its prey that I had heard weeks ago. It sounded even better the second time around. Soon enough, they were done.

I sighed heavily, not realizing I was shaking until I let out my uneven breath.

"You okay?" Emily asked as we stood.

I feigned a smile, the one she had believed for weeks until she learned the truth.

"Yeah." I nodded.

Jack was by my side instantly, his eyes wide with desire, quickly putting his hand behind my neck and pulling me in for another passionate kiss. I forgot there was a room full of people until we parted and I saw several people staring from the corner of my eye.

"I'm fucking wound up. I need you right now," he growled quietly.

I nodded, heat rising in my chest. I felt the exact same.

Jack took my hand and pulled me out of the room and into the hallway. We entered a private bathroom, and he locked the door behind us before pushing me against it and holding my arms up beside me.

"Everything I felt while writing those songs came back to me. You fucking destroyed me, Hana," he spit out angrily, yet his hard erection pressed against me eagerly.

Tears started running down my cheeks.

"I know." I nodded, my heart desperately trying to jump out of my chest.

"And now you're all mine and you're still destroying me." His confused eyes scanned my face as he said the words.

His grip tightened against my wrists. I nodded again, emphatically turned on even as fear rose in my chest.

"You know you still belong to me, don't you? You know that you love me more than him," he stated straightforwardly.

"Yes, baby. I do." I started to cry. The realization suddenly hit me, and it was terrifying.

Jack quickly let go of me then pulled down his zipper while I eagerly stripped out of my jeans. His erection sprung free before he took my wrists again and slammed me against the door. I wrapped my legs around him as he thrust inside of me, his hips slamming against me while he furiously fucked me.

"Come on, sweetheart. Show me," he said into my ear.

I felt my orgasm building as he continued to thrust, my moans and his grunting loud enough for the whole building to hear.

"Come for me. Now," he ordered forcefully.

His voice pushed me over the edge, and I came loudly, my legs pulling him closer to me as my whole body exploded with pleasure. It wasn't long after that Jack moaned into my ear and his hot breath turned into bites on my shoulder as he came inside of me. When he finally released my wrists, I wrapped my arms around him and started sobbing. He held onto me tightly, knowing exactly what was happening: He was taking control over me again. And I was letting him.

Michael

Jack kept stealing Hana away from me during the day. She wanted to tag along to his band's promotion for their album, and I wanted nothing to do with it. I heard their single; it was fine, but I wasn't exactly their biggest fan. I was more of a classic rock guy. I loved that Hana was a fan of all the old bands that I liked. But I could also tell that Jack being in a band made him even more appealing to her. So very typical, it was a bit disappointing.

But Hana's time away allowed me to figure out how I was going to get Jack out of the picture for good. I knew money could buy most things, but I wasn't sure where to start. Under the guise of getting "business things" done, I used my time to look through violent criminal records from the NYPD. I asked my old friend, Officer Daniel, for some help, and he didn't question anything when I gave him a few thousand dollars. He pointed me in the direction of a few men he had recently detained but were bailed out. I was scheduled to meet with the one who had the most violent past; he was suspected of domestic violence several times and assault with a deadly weapon. Offering him fifty thousand dollars for a small favor was too easy.

When Hana and Jack walked in, the smile on his face

repulsing me, I quickly hid away my laptop.

"Hi, babe. How was your day?" Hana sat next to me on the couch while Jack didn't even bother to look at me as he went upstairs.

"Boring." I smiled at her, putting my hand on the couch behind her.

She narrowed her eyes as she ran her hand through my hair. I loved how comfortable she was feeling with me again.

"So what exactly is this business stuff you're wanting to do instead of spending time with me?" she teased, giving me her sweetest, saddest eyes.

I sighed, feigning boredom. "Boring business stuff you don't want to know about, but it can give us more than you've ever dreamed of," I said as I put a strand of hair behind her ear. I wasn't exactly lying by being vague like this.

She nodded and then bit her lip; I could tell she was thinking of something, and she seemed nervous.

"I have a proposal," she finally said with her crooked smile.

She still gave me butterflies when she did that. I had never gotten butterflies before I met her.

I raised my eyebrows at her. "I thought I was the one that was supposed to propose? Again?" I teased, but it stung a little as I said it.

She smiled and rolled her eyes. She'd pay for that later.

"I want all three of us to go on a date."

Fuck.

"I think we all need to spend more time together. All of us. Otherwise you two will just quietly hate each other while you pass each other in the hall," she explained further, as if that would make any difference.

This was the last thing I wanted to do, but I had to cooperate.

It would be easier for her to believe Jack's death wasn't my fault if I did.

I put my hand to her thigh and nodded. "Okay, baby. Whatever you think is best."

She laughed as if I had just made a joke. I didn't care; seeing Hana laugh was my favorite thing in the world.

"That was way too easy." She shook her head at me. "What do you have planned, huh?" she teased.

If she only knew.

"All I really plan to do is bend you over this couch so I can spank you for rolling your eyes at me."

Her eyes filled with lust. I loved the effect I had on her—getting her excited just by talking dirty to her. She quickly stood and slowly backed away from me, a smile creeping on her face.

"Before you can distract me, I'm going to get ready so we can all go out." She turned on her heels and ran up the stairs.

I couldn't help it—I started chasing her. She squealed with delight as she realized I was inching closer to her, her little legs not nearly long or fast enough to outrun me. Her blonde hair swayed behind her, flying across her shoulder as she looked back at me with an excited grin. Jack opened his door as we passed his room in the hallway, and I caught up to her and lifted her from behind, her squeal quickly turning into laughter.

"You win, you win." She tapped on my forearms, out of breath from laughing.

I eased her down as I smelled her hair, not quite letting her go yet; I wanted to bask in her happiness forever. It made me feel normal.

"Does this mean we're going out?" Jack asked, irritation

clear in his voice.

I sighed as I let go of Hana and closed my eyes, trying not to let his presence ruin everything. She turned around and put her hands to my arms, holding on for balance as she looked at Jack over my shoulder.

"Yes. Get ready." She laughed, then looked up at me.

I couldn't stop staring at her. She was so bloody beautiful. I started to doubt myself and my plan; she wouldn't be the same without Jack here. It was obvious that he brought out some carefree, cheerful version of Hana that I didn't see often. For some reason, she loved him all too intensely. Did I want to ruin her happiness? Could she get past it? I worried that she might have loved him more than I thought. What if she never recovered from his death? What if it made her want to die as well?

She looked up at me as she pulled her brows together, concern clear in her eyes. "What are you thinking, baby?"

I gave her a small smile and shook my head. "Nothing, babe. Go on, get ready." I kissed the top of her head and let go before I walked into my room.

"Hey," she called behind me.

I turned, and she stood at the doorway, hands on her hips. She was so cute when she tried to look tough.

"Really? What's wrong?"

I forced a smile. I had to pull myself together. "You just make me so happy, Hana. I can't believe we get to be together again."

She bit her lip and looked like she was going to cry. She slowly walked toward me and put her hands to my cheeks, searching my face as if the words were all over my face.

"I love you." Her voice was almost a whisper, and she looked

as if she was torn inside as well.
 "I love you too. More than you'll ever know."

Hana

Michael and Jack seemed to be in their heads lately. I knew they were struggling with this, and I needed to do something about it before it all imploded. Suggesting a date night seemed harmless enough. Maybe even having a couple drinks could loosen us all up. Of course, if Michael let me.

My boys were so vastly different—it was obvious by their date night outfits of choice. I walked down the stairs and eyed Michael sitting on the couch in his black jeans, brown suede boots, and brown polo shirt, completing his look with a silver watch. I spotted Jack on the downstairs patio on his phone. He wore black jeans, black boots, and a very well-loved, worn-in band T-shirt. I wouldn't change a thing about either of them.

Once Michael noticed me, he stood with a warm smile on his face.

"Hello, beautiful." He walked toward the stairs and took my hand, twirling me around.

I wore a casual, white midi dress with my usual pointed black boots and a black pleather jacket, but the way he looked at me made me feel like I was fucking Cinderella at the ball.

"Your red lips just…" He shook his head at me as he sighed. "I want to see them around my cock later." He moved closer to me, putting his hand under my chin.

There was a strong, abrupt swell in my belly that shot straight to my pussy. Suddenly, the patio door swung open. The way Jack looked at us somehow made me feel like I was doing something wrong.

"Having some foreplay, are we?" he jested then looked to me as he put his hand to his heart. "My love. You're stunning, as always." He flashed me his famous Maynor dimples that made my heart flutter.

My cheeks burned from the flattery as I cleared my throat. This was either going to be an amazing night, or it would end up going terribly wrong. Honestly, I wouldn't be surprised if both happened.

"Follow me, boys. We're going to have fun tonight."

* * *

I hailed a cab, and we headed north toward my old neighborhood. I wasn't sure if I would ever get used to having both Michael and Jack next to me; I was especially not used to having each of them rubbing my thigh, knowing they were working me up, as if they were working together.

We didn't have enough time to recreate our fun Uber ride, though. After only a few minutes, we stopped at a new place I kept hearing about with a rooftop bar and amazing appetizers. Michael held the door open for me as Jack quickly grabbed my hand and guided me inside.

"Thank you, baby." I made sure to acknowledge him, resting my hand on his strong arm as we waited for the host to seat us.

Surprisingly, he gave me a content smile before he quickly handed the host something. "Put us at your best table, please."

HANA

Oh. The host quickly nodded and led us outside, seating us at a small, square table with three chairs surrounding it. It gave us a beautiful view of the sparkling New York lights over the river.

I quickly opened the menu, knowing I wanted a drink and hoping they would too. I glanced over at Jack as he eyed the menu intently, seemingly lost in his thoughts. When I looked over at Michael, he was staring at me, watching me. I blushed as I looked back down at the menu. They were both being so quiet, and I knew I had to break the ice.

"I'm glad you both agreed to come out with me tonight." I first looked at Michael then Jack.

Jack quickly grinned at me. "Of course, sweetheart." He held his hand out for me on the table and gently squeezed as I placed mine on his.

I couldn't forget to acknowledge Michael as well. I turned to him and put my hand on his thigh, rubbing around in circles.

"Careful there." He smiled, almost surprised. "I'm not sure the other guests would appreciate me lifting up that dress of yours and making you come loudly with my hand."

I looked down and tried to contain my smile, not able to look at Michael for very long. I was startled when our server came up to us with a pitcher of water, pouring some in each of our glasses that were already on the table.

"Can I start you with any drinks?" he asked as he glanced at each of us, stopping at me.

I quickly nodded. "Yes, I'll take a glass of the rosé." I looked back at Michael and almost dared him to say something.

"Whiskey, neat," he responded, not breaking eye contact with me.

"Just a gin and tonic for me, thanks," Jack told the server.

The server nodded and walked away.

"Are we partying tonight or what?" Jack quipped.

I laughed and shrugged. "Maybe that's what we need to all get along." I put my elbows to the table and rested my chin on my hands, staring out at the beautiful view.

"Funny, are you not supposed to be sober? With your past heroin addiction?" Michael asked dryly.

My shoulders tensed. "Please," I quickly interjected, turning to Michael. "Can we not be bitter to each other? Just for one night?"

Michael almost looked like he was pouting. His eye twitched before he looked away from me and at the city skyline. It was quiet and awkward for a moment before the server came back with our drinks. I quickly took a gulp of my rosé and sat back on my chair, resting my arm up on it and crossing my leg toward Jack.

"I think we should all vacation to the west coast this summer. Before touring starts, of course," I said to Jack, desperately trying to change the subject.

He smirked at me as he took a drink. "That sounds quite nice." He nodded.

I turned to Michael as he stared out at the skyline. "I've never been. My mum always wanted to see Hollywood. She thought it would be so glamorous." His tone was distant and sad.

My heart broke for him. The anniversary of his mother's death had just passed, and I somehow had forgotten all about it. I even missed his birthday, although I had thought of him all that day.

"I'm sure she would have loved it, baby." I gave him a small smile, putting my hand atop his.

I cleared my throat, thinking of something Michael and Jack had in common.

"Jack lost his dad around that age as well." I turned to Jack as I spoke, and he stared down at the table, his brows pulled together.

He shook his head. "No. My dad killed himself. You can say it, Hana." He looked up at me with somber eyes then turned to Michael. "I found him hanging in our bathroom. How did your mum die?"

It was as if he was challenging him. I turned to Michael slowly; he was narrowing his eyes at Jack, his jaw clenching.

"Slit her wrists in the bathtub. Any other burning questions you're eager to ask me?"

Fuck.

"Ah," Jack responded. "That explains why we're both so fucked up, doesn't it, mate?" He was smiling at Michael as he spoke.

I took swigs of my rosé to finish it.

"Hana," Michael scolded me.

"I'm sorry I brought it up." I shook my head at myself. "That was stupid. Why would I think that talking about your dead parents would be a good idea?"

Jack put his hand to my thigh. "It's okay, sweetheart," he said quietly.

"Excuse me? Could I please have another glass?" I motioned to our server, holding up my glass.

Now I felt like *I* was spiraling. I couldn't imagine this working out. Why was I forcing them to do this? They hated each other and they would always hate each other. But what other choice did I have? If I chose one, the other would be heartbroken and fly off the rails again. I didn't think either of them would be okay without me. All I could imagine was Michael hovering over me the day he took me and Jack's dark eyes watching me from across the room in the music studio. How could I ever do that to one of them again?

The server quickly took my glass and disappeared.

"Maybe we shouldn't be here. Maybe you're both right. Maybe it should be like, a joint custody thing? I could split my time between both of you?" I turned to each of them, speaking quickly.

"I don't want to split any time with you," Jack quickly answered. "You're my fucking wife."

Michael scoffed. "Your wife that you *forced* to marry you."

"Oh, fuck off. She would have married me anyway. She would have been the runaway bride at your wedding, running back to me," Jack responded bitterly.

"Please," I muttered quietly. "Stop."

"Wouldn't it have been nice to give her a choice on the matter? How would you know what would have happened?" Michael kept prodding.

Jack laughed. "Because I know. She always kept running back to me and she always would have."

I stood quickly, making my chair fall to the ground behind me as I grabbed my jacket and stormed off. I knew everyone on that rooftop was staring at me, and my cheeks burned with rage and embarrassment. For a split second, I considered running away to some place neither of them would ever find me. They would *always* fight over me. I would *always* be torn apart. Why couldn't I just fucking choose one?

"Hana." Jack was behind me, walking out of the restaurant door with me. "I'm sorry. We shouldn't have kept on with that."

I kept walking, ignoring him. I turned and saw Michael walk out, following behind us.

"This isn't fair," I cried, tears streaming down my face. "Why can't you both just let me make my own decisions? Why can't I fucking be free?" I pressed the elevator button continuously, the impatience in my chest feeling like it would crack my lungs apart.

"Free, Hana? You *are* free. You're free to do whatever the fuck you want," Jack responded harshly. "You're free to leave me. You're free to leave Michael. You've had this power the whole time, damnit!"

I turned to him and shook my head. Tears were streaming down his face now as well. "I'm powerless with you two. Even when I've been given it, I won't ever be able to use it."

His eyes widened.

"Hana, maybe we can all calm down and talk at the apartment," Michael said gently beside us.

"No." I shook my head again. "You two stay here. I need space. I need time alone."

The elevator doors pinged open, and I quickly walked in. "Don't follow me."

I watched their confused, hurt faces as the elevator doors closed.

Emily

Adam and I were watching reruns of a trash TV show, both of us mindlessly on our phones and only half-paying attention to the show, when I suddenly heard something odd in the hallway. I quickly grabbed the remote to turn down the volume.

"What's wrong?" Adam looked up at me.

"Shhh!" I looked around our apartment as if that would give me the answer.

It sounded like sobs coming from one of our neighbors.

"Do you hear that?" I asked Adam as I stood and investigated.

"Someone crying?" he wondered aloud.

I quickly went to the front door and looked out the peephole.

I gasped. "Oh my God." I opened the door, finding Hana slumped down on the floor against the wall and sobbing into her knees.

"Hana!" I sat down in front of her, taking her hand. "Hana, are you okay?"

I swear I started seeing red. If one of them hurt her, I was going to prison for murder.

She shook her head no, still sobbing uncontrollably.

"Did they hurt you? What happened?"

I saw Adam in the doorway and I shooed him away, trying

EMILY

to give Hana privacy. I didn't know what else to do other than put my hand on Hana's back and rub around in circles. Something was going on, and I needed to know what it was so I could take action. But first, I needed to make sure my cousin was okay. Seeing her this way broke my heart, and I started to cry too.

"Han," I said quietly as her sobs lessened, her breath hiccuping in her chest. "Come inside. Let me get you some water."

She shook her head again, finally looking up at me. Her tear-soaked eyes were red and puffy.

"I can't bother you with this, Emily. You won't understand. I just…I didn't know where else to go." Her voice was small and shaky.

I sighed. "You don't have to talk. Just come inside. Who knows what the fuck kind of germs are on this shit hole floor."

I got a smile out of her. She finally nodded and took my hand, both of us getting up and slowly walking through the door.

Adam sat casually at the kitchen table, looking down at his phone before looking up at us. I shook my head at him as I guided Hana into the privacy of our bedroom. I closed the door behind us as she sat at the edge of the bed, throwing her purse on the floor. Our bedroom was an absolute disaster, but Hana didn't even seem to notice.

"We all went on a date at the new rooftop bar near Greenpoint," she started, still looking down at the floor. "They wouldn't stop fucking bickering. It made me realize that this was never going to work."

She looked up at me with hesitant eyes and shook her head. "Why can't I just fucking pick one, Emily? What's wrong with me? I can't live without them."

I would never understand her love and loyalty to those two men who pretended to be perfect—she knew that. But she still wanted to confide in me. She trusted me, and I had to listen; I had to be her rock.

"Nothing is wrong with you, babe. You're perfect." I smiled as I sat next to her.

She snorted and looked over at me.

"You're just so loving and empathetic, Han. It's your best quality and your worst quality." I shrugged.

She didn't respond; she only looked down at the floor, lost in her thoughts.

"I remember thinking Michael was so fucking perfect. He was handsome, intelligent, and just...he treated me *so* well. He took care of me." She started crying again. "And that image of him just fucking shattered when he took me. He was like, a different person. He's changed but somehow he's still the same. And I still love him so much." She shook her head and started laughing. "And with Jack...God, he was so fucking sweet and romantic and just...I knew he was a tortured artist. Honestly, I almost wasn't shocked that he took me. Then I fell in love with him more than I ever thought was possible."

She finally looked up at me. "You see it too, don't you? The way he loves me, the way I love him? And with Michael? Tell me who I'm supposed to be with because I can't do this on my own."

I gulped. Of course I saw it, with each of them. But I couldn't possibly help her choose. I jumped at a quiet knock on the door and Adam appeared, wide eyed.

"Um, Hana? Jack just asked me if you're here. Do you want me to ignore it?"

Hana let out a laugh. "He knows I'm here, don't worry. You

can tell him."

Adam looked at me, confused, then nodded and closed the door behind him.

I tried not to sound judgmental when I asked her, "Is he still tracking you?"

She nodded and bit her lip as she stared down at the floor. "They both are."

* * *

Adam let Hana and I have the bedroom that night after she decided to stay. I went to hang out with Adam on the couch while I waited for her to shower, and it was clear by the look on his face that he was concerned.

"What happened? Is she okay? Did Jack hurt her?" he whispered to me frantically, eyeing the bathroom door.

Ever since he found out about Jack, he almost seemed afraid of him. Jack briefly spoke to him about how he and Hana were trying to "add Michael into their relationship," but Adam couldn't bring up literally *everything* else.

I shook my head as I sighed, eyeing the bathroom door as well.

"No, no one hurt her. They all went out and it ended with Jack and Michael arguing, and it kind of sent Hana into a panic attack. She's…she thinks she needs to choose between them."

Adam sighed and crossed his arms as he leaned back onto the couch.

"Well, she should. And it shouldn't be Michael," he huffed.

I turned to look at him, feeling like my eyes were going to fly out of their sockets. "You think she should be with *Jack*?" My face twisted with disgust.

Adam threw up his hands. "They're married. Like, she *wants* to be married to him now, right? If she ever left him, I know for a fact that he would kill himself. He's told me."

I narrowed my eyes at him. "So just because he's threatened to kill himself, you think that gives him the right to guilt her into staying with him?"

He shook his head again. "No, Em, I don't. But I've been thinking about this a lot, and I know Jack has done some fucked up shit, but it's her decision to stay now. Like, she's a grown fucking woman and she can do what she wants. Michael threw himself back into the picture and now he's fucking up their whole dynamic."

I was shocked that Adam was defending Jack. I knew they were best friends and all, but *this*? Did I even know my own boyfriend?

"I'm so fucking confused." I stood. "How are you defending his actions?"

Adam scoffed and stood in front of me. "I'm not, Emily. How are you supporting your cousin's decision to be with both of those fucking psychopaths?"

I didn't realize that the bathroom door was wide open until I turned around, seeing Hana slam our bedroom door behind her.

"Fuck!" I yelled to Adam then stomped to our bedroom door, finding the handle locked.

"Hana! I'm sorry. Please, let me in," I called out.

I could hear her clattering around before she opened the door in my borrowed sweats and T-shirt. She came bursting through with her clothes in one hand and her purse in the other.

"Han." I followed her to the front door. "Please, let's talk.

EMILY

You can't leave, it's fucking 2 a.m.," I continued.

"Let me make my own fucking crazy decisions, Emily. But don't you dare fucking judge me anymore."

The door slammed behind her.

"Fuck!" I turned to Adam. "Call Jack. Make sure he gets her home safe."

I thought about what I had said. *Jack* and *safe*, two words that didn't belong together in the same sentence. Yet here I was, knowing that Jack would stop at nothing to make sure she was okay. He would protect her, at least from the outside world. I knew all of those months ago that it was true. He worshiped the ground she walked on. He was obsessed with her.

And then I realized Hana felt the exact same about him.

Hana

I found myself walking toward the train station, not really sure of my destination. Where was home? I didn't know Cobble Hill all that well, but I knew the L train would take me where I needed to go.

I felt hopeless and broken. I hardly recognized myself as I watched my reflection in the subway windows as it traveled through the tunnel. Since when did life become so hard? I dreaded every day because I didn't know what to expect. Before all of this, when I was with Michael, life was predictable. I felt safe and secure. Would I still feel that way if I chose him now? I used to think he was perfect, which was intimidating. I didn't feel 100% myself around him. But now? My perfect Michael was flawed. *Very* flawed. Was that a good thing?

Things were the exact opposite with Jack. We didn't exactly start our relationship in the most ideal way, but being with him was exhilarating. Even though I knew the darkness in him was easily switched on and off, I felt connected to him. I literally felt a sting in my chest when I thought about being without him.

I didn't realize I had missed my stop until I heard the automated announcement of the Bedford Ave stop. I mindlessly exited the station and walked toward mine and Billie's old apartment. The lease didn't run out until June, so I figured she would still be there. I sent her my portion of rent and bills every month, probably way too much. But I never heard a peep from her.

The codes to get in were the same. I walked into the lobby and up the stairs until I reached our apartment. It felt surreal knocking on my own door. I still had a key, but I didn't want to intrude. I heard some shuffling around before the door opened. It wasn't Billie—a gorgeous blonde with blue tips answered, smiling at me with wide eyes. She appeared to be in her pajamas, looking right at home.

"Hana?" she asked me with knowing eyes.

I must have looked like a deer in headlights.

She laughed lightly. "Sorry. I'm Billie's roommate. I've seen pictures of you around here." She turned to look at the apartment then back at me. "Come on in. Billie's still up. I'm sure she'd love to see you," she suggested.

I looked around. The place was exactly how I remembered it. Billie and I had decorated it ourselves. I felt a pang of jealousy as Billie's new roommate sat comfortably on the couch.

"Um, sorry. How exactly did you meet Billie?" I asked, awkwardly standing at the foot of the couch.

She hesitated for a split second, tugging her long sleeves further down to her hands and fiddling with a ring on her right hand.

"We have mutual friends." She adjusted her body to put her legs up on the couch. "You know, I thought you and Billie weren't on great terms." She lifted her eyebrow knowingly.

I crossed my arms. "Billie and I will always be friends," I argued, not even sure why I felt the need to defend myself. "Excuse me."

I turned and went directly to Billie's room, lightly tapping on the door. After a few seconds, she opened the door; I had never seen her look so shocked before.

"Fuck, you were not what I was expecting." She laughed, widening her eyes.

I froze. *Shit, this was a bad idea*. But then she quickly wrapped her arms around me and gave me the longest hug; relief flooded through my body, loosening my limbs. I didn't even realize how tense I was.

She let go of me and kept her hand on my shoulder. "Come on." She gestured into her room.

I crossed my arms as I entered her room. I instantly felt like I was home as Billie sat on her bed and eyed me while I casually paced her room.

"I'm sorry for barging in so late," I started. "I just…I didn't really know where else to go."

Billie immediately frowned. "What's going on?"

I sighed as I shook my head. "Where do I even start?" I asked, more to myself than to her, as I looked down at the floor, still pacing nervously.

"Why don't you sit and relax and start whenever you're ready," Billie offered, her tone gentle and caring.

I nodded and quickly sat down next to her on the bed.

"Michael and I…and Jack," I started then began to laugh. "I'm making them share me. But they both hate it and they both fucking hate each other. And I'm so fucking selfish and idiotic for even thinking this could work out."

Billie was quiet as she took it all in. "So let me get this straight. You're in a poly relationship with Michael and Jack? Since when?" she asked calmly, no hint of judgment in her voice.

I sighed. "I wouldn't exactly call it poly. I'm basically forcing them to share me. And you don't even want to know what Michael did." I put my face in my hands, the shame and guilt overwhelming me.

"I'm all ears, Han," she finally responded.

I looked up at her and shook my head. "I can't drag you into this again, Billie. You don't deserve to be caught up in this mess. You were right to cut me off before." I started to cry as Billie watched me with concern and her knowing, caring eyes.

"You don't need to give me all the dirty details if you don't want to, Han. But I just want you to know that I'll always be here for you. You are never, ever alone."

With that, I began to sob, and Billie swiftly took me into her arms and held me, letting me get everything out. There had been so much tension between Jack and Michael, so much worrying that one of them would snap on the other. There was a sense of impending doom that neither of them would be able to take it and just off themselves, each other, or me. I had the sense that they would call my bluff; if one of them took me again, I don't know if I'd really kill myself. I was almost hoping that one of them would do it anyway so I wouldn't have to choose anymore.

I needed time to reflect by myself, or at least without them there, but I knew they were both too damn needy and impatient to let me do that. After crying on Billie for what felt like hours, I texted both of them to let them know I was staying with Billie and I would be back the next day. She didn't poke and prod for answers or information; she quietly lay next to me, stroking my hair until I cried myself to sleep.

***

Billie was gone by the time I woke up. She left a note on the nightstand letting me know she was at work and to stay as long as I needed to. I also had several texts from Michael and Jack. They both acknowledged that they wanted to give me space, but they couldn't stand to have me gone for very long. Jack sent me a picture of himself at our apartment, his big blue doe eyes sad as he held onto my pillow. I smiled and rolled my eyes. And then I received a text from Michael as I held my phone in my hand: **Hana, please give us another try. I'm sorry we were both acting like children. I spoke with Jack and he's agreed that we should all meet back at the apartment.**

I immediately dialed Jack, almost not believing Michael.

"Hello, love," Jack answered excitedly.

"Hey, babe. Michael said you agreed that we should all meet back at the apartment?"

Jack hesitated for a moment before he spoke. "Yes. I know I feel awful about bickering with him when all you wanted was a nice night. We really need to try harder. For you, love," he explained, his voice so soft and sweet.

For a split second, I thought maybe things could work after all.

"Come home to me, sweetheart. We can go to Michael's together."

I smiled to myself. "Okay." I nodded, as if he could see me.

"Hurry home. It's been too long since I've been inside of you, my darling wife," he growled into the phone.

I was instantly wet. "I'll leave now."

I put on my shoes and jacket before I opened Billie's door

and found her roommate lounging on the couch, looking up at me intently.

"Good morning," she said sweetly as she smiled.

Her voice was raspy and gravelly, as if she had been smoking or crying all night. I wasn't sure if she sounded like that last night, or if I just didn't notice it because of how distraught I was.

"Hey, good morning." I smiled back, heading for the front door.

"Um, hey, Hana?" She stood and slowly walked toward me as I stopped and turned around.

"I need to tell you something about Michael." *Wait, what?* "My name is Jackie."

My heart dropped. My hands shook as I clutched my purse, my heart racing wildly in my chest. Jackie…Michael's ex. The woman that accused him of such horrible things. *Why is she here? What is going on?*

"You're…*Jackie*," I said knowingly.

It was not lost on me that Jackie probably sought out Billie to get closer to me. The thought of her pretending to know nothing about me made my stomach curl. Maybe she even knew *too much* now.

"So you've heard of me." She smiled, stopping in front of me and observing my face.

I nodded.

"I was supposed to approach you at the Bowery next week, but I couldn't wait any longer. Especially since you just showed up here," she explained as her eyes began to fill with tears.

"You were going to the show?" I asked, confused.

She nodded, fidgeting with her ring again. I now realized it was exactly the same as the one Michael had given me.

"Jack asked me to approach you there," she explained.

So Jack spoke to her too?

"Why did he want you to approach me?" I interrogated, almost angry at Jack now. *Why the fuck would he want me to see Jackie?*

She looked down at the floor and tugged on her sleeve. "Like I said, I need to tell you something about Michael."

Please don't. Please don't tell me. It can't be true.

My knees buckled and my heart broke as she lifted her sleeves then her shirt. And at that moment, I knew I had fallen out of love with Michael.

Michael

I paced around the living room as I waited for Jack and Hana to come. I hadn't heard from either of them for over an hour, and neither was answering their phone. Something was going on. What did Jack do? Had he taken her away from me once again? I tried looking at Hana's location, but the app showed that her location was unavailable. I couldn't sit around and wait any longer—I dialed Billie, the last person she was with.

"Hey, Michael?" she answered after a few rings, confusion clear in her voice.

"Hey yeah, hi, Billie. I know Hana stayed with you last night. Do you have any idea where she is now?" I tried not to sound panicked.

She sighed. "No, I don't. My roommate said she left late this morning. Don't you think she would have let you know where she was if she wanted you to know?" Her tone was full of disdain and judgment.

"I'm not sure if you have forgotten or not, but Jack has a tendency to take Hana whenever he pleases," I spit out.

There was silence on the other end for a moment.

"Sorry, Michael. I don't know where she is," she finally replied.

I ran my hand through my hair. "Does your roommate have

any idea where she went?"

There was a knock at the door. I held my phone to my ear as I looked through the peephole and waited for Billie to respond. I started seething with anger when I realized who was on the other side of the door.

"No. I gotta go, Michael," Billie responded and hung up.

I quickly pocketed my phone and opened the door.

"What are you doing here?"

She seemed genuinely shocked that I was speaking to her this way; her eyes widened as she started to frown. She tried to mask it with bravery, but she was failing miserably.

"She's not coming back. All you have left is me. She knows who you really are."

I stared at her. *What did she do?*

"What the fuck do you mean, Jackie?" I spit out, my hands automatically forming into fists.

She scoffed. "What do I *mean*? Do you not remember these?" She lifted her sleeves, exposing her scars. "Do you not remember forcing me to be your slave? Bribing me to stay? Fucking mutilating me?" She was shaking now.

"You told Hana all of this?" My mind was blank; all I could think of was killing this fucking traitor.

Jackie nodded. "She was terrified, Michael—"

I grabbed her by the throat to shut her the fuck up. "Jackie, little girl. Is that what you call me?" I guided her inside, slamming the door shut with my foot.

Her eyes watered as she shook her head. "I'm sorry, daddy," she breathed out.

"Where is she?" I squeezed harder.

"I don't—I don't—"

I had to let her go if I wanted any answers. I released my

hand, and she gasped for breath.

"I don't know. Does that matter? You have me now. I will serve you, daddy. I love you." She inched in closer to me.

I scoffed and rolled my eyes. "Do not speak unless you're spoken to, Jackie. On your knees," I instructed.

She thinks I still want her? She really was fucking delusional. She looked up at me with her wide hazel eyes as she got on her knees. She looked so fucking eager. It was something I used to love about her, but now it repulsed me.

"Eyes on the floor."

She did as she was told.

"You're willing to serve me completely? Do as I say?" I slowly walked around her in circles. Her chest rose and fell quickly.

"Yes, daddy."

I thought for a moment. "Call Hana. Tell her you're a fucking liar. Make her believe you."

She was silent for a moment. "I can't. Then she will take you back," she cried quietly.

"So you won't obey me. Not a very good little girl, are you?" I hissed angrily.

She continued to cry. I took her by the hair and threw her on the floor. She thought she could ruin me and Hana? I would make her pay.

"Please, daddy," she cried pathetically from the floor.

"Shut the fuck up!" I yelled, making her flinch. "You have ruined fucking *everything*, Jackie. You think I would want to be with you after you sabotaged my relationship with Hana? How fucking daft are you?"

I punched the wall in the walkway. I was tempted to tie her up, force her to stay in a cold room upstairs, alone and afraid. But I needed to be a better man for Hana. I needed to show her that I was a changed man. Perhaps I could even convince her that I never did those things. Whatever it took, I was going to find Hana and make her believe me. She would be mine, Jack would be dead, and I would be the man that Hana had worshiped since the first time "sir" came out of her mouth.

Jack

I had been refreshing Hana's location practically every minute for hours now. I could see that she was almost home. I was eager to have her back to me.

I looked out the window from the living room, looking for any sign of her. *Not yet.*

When she left last night, I was fucking terrified. She was so upset, and I hated the way she looked at me as the elevator doors closed, taking away my Hana. It took everything in me to not physically follow her, but I did check her location to make sure she got to Emily's, or wherever she was going, safely. I had nothing to say to Michael; he was the one that started this whole tiff that could have easily been avoided. I even tried to shut my mouth, but he wouldn't budge. I quickly took another elevator downstairs, letting Michael take care of the bill. Of course the elevator had to stop on nearly every fucking floor on the way down.

I texted Hana as I walked toward the train station: **I'm sorry, love. That was ridiculous. I will do better, I promise.**

I nearly chewed my lip off as I watched Hana's location go from Williamsburg to Cobble Hill, verifying my theory that she was going to Emily's. That's when I texted Adam. When he let me know she was there, I sluggishly made my way back to our apartment. I hated walking into it alone. I hadn't realized how much I truly needed Hana's attention, or at least for her to be in the same vicinity as me. I hadn't realized how much my happiness depended on her, and it hurt like hell knowing she wasn't close to me. I wrote her a long letter describing everything I loved about her. I lay in our bed, hugging her pillow. I sent her a picture of myself holding the pillow close to my face, telling her how much I missed her. I sent her voice notes telling her that she was the love of my life. I couldn't believe I was actually letting her be away from me this long. Each minute that passed made my heart sting just a little more. Eventually, I fell asleep after jerking off to our sex video.

I woke up with a text from Michael the next morning: **Let's be civil for Hana. Why don't we all meet at the apartment today?** *This fucking twat.*

I responded: **Yeah mate. We'll see you there later.**

I checked Hana's location again. She was at her old apartment? She was with Billie? Fucking great. The way Billie hated me, I could only hope she hadn't swayed Hana's opinion of me. We had been through too much for her to listen to her friend that she hadn't talked to in months. Billie had no idea what our love was like now. No one except Hana and I knew that.

Shortly after Michael's text, Hana called me. I had never felt so fucking relieved. She wanted to make sure Michael wasn't lying to her—that was a good sign. She was starting to trust him less. Having Jackie approach her at the show was sure to work, and Michael would finally be out of our lives for good.

Only twenty minutes or so later, Hana was calling me again. I was all showered and ready for her to come home to me, so I answered cheerfully.

JACK

She was sobbing. I was immediately irate at whatever it was that made her cry like that.

"Hana? What's wrong?"

"Jack," she finally let out between sobs. "It's fucking true. You knew it, didn't you? Why didn't you tell me you saw proof?"

I could barely understand her. "What, sweetheart? What do you mean?" I prodded. It was about Michael, I already knew that. But how did she know?

"Jackie showed me. She's Billie's fucking roommate. They're both fucking crazy," she cried. "I can't go back there. I can't look at him again."

Jackie was Billie's roommate? *What the fuck?* This Jackie was sneakier than I thought.

"I know, sweetheart. I was waiting for the right time to tell you. It's despicable, isn't it? Come home, where are you?"

"I'm in a cab. I'll be home in five." She was finally calming down.

"Okay, love. I can stay on the phone with you if you'd like," I offered.

"No, I just…I need to process this. I'll see you soon." She hung up.

I smiled to myself. She didn't want to look at him again? It fucking worked. I had won.

Hana

It felt like my life and everything I knew were crumbling beneath me. My *perfect* Michael was just one big act; in reality, he was a fucking monster. How could he do such a thing? The way Jackie described every detail with tears streaming down her face made me want to die. I had seen a glimpse of this Michael, but he explained it away by pleading temporary "madness." How could he explain doing this to Jackie well before we were ever together? He lied to me about *everything*. He pretended to be some victim of a crazy girl who was obsessed with him. How in the fuck would I ever believe a word he said to me now? Did he ever actually love me, or did he just want someone to control? Would it have gotten to that point? If I didn't obey him, would he have become this deranged psychopath who would want to "ruin" my body too?

I knew for a fact Jack was nowhere near perfect. He acted on impulse, he had anger issues, he was volatile and impatient and stubborn. But he always knew when he was wrong. He didn't pretend to be a saint. He was completely himself, and I loved him for everything he was. What the fuck did I love about Michael? I didn't even know him anymore. I loved that he took care of me, or was that him subtly trying to control me? I loved that he was so confident, or was that just grandiosity? I loved that he showered me with gifts and worshiped my body, or was that just a ploy for me to behave? He could so easily control me with how much I desired him. What if we only had lust? What if this was never love after all? Did he even know how to love?

I sobbed in the elevator all the way up to mine and Jack's apartment. I opened the door and found Jack waiting for me in the hallway, immediately opening his arms and embracing me tightly. If he had never approached Jackie, I would have continued living with a psychopath. Jack was my knight in morally gray armor.

"I'm so sorry, sweetheart. I know this must be too much to bear," he said softly as he continued to embrace me.

"You tried to tell me. I didn't listen." I sobbed into his chest. "I'm so sorry."

"Don't be sorry, love. I just love you so much. I would do anything for you," he responded, grazing his lip over my earlobe.

It had been too long since Jack and I had made love. I knew it when I started getting wet just hearing his low voice whisper into my ear. I needed him right then and there.

"Fuck me, Jack. Make me forget about all of this," I pleaded, letting go of him and putting my hands to his stubbly face.

Jack licked his lower lip before grabbing my legs and pulling me up against him.

"I will fuck you so hard you'll forget your name, love. How's that?" he growled.

He didn't wait for an answer; he fervently pressed his lips to mine as he backed me against the wall. My hands ran through his hair, my hips desperate for his hard cock that I felt between my thighs. He took me into the kitchen and set me onto the counter, throwing anything off that was in our way. Glass shattered on the hardwood floor as Jack lifted my dress off and immediately put his mouth to my nipple, teasing it with his tongue. I ran my hands through his hair as I closed my eyes, needing my mind blank and only the feeling of pleasure consuming my body.

"I love you, Hana," Jack whispered as he trailed kisses from my breasts to my chest, then up to my neck, making me squirm with need.

"I love you, Jack. I love you," I whispered back, pulling him closer with my legs.

"I will protect you, my love. You're my wife and I will die for you if I need to," he breathed, focusing on my neck as he took my breast in his hand.

Tears streamed down my face. "I know, Jack." I pulled him close again, putting my lips to his shoulder. "Please. I need you."

Jack quickly took his lips off me and pulled down his jeans and boxer briefs, pulled me closer to the edge of the counter, and quickly slammed himself inside of me. I screamed with relief as he thrust deep inside of me, his rhythm quick and feral.

"You're mine, Hana. My wife," he grunted, digging his nails hard into my hips.

"Always," I moaned, my head falling back with pleasure.

Jack quickly pulled out of me then lifted me up, turned me around, and bent me over the counter. He pulled my hair with one hand as he entered me then put his other hand to my clit, rubbing furiously. My release continued to build as I pushed my hips against him. My hands slid across the top of the counter as I tried to push back into him further.

"Come for me, sweetheart. Tell me you're mine. Scream my name," Jack ordered, pumping even harder now.

"Jack. I'm yours, baby. Fuck, Jack!" I moaned with pleasure from my orgasm, my pussy clenching against him, needing more.

Jack didn't slow his fingers on my clit, forcing another orgasm, and I screamed again as I rode his fingers and cock.

"Baby. I need you to come inside of me. I need all of you inside me," I moaned, desperate for the feeling of his warmth inside of me.

"Oh, fuck yes, Hana," he grunted. He moaned loudly, and his warm cum started leaking down my thighs as he slowed his thrusts.

"Jack," I whimpered, tears streaming down my face again.

All I could see, now that my mind returned to its racing thoughts, was Michael's angry glare and Jackie's scars. I needed Jack and I to get away, to run from this mess I created.

"Sweetheart." Jack pulled out of me and turned me around, a look of concern washing over his face as he noticed my tears.

"We need to leave. We need to get out of here. I can't see Michael again. He will look for us and I can't lose you," I cried, sheer panic arising in my chest.

Jack took my face in his hands, forcing me to look at him. "Hana. There is no reason to be afraid. I will protect you, my love," he assured me confidently.

I shook my head quickly. "No, no. We know what he's capable of. He will hurt us. Please, we need to get out of here," I cried, holding onto Jack's shoulders.

Jack's eyes went dark. My scary Jack was emerging, and for once, it was a good thing.

"We're not hiding, love. We need to confront him; we need

to tell him you're done with him," he growled, and I could tell he took pleasure in saying those words aloud.

I knew he was right. I needed to tell Michael face to face.

Suddenly, there was a knock on the door. I was nauseous with fear—I was positive it was Michael. I blocked him on my phone so he couldn't contact me or track me.

Jack quickly stormed into our room, and I instinctively followed. I watched as he opened the safe and pulled out his gun.

"I thought it was at Michael's." I shook my head, trembling as I watched Jack put it into the waistband of his jeans.

"I got another. Just in case," he explained then stormed back out into the living room.

I followed as Jack went to the front door and looked out the peephole. He looked back at me with confusion as I stood behind him.

"It's Jackie," he whispered, eyeing me for approval to answer it.

She must be in trouble. Maybe she was fleeing from Michael. I didn't even question that she knew where we lived. "Open it," I whispered back.

Jack flung the door open, and there was Jackie, her arms crossed and her face covered with fear. And then it all happened so quickly that I couldn't even blink or comprehend what was happening before me. Michael appeared, slammed his fist into Jack's face, and then Jack fell onto the floor, unconscious.

"Jack!" I cried, quickly leaning down to him.

Michael's hand pressed against my mouth, but it wasn't just his hand—there was something in it that made my head spin. Then, as a recurring theme in my life, everything went black.

Hana

I woke up with my wrists and legs bound, lying in fetal position on something soft. A bed? I couldn't open my eyes yet. I knew I was naked when something above me caused a chill over my bare skin. My head pounded with a furious headache, and my mouth felt like a cotton ball. I suddenly felt a hand on my head, softly stroking my forehead and hair. I knew by the smell of his cologne who it was. I suddenly remembered what had happened: Michael knocked Jack out. Now I was sure he had taken me again.

"Hello, sleepyhead," Michael whispered, his fingers softly stroking my cheek.

My eyes finally fluttered open; we were somewhere dark, and I could hardly see Michael at first.

My eyes finally focused on him. There he was, a faint smile on his lips as he observed my face. I looked around as my eyes adjusted more to the darkness. It looked like we were in a furnished basement of a house, but I had no idea where.

"How are you feeling?" he asked softly, getting closer to me on the bed.

A tear streamed down the side of my face.

"I'm not sure what's going on, Michael," I whispered, struggling to sit up.

He sighed loudly as I sat up to lean against the wall.

"Well, Hana. I realize what you must think of me after what Jackie told you. I needed to show you that I'm not that man anymore."

I didn't know if Michael realized it or not, but fucking kidnapping me and tying me up again wasn't making a very good impression.

"So it *is* true?" I asked wearily.

He rubbed his forehead, seemingly with frustration, before he looked at me.

"I didn't know who I was until I met you, Hana. I did some terrible things in my past. I was a broken man and you fixed me. Until you left me," he explained, his gray eyes dark, and not just because of the lighting. "And then that man came back. But I'm not capable of things like that when I'm with you."

My heart felt like it was literally breaking. The man of my dreams wasn't real—he was a facade used to hide a monster from me for all those months. And I had cried over him for weeks while he was out there mutilating an innocent woman.

"Michael." I started to cry. "You don't need me in order to be a good man. You don't need me to redeem yourself."

His jaw began to clench. I realized my hands were shaking as I wrung them together. I feared he was going to hurt me the way he hurt Jackie.

"Please don't hurt me." I started to sob into my hands at the mere thought of Michael doing anything to me; it would be more heartbreaking than anything.

"Hana." He put his hand to my shoulder, and I flinched, which only made me cry more. "I'm not going to hurt you, baby. I would never," he whispered before putting his lips to my shoulder.

I tried to calm myself down. I needed to get out of this situation. I needed to fight, either with kindness or by outsmarting him.

"Baby, this rope hurts me." I looked up at him, holding up my hands, my eyes burning as I stared into his concerned eyes.

He shook his head knowingly at me. "I can't have you hurting yourself, Hana. I can't let you leave," he responded sharply as he got off the bed and stood.

"I'm not going to leave. Why would I leave you? You're perfect." I lifted my hands to him. "I won't hurt myself, I promise. I just…keeping me tied up like this, against my will? Are you really going to keep me like this?"

I saw his mind working as he stared at me with his hands on his hips. Of course I wanted to leave. He *was* going to hurt me, I was sure of that. I didn't know when he would snap, so I needed to think quickly.

"Hana." He knelt down beside the bed, his voice calm and quiet. "I would love to keep you like this, but I'm not going to. But you need to earn my trust again, my love. I know what you're thinking—you hate me right now. But I know for a fact that even when you hate someone, you'll spread your fucking legs for them."

His eyes were boring into me, a glare that I had only ever seen at the house in Greenwich.

"I don't hate you," I responded, my voice shaky.

He smiled at me. "Good. So you'll obey me then, won't you, baby?"

"Of course, sir." I nodded.

He licked his lips. "There's my good girl." He stood and began to unbutton his jeans. "I'm going to fuck you and plant my seed in you. Every. Fucking. Day."

Wetness pooled between my thighs, an ache for him that would always be there. I hated myself. His cock sprung free before he removed his shirt in one quick motion, revealing every glorious part of him. He grabbed my feet and forced me onto my back. He hovered over me and put his lips to my shoulder then my neck, making me squirm.

"I'm going to make you mine again, Hana. Once I put a fucking baby inside of you, you'll never be able to leave."

Tears welled in my eyes again, but before I could process what he had told me, he lifted my legs and plunged himself inside of me.

"Fuck, you're so wet. You're a fucking whore, aren't you? You're so scared and so fucking wet for me," he moaned, pumping quickly.

His cock hit my g-spot perfectly. I didn't want to give him the satisfaction of me coming so quickly so I tried to hide it. I bit my lip as I moaned, clenching my eyes shut.

"Did I say you could come, Hana?" He slowed his thrusts.

Fuck. "No, sir. I'm sorry. I couldn't help it," I cried.

Michael chuckled. "This is why I fucking love you, Hana. You're so easy to crumble under my touch." He started to quickly pound me again, smiling down at me deviously.

I hated that he was right. I hated how wet I was for him even after learning he was a monster. Even after he had chloroformed me and brought me to wherever the fuck we were and bound me with rope with no intention of ever letting me go.

"Come again for me, baby. I want to see your face blinded by pleasure while I come inside of you."

I hated my body and myself as Michael hit the perfect spot

again, making my pussy clench around him as I came quietly while he pounded me.

He chuckled again. "That's right. I'm gonna make you come every single fucking day, whether you resist it or not."

He grabbed my hips as my bound legs rested on his chest and moaned loudly as he came.

He slowed his hips and grabbed a pillow from the top of the bed then rested it under my ass so my hips were lifted. I knew this old trick—he was trying to help plant his seed in me, get me pregnant easier.

"Sir," I said quietly as I watched him grab a bottle of water from a small fridge across the room. "Do you think getting me pregnant against my will makes me think you're a better man now?"

I wanted to get into his head. I wanted to try to at least attempt to get out of here and see Jack again. I had some small hope he would find me, but I wasn't optimistic. Or maybe it would be like the Double Tree in Jersey all over again. I secretly hoped Jack had implanted some sort of tracking device in me while I slept. *God, I hope so.*

I watched as Michael slowly walked over to me and smiled. He was fully nude and his semi-hard dick moved around, making my pussy twitch involuntarily.

"Baby, I know you want to bear my children. I know you've always imagined having little Michael juniors running around," he said quietly, sitting next to me on the bed and stroking my hair.

Tears started to stream down my face. "That was before I knew who you really were," I spit out, adrenaline making me shake as I gained the courage to speak my mind. "How could I have a child with someone who fucking mutilates women? I would never—"

Almost instantly, Michael's wild, angry eyes were mere inches from me. He grabbed my face, squeezing my cheeks with his thumb and fingers.

"Hana, if you ever want to get out of this fucking rope, you better watch your fucking mouth," he spit out. "You really need to be on my good side, my love, unless you really want to see how fucking cruel I can be. You haven't seen anything yet."

His eyes were wide and clouded with a rage and malice I had never seen before. My heart sunk deep into my belly with a fear I had hardly experienced, and the fact that I felt that fear from Michael made it even worse.

"Yes, sir." My shaky words were barely audible.

Michael's eyes were soft again. "Good, my sweet girl. I'm glad we have an understanding."

He got up and softly grazed his fingers against my breasts and collar bone, then to my belly and above my pubic bone.

"You're so lovely. I can't wait to see your belly swell."

It was so easy for him to turn. It was as if he hadn't heard a single thing I said, or it just didn't bother him. He knew I didn't have a choice.

"I love you, Hana." He smiled down at me as he started to stroke himself again.

The heat deep in my belly shot straight to my pussy. It was happening all over again—I was being held captive. And I would never see Jack again. I started to cry as Michael lifted my legs and thrust himself inside of me. And I knew if I was ever free again, I would make sure Michael could never hurt me, or anyone else, ever again.

Jack

Groggily, I tried to open my eyes, realizing my left eye was unable to open. I shot straight up with a gasp as what had happened sunk in.

"Hana!" I shouted, searching the apartment and praying to whoever was listening that she was safe and in our home.

My heart crumbled in my chest as I realized she was gone.

"Fuck!" I screamed.

My knees buckled underneath me. "Fuck!" I yelled, my chest heaving as tears streamed down my face.

I had to take action immediately. Jackie was involved—I needed to get to her. *She's at Billie's apartment.* I sprung to my feet, feeling my gun still securely in the waist of my jeans, and shot out the front door. I immediately dialed Billie as I took the elevator down. I was shocked at how quickly she answered.

"Jack?" She sounded surprised to hear from me.

"Billie, Hana is in trouble. Michael has taken her against her will. Jackie helped him."

There was silence. "Billie!"

"*Jackie* helped him? My roommate Jackie?"

"Yes!" I huffed. "She's Michael ex. I assume she wanted to be closer to Hana and Michael through you. Where is she?"

"She's uh—fuck, I don't know! Let me call her," she replied nervously. "What do I say?!"

"Tell her it's an emergency. Tell her the landlord is kicking you out. Make something up, Billie!" I didn't have any patience. I couldn't when Hana's safety was on the line.

"Okay!" she snapped. "Then what?"

I was already out the lobby's door, racing toward a cab.

"I'm on my way. I'll take care of it."

I already had a key to Billie's apartment; Jessica got one made when I started watching Hana the first time. Speaking of Jessica, I needed to fill her in. Maybe she could help find Hana. I quickly dialed her as I got into a cab.

"Hello, brother," she answered cheerfully.

"Jessica, Michael took Hana. Jackie helped him. He fucking sucker punched me and took her," I explained, my voice shaky; saying it aloud more and more made it start to sink in even deeper.

Jessica gasped. "No…"

"I'm on my way to Billie's apartment. Your friend Jackie is her roommate—did you know that?" I was angry and desperate to point the blame at anyone I could.

"Of course I didn't know that, Jack! Jesus Christ. What can I do to help?" She sounded frantic as well.

I put my hand to my forehead. "Fuck, I don't know. See if Michael has any other residences he's associated with. Call his aunt and uncle, every single person he knows. Just fucking find out everything you can," I ordered.

"Okay. Okay, Jack. Please be careful." Her voice was shaky and hesitant.

"I will, Jess. I love you." If I got myself killed somehow, I needed her to know that.

Her breath hitched a little. "I love you too, Jack."

I hung up as the cab pulled up to Billie's apartment. If Jackie was there, she was a lot more idiotic than I thought. I jogged upstairs, stopped in front of their door, and unlocked it. I quickly searched Jackie's room. It was fucking empty. I went into Billie's room and then the bathroom. Empty. I slowly walked into Jackie's room again, waiting for her impatiently. I sat on the bed and looked at my phone, waiting for any word from anyone. Why didn't it cross my mind before to call the direct source of this destruction?

It rang three times before he answered. I shot up off the bed.

"Hi there, mate." He sounded so smug, fucking bastard.

"Tell me where you are. Where the fuck is my wife?" I snarled into the phone, my face on fire with anger.

"She's with me. She's not yours anymore, Jack."

I could hear crying in the background. It hadn't sunk in that I may never see her again, but it hit me now. I started to panic. *Fuck, I should involve the police.*

"Once I find you, Michael, I'm going to fucking kill you," I snapped.

The bastard laughed. "Okay, Jack. Good luck with that." He hung up.

I wanted to crush my phone in my hand. Red clouded my vision as I heard the front door open. I swung Jackie's door open as the front door shut behind her, a look of pure shock on her face. I walked right up to her, pushed her against the wall, and pressed my hand up to her throat.

"Where the fuck is she?" I growled, my body shaking with rage.

She stared at me with her wide eyes.

"I don't know. He didn't tell me. He just used me to get you to open the door," she cried, tears streaming down her face. "He had a cab waiting. I followed them downstairs as he carried her and he left me on the street."

"What cab company was it?"

I squeezed her throat harder as she shook her head.

"I—I—I don't know. It—"

"Think, Jackie!" I shouted.

"It was yellow. Yellow Cab," she cried.

"Are you fucking positive?"

She nodded, her eyes terrified. *Good. She deserves to feel that way after helping someone kidnap my wife.*

I finally let go, and she coughed out for breath, sliding down the wall and crying.

"Does Michael have any other houses? Tell me everything you know," I told her as I paced around the living room.

She stayed on the floor, crying as she put her knees to her chest. "He doesn't tell me anything. All he's done is use me. He doesn't give a shit about anyone except himself."

She was angry at him. This was good.

"Tell me, Jackie." I leaned down to get closer to her. "Do you still love him?"

She looked up at me and blinked. She began to shake her head no. "He's a fucking monster."

I grew excited. I was playing nice guy now. "Would you tell the police what he did? Would you help me find Hana?"

She bit her lip and looked down at the floor. I was patient while I waited for her to answer.

"Yes. I can't have him reeling me in over and over. He'll fucking kill me one of these days."

I tried to contain my excitement. "Good, Jackie. Come with

me to the police department." I stood and held my hand out for her.

She seemed to think for a moment. "Okay." She grabbed my hand and let me help her up.

We walked out the door together, and I quickly texted Jessica: **Jackie is coming to the police station with me. She's telling them everything.**

Jessica responded quickly: **Oh thank God. I've talked to Michael's aunt and uncle. They are shocked to learn of his behavior. They are trying to contact him now.**

I smiled as I read the text. We were going to bring this fucker down, and I would have my wife back—all to myself.

Emily

Hana's phone kept going straight to voicemail. Did she block me? I didn't want to bother her but I *did* want to apologize. I wanted to support Hana's decisions, no matter how outrageous they were. I just didn't want her to get hurt.

And fucking Adam—he seemed so unfazed by all of this. Did I even know my own boyfriend, the man I was living with?

As I paced our living room, trying to call Hana for the 175th time, my phone rang with a call from Billie.

"Billie?" I answered, looking in the mirror at my confused face.

"Em, Hana's in trouble," she started. *Oh fuck.* "Apparently Michael has taken her. Can you fucking believe this is happening *again*? What the fuck is wrong with these men she gets involved with?"

I immediately started to sob. "Are you fucking kidding me?" I asked, more to myself than Billie. I didn't know if my heart could take any more of this.

"Who told you this? Jack?" I inquired, grabbing my coat to head out into the city, unsure of where I was going.

"Yeah. I guess my fucking roommate, Jackie, is Michael's ex. She helped him take her. I could fucking kill both of them myself." Her voice cracked.

EMILY

"I'm coming over. Are you home?" I quickly walked down the stairs of my apartment building.

"Not yet. I'm on my way, though."

"I'll see you there." I hung up and dialed Jack.

He answered right away. "Emily. Good timing."

"What the fuck is going on?" I yelled into my phone.

"Michael took Hana. Again! I have no fucking idea where they are. However, my new friend Jackie and I are headed to the police station. Fancy meeting us there?" He seemed so calm.

"Um, yeah. How would I help?"

I had little faith in the police. They were fucking useless before.

"You can tell them what he did to her before. What she told you. Of course, leave out anything that puts me in a bad light." He laughed nervously.

"Yeah," I sighed. "Yeah, okay."

I didn't know why I agreed, or why I let Jack off the hook. Maybe because I was desperate to make sure Hana would get home safely, and if talking to the police and working with Jack helped, I'd do it.

"We should get Hana's parents involved. The police listen to rich people. Once we find Hana, Uncle Dan will have him in prison for fucking life."

I tried to think of all the resources I could provide and sometimes having money like our family did could get things done very quickly.

"Okay, you're right. Thank you, Emily. Meet us at the station—90th Precinct. " He sounded relieved.

"Okay." I nodded. "I'll see you there."

I texted Billie to give her an update as I hailed a cab.

Hana

I wasn't sure how long I'd been tied up for. It felt like days had gone by. We had a routine I was starting to get used to: Michael would wake up beside me then he would fuck me and make me come over and over again before he would come inside of me. The light of day shining through the small windows above the bed confirmed my theory that we were in a basement. It looked like it was in a brand new home. There was a couch in front of a TV on the wall. There were stairs that led up to the house where Michael would disappear for only a few minutes at a time. He let me take baths with him at night; he would remove the rope from my wrists and ankles after he carried me into the bathroom. It was a bare bathroom with absolutely nothing in it besides a bath, toilet, and sink. Not even a mirror. Was that on purpose? As he bathed me, he would slowly rub his hands around my tits and turn me on, making me hate myself even more. He would try to make conversation, acting as if everything was normal. I was far too depressed to give him anything good.

"Hana," Michael whispered in my ear as he carried me to bed, and I finally realized that I didn't have any rope binding me. "Let's talk."

He laid my naked body onto the bed and lay beside me,

rubbing circles on my belly.

"Tell me you love me, Hana," he ordered quietly.

I looked up and shook my head, but the words still came out. "I love you, Michael." My voice was hoarse from my incessant crying over the last few days.

He looked down at me angrily. "Say it like you mean it."

I sat up and rubbed my wrists with my hands, looking at the red, raw skin that the rope had left me with.

"I can't, Michael. I don't mean it anymore."

I didn't want to be his obedient, compliant submissive anymore. I didn't want to please him anymore. I loved the idea of Michael and I loved his gorgeous exterior, but I hated him. All I wanted was Jack, and now I was certain that was never going to happen. If Michael killed me for "misbehaving," then so be it. I didn't want to live without Jack. If I were presented with something I could use to hurt myself, I would do it. I would try to kill Michael first, but then I'd do it.

Michael sat on the edge of the bed, shaking his head as he let it hang in front of him. "Oh, Hana. You don't mean that," he said as he looked over at me, his malicious glare staring right through me.

I wanted to die, but I was still afraid of him hurting me. My heart raced with sheer panic. I couldn't move or speak; I just silently waited for my punishment.

Michael shook his head at me as he stood and put his hands on his hips.

"Nothing to say? You don't want to apologize or beg on your knees for forgiveness?" His voice was loud and his eyes were wide.

I started scooting back against the wall, hugging my knees into my body and shaking my head. "No," I muttered.

He was silent for a moment as he narrowed his eyes at me. Was he thinking of a fitting punishment? And then a sinister smile appeared across his lips. I watched him walk upstairs, slam the door shut, and then come right back down with a belt in his hand. He already had one side wrapped around his fist.

His eyes were wild with pure anger. I didn't see any amusement or lust in them, just sheer animosity.

"Still a 'no,' Hana?"

I started to cry. I needed to be strong, but I felt myself crumbling again. I didn't know what to say—all I did was watch him stare at me with hatred in his eyes. And then a fucking grin appeared on his face again.

"Last chance, Hana. Anything you want to say to me before I punish you in every way I desire?"

"Fuck you," I said between sobs, my breath hiccuping and my whole body vibrating with panic and fear.

He grabbed me by my hair, pulling so hard that he lifted me onto my feet, and then threw me on the ground. I landed on my knees and shins, immediately feeling the pain from the throw. I started to move across the floor to try to put space between us, but he didn't waste any time grabbing my feet and dragging me toward him. I began to kick at him as I felt something plastic wrap around my ankles, but my attempts were futile. As he turned me over, I realized he had wrapped zip ties around my ankles; I looked up at him and I didn't even recognize him anymore. His face contorted into something evil. He took another zip tie and wrapped it around my wrists as I screamed at him. He took my restrained hands and quickly walked me to the bed before throwing me down. I didn't even have time to process any thoughts, all I felt was the stinging pain of his belt across my ass. He didn't waste any time before giving me a second and then third blow. All I could hear were my own sobs as he repeatedly hit me, each blow hurting more than the last. I finally heard him drop the belt and grunt loudly before taking my hips and quickly thrusting inside of me, his pounding violent and wild.

"You're mine, Hana," he growled before grabbing my hair with his hands and lifting me up, my back now parallel to his chest. "No one will find you, Hana. You better start behaving, or this is what you'll get every night."

He didn't just simply cum inside of me and be done with me; he made sure to reach around and finger my clit, knowing exactly how to get me off. He took pleasure from knowing how badly I tried to resist him, yet would crumble each and every time. As I came, my cries mixed with my moans, he laughed in my ear and threw me back onto the bed. I felt his warm cum inside of me as he slowed his hips, and all that kept repeating inside of my head was *die, Hana. Kill yourself*. I screamed out as I cried, "I can't!"

Michael chuckled to himself as he pulled out of me, not even fazed by my outburst.

"It'll only get worse from here on out, Hana. If you're smart, you'll start acting like my good girl again."

I feebly lifted myself off the bed, looked over at him, and vomited all over the perfect gray carpet. I started to get lightheaded as I turned and noticed Michael's angry eyes watching me, and then I fell back onto the bed, everything finally silent and dark.

Hana

Michael tried to be nice to me after he beat me with his belt. I could barely move with how depressed I was. I would watch Michael read and then I would fall asleep. I watched as he ate, watched TV, worked out, and all I could do was lay on my stomach and watch him before I fell asleep again. I couldn't eat. I woke up to him fucking me and I would just lay there until he turned me on my back, used the wand or his fingers to stimulate my clit to make me come, and then came inside of me. He would always prop my hips up to keep his cum inside of me.

I gave up any hope of seeing Jack again. He would have found me by now. It had to have been at least a week since Michael took me. I wondered what Jack was doing. Would he move on without me? Did he kill himself because I wasn't there? I wanted to join him. I needed to see him again, whether it be in hell or not.

I started fantasizing more and more about death. When Michael fucked me, I prayed he'd hurt me so bad that it would kill me. Ever since he beat me with his belt, he wasn't the same. *I* wasn't the same. All he cared about was fucking me, holding me captive, getting me pregnant, and making me "his." I felt disconnected from my body. I could see myself from above, lying in bed, Michael digging his nails into my flesh as he fucked me. The sight of him only repulsed me now. How could someone so beautiful be so evil? My body would betray me daily, my pussy wet for him even when I could barely move. He was right when he said I crumbled under his touch. My body never failed to respond to him. I hated myself more and more.

I opened my eyes to the sunlight shining through the small window, my hands and feet no longer bound. Michael took my hands and lifted me, making me sit up on the bed. He had a dress in his hand—a white summer dress. He put it over my head, and I lifted my arms, looking down at my clothed body. My bones felt weak. I didn't know if I could walk—I could barely sit up. I guessed that was the result of me refusing to eat.

Michael lifted me in his arms, holding me against his chest with my legs dangling over his arm. He sat me down on the toilet and brushed my teeth as he did daily—he did take care of me in that way, making sure I was clean. But it was different this time. He was clothed too, in jeans and a T-shirt, and he had trimmed his growing beard so it was now only a stubble. I felt an ache in my chest as I watched him in front of me. *Why couldn't things have been different? Why did he have to end up being a terrible monster?* He brushed my hair, put some flats on me, and then helped me stand.

We slowly walked up the stairs and into the house I had wondered so much about. It was a beautiful house with perfect natural light shining through, a grand staircase and beautiful hardwood floors. But there was no furniture—it was empty. Michael didn't bother to give me a tour, he just led me outside, the bright light blinding me as he held tightly onto my hand.

My legs felt wobbly as I found my footing. I heard the sounds of nature all around and felt the sticky heat on my skin as if it had rained earlier. As my eyes adjusted, all I could see was the big house we just came out of and literally nothing else around except for trees and wild grass. There was a dirt road that led to the house with no paved road in sight. I didn't bother to ask where we were as he opened an SUV door for me. *Where did that come from?* He helped me in the car and then quickly went to the driver's seat. *Michael can drive?* As he started the car, I began to feel something again. Fear? Hope?

"Where are we going?" I asked quietly, holding onto my seatbelt that felt like it was digging into my clavicle.

I looked over at Michael, and he said nothing; he kept his gaze forward as he sped down the dirt road with his jaw clenched. I looked back at the road and felt nauseous, the bumps making it hard to keep still in my seat.

"We're finding another house. We can't stay in one place too long. You're lucky I didn't chloroform you again," he said bitterly, as if I had just asked him something offensive.

I shook my head, not bothering to look at him as I watched the road.

I was never going to get out of this. *Now is the time. It's the perfect opportunity.* We finally pulled onto a paved, two-lane highway with more trees lining each side. It was quiet for too long, and I laid my head against the window, pretending to sleep but keeping my eyes slightly open. *He won't expect it this way.* I finally saw a car approaching from the other way. I didn't know if I had enough physical strength, but I was going to fucking try with all my might. I didn't even have time to second guess myself. The car was about to pass as I quickly shot my head up from the window, took a hold of the wheel, turned it toward the other side of the road, and waited for this nightmare to finally end.

Jack

Nine days earlier.

"He fucking what?" Dan, Hana's father, responded after I explained the situation. He sounded fucking furious.

"Kidnapped her, Dan. I'm on the way to the police station now with his ex-girlfriend who is willing to corroborate our story. Emily is meeting me there as well," I explained further.

"I'm on my way too," he replied, his southern accent almost humorously different from my British one.

I looked over at Jackie as she stared out the window, still visibly shaking.

"I'll see you there." I hung up and put my hand to Jackie's shoulder. I needed to be kind to her, especially after all she had been through. Plus, I needed her help to put Michael in fucking jail.

"You alright?" I asked quietly as she gazed over at me, seemingly no light in her eyes.

She shook her head no. "I will never be alright." She turned to look out the window again.

I almost rolled my eyes at her dramatic response, but I knew I must have sounded the same way when I thought I would never get Hana back. I knew what it was like to get your heart

JACK

broken, to have no hope. However, I didn't know what it was like to be tied up and have my skin carved into.

We pulled up to the police station, and I nearly ran in. I demanded to speak to the same officer I spoke to before—he knew the history of my wife being taken. I had gone into the station when we got back into the city from Greenwich, explaining that I had misunderstood the situation. I only hoped they would take me seriously again, but I was confident bringing in others to corroborate would make it even more urgent.

I explained in great detail what had happened when I answered the door for Jackie. I explained Hana's learning of Michael's past from Jackie. Jackie was taken into a private room to speak to another officer, giving her all the horrid details of her and Michael's past.

"Has anyone found my fucking cousin?" I heard yelling from the front of the station and immediately knew it was Emily—the woman had no filter.

I stood, motioning her over, and she pushed past the cops with Dan right behind her. His cowboy hat, big gray-and-white beard, and cowboy boots stuck out like a sore thumb as he marched up to me, his mere presence demanding attention.

"Son, your eye looks terrible," he said to me then turned to the officer. "Now who the fuck do I need to speak to in order to get my baby girl back?"

* * *

Three days had gone by, and nothing was happening. The police had some information, but they weren't doing anything with it. They knew about Michael's house in Greenwich, his apartment in Williamsburg, and apparently even his aunt and uncle's residences as well. They found out that they had indeed taken a Yellow Cab, but it was to a public parking garage in Queens. They managed to get footage from the surveillance camera on the property. He had been driving a costly SUV, but the plates were deliberately covered. His phone was last pinged at that parking garage. And that was it.

His and Hana's faces were plastered all over the city and surrounding states. The missing persons flyer seemed surreal as I passed by it in the subway station every day.

My heart was broken into pieces. I felt hopeless. I wanted to keep looking for Hana, but I had no idea what else to do. All I kept imagining were the horrible things that fucking monster was doing to Hana. I knew I wasn't an angel—I knew I did terrible shit to her. It was out of passion; nothing was ever deliberate aside from planning to bring her to my loft. I was desperate for her to stay, and I did what I could to keep her. I never planned on killing anyone; I didn't *want* to hurt anyone. I was surprised that she had stayed, that she didn't fight harder, that she fell in love with me so quickly. And I knew I had issues, I knew I needed to be in fucking therapy and get through my years of trauma and addiction and anger. But Michael? He had done things to Jackie that were methodical and sinister.

And apparently he had done things to other women too.

Two other women went to the police after they saw that Michael was wanted. They told similar stories to Jackie's and they even had the scars to prove it. It was proof that he was a psychopath.

On the seventh day without Hana, I started to believe that Michael had taken her into the woods and killed her and then himself. I could understand the notion; if he couldn't have

JACK

her, no one could. I felt the very same way.

I found myself sinking into a deep despair. Michael's whole family had tried to reach him to no avail. They had to be gone. I didn't want to live in a world where Hana didn't exist. I could never go on without her. How could I ever possibly get over the loss of my one true love?

On day nine, I had my suicide planned. I had decided that if she wasn't back to me within the next few days, I would take my gun and end it all. The pain of being without her was too much to bear. I had told Hana I would die for her. It was still true.

I had fallen asleep in my loft on the cold, hard floor after painting nearly a dozen portraits of Hana. I needed her beauty to live on in the world. Maybe Jessica could sell my paintings and be set with money for a lifetime. I wasn't worried about leaving my sister—she was strong. She would be okay. She was always the most level-headed sibling. And my mum and brother? They'd be fine. Everyone would be just fine without me.

I woke up to the buzz of my cell phone vibrating on the floor beside me. Dread consumed me when I realized it was the police calling. They had to be calling to inform me that they had found Michael and Hana in some wooded ditch, their flesh rotting into the Earth.

I hesitantly put the phone up to my ear after I answered. My sweaty, shaking palms nearly dropped it.

"Hello?" I answered, holding my breath, feeling a hole directly in my heart.

"Jack Maynor? It's officer Hanson. We've found your wife—she's alive."

Hana

I woke up to a steady beeping noise, my head feeling like I had a ton of bricks on each of my temples. I could barely open my eyes; my eyelids felt too heavy, like lead was keeping them shut. I tried to speak but my mouth wouldn't open. *Am I dead?*

"Hana?"

My heart leapt through my chest—*oh thank God, we're reunited, the afterlife does exist.* I felt his warm hands on my cheek and arm, the weight of his body next to mine. I could smell the paint on his clothes.

"Jack," I croaked, using all of my strength to muster up the words when what I really wanted to do was jump up and into his arms.

"Sweetheart, I'm here. You're okay. You're gonna be okay," he said quietly, his voice shaky. "You're in the hospital. I'm not leaving your side."

With his reassurance, I let my mind drift to a dreamless sleep.

* * *

I woke up suddenly in sheer panic, gasping for air. Was I still with Michael? Where was I? I came to when I realized that

HANA

Jack was right next to me, taking my hand and speaking calmly to me. I didn't register what he said; all I could do was break down in tears as I turned and saw my doe-eyed, beautiful husband next to me.

"Jack." I sobbed, squeezing his hand with mine.

"Hello, sweetheart." He smiled, tears welling in his eyes.

"Is this real? Am I alive?" I asked, still feeling spacey and out of it; I was sure I was drugged up on something, especially after feeling the IV in my hand when I squeezed his.

Jack chuckled next to me. Fuck, I missed his laugh. I missed his voice. I missed *him*.

"Yes, love. You're alive. You've been practically asleep for almost two days, though," he explained. "I haven't left your side. Except for the loo." He smiled, revealing the dimples that I loved so much.

Tears streamed down my face as I laughed. My ribs hurt with the motion, making me wince.

"What happened?" I asked curiously.

Jack sighed heavily. "What's the last thing you remember?" His face was serious again.

I shook my head. It came back to me suddenly. *Oh fuck.*

"I...I tried to crash us into another car." I stared at him, horrified.

Jack nodded knowingly.

"Is he...?" I asked after a moment. I don't know why I asked, or why I cared, but I needed to know.

Jack sighed again. "He's fine, Hana. He's in the county jail, though. He walked away from the accident barely scathed," he explained, looking disappointed.

It was over. *Oh my God.* No more choosing, no more guilt, no more second guessing myself. The horrible monster was out of my life. I still felt a twinge deep in my chest; was I mourning the loss of the person I thought I loved?

"What about…the other car?" I suddenly felt tremendous guilt. All I thought about was ending mine and Michael's lives, not anyone else's safety.

"They swerved out of the way. They're fine. You and Michael spun into a tree," Jack explained quietly.

I could see Jack's mind working, keeping something back from me.

"What?" I asked, suddenly nervous.

He hesitated. "I never thought I'd see you again," he breathed out. "I almost took my own life, Hana."

The beeping on the monitor quickly sped up, a reflection of my heart almost exploding with sorrow.

"I thought you would have. I wanted to go too if I couldn't see you again," I cried, realizing I was squeezing his hand again.

Jack shook his head, his tears finally releasing. He put his hand to my cheek and leaned down to get closer to me.

"I would have followed you, even in death, my love."

He pulled me in for a kiss, his lips desperate as he lifted me and held me close to him. I used every single last ounce of my energy to kiss him back. The pieces of my heart were finally together again.

Hana

The weeks had gone by in a blur. Jack and I started to put our lives back together, regaining a sense of normalcy. Or at least, whatever normalcy we had before. We had talked to the police countless times, and I had chosen to testify against Michael when the time came. It broke my heart to learn that Jackie wasn't his only other victim. He had done things far worse to other women who came forward. I had to recount my time with him multiple times. It was a nightmare I had to relive over and over. But I wanted to get it done—I didn't want Michael to get off easily. The best case scenario had him in prison for forty years; the minimum was fifteen years. And the worst case scenario was that he wouldn't get convicted. However, my attorneys and I were confident he would be. Jack also said he would easily kill him if he went free. I thought that was romantic.

I discovered that Michael was going to hire someone to kill Jack while all three of us were "together." When his plans changed, he paid someone to find a list of houses that went unfinished in the last stages of the building process, essentially being abandoned. Apparently, he had held me captive in the Hudson Valley, less than a couple hours from the city.

I was going to therapy. I was taking my meds again. I was

on birth control—thank God Michael didn't get me pregnant. Jack and I were cozy in our Williamsburg apartment; we still stayed up way too late and I still drank from time to time, but surprisingly my mental health remained in a good place.

Jack was getting ready for his summer tour with Chaos Catalyst. Everything between him and Adam seemed to be swept under the rug—they were the best of friends again. Emily was around a lot too, even Billie. We had dinner dates and went to gallery openings and the guys' shows around the city together. Jessica was over every other day, bringing us food or random gifts. She was acting off Broadway now and she seemed happy. We all seemed to be okay again.

My twenty-sixth birthday was approaching. Jack had something planned, but he wanted to surprise me.

After his show one night, Jack and I went to the loft so he could "pick something up."

"I'm not sure I believe that you need to just pick something up." I side-eyed him as we strolled down the street toward the loft.

He looked over at me and grinned.

"Sweetheart, do you think I'm trying to trick you? I'd never," he scoffed mockingly at me.

We could joke about the start of our relationship; our dark humor amused us and frankly, if Jack had never forcefully whisked me away, I'd still be with the monster.

"You're right, baby. I shouldn't even question it," I jested, my lips curling up into a smile.

We walked into the loft where it was dark and quiet, and I was surprised that when Jack flicked the lights on, no one else was in there. There were only red roses spread across the floor with a round table in the middle of the loft, a black cloth covering it and a single candle in the middle.

I turned to him, confused.

He grinned at me. "Surprise!"

I shook my head at him. "What is this?"

Jack walked over to the couch on the side of the room and pulled out some canvases behind it.

"It's a personal viewing of all the paintings I did of you." He seemed nervous; he had four or five medium-sized canvases, the art still turned around in his hands so I couldn't see.

"Are they X-rated or something?" I teased. "Are you going to show me or just keep them hidden like that all night?"

Jack gave me his perfect, dimpled smile.

"I just wanted to explain exactly how I felt while painting these," he started, gently setting them next to the table and slowly walking toward me. "It was a few days after you were taken that I started these. The first one was a portrait done with oil paint, and all I imagined was the look you have when you're upset or mad. I imagined you fighting. So this was the result."

He picked up the first canvas and there I was, a perfectly painted portrait with my brows pulled together, my lips slightly parted, and my green eyes boring right back at me.

"Jack." I walked toward him, gently grazing the canvas with my fingertips. "This is amazing."

He put it down and grabbed the next canvas. He looked so serious and sullen.

"This is the next one," he started as he revealed another portrait of me, this time looking terrified; I was frowning, my eyes wide as I looked up in the distance. My heart sank—he probably knew this look well.

He shook his head, tears welling in his eyes. "I hated that I so easily knew how you looked when you were scared. And I hated thinking that's how you were feeling."

There was a sting deep in my chest. We had come so far since that first day here in the loft. All I wanted then was to escape and run back to Michael. Now I wanted to escape any memory of Michael and never leave Jack's side again.

He continued before I could say anything. He grabbed the next canvas and held it in front of him. It was me, smiling widely in a laugh, my eyes closed.

"A week had passed and all I wanted to think about was your beautiful, happy, smiling face. Your sweet smile was on loop in my brain," he explained with a faint smile. "I thought you were gone and this is how I wanted to remember you. This is how I wanted the world to remember you."

A tear shed down his cheek, and he gulped, staring at me with his big blue eyes.

"Thank you, Jack. These are all so beautiful." I put my hand to his face and smiled as the tears fell down my face as well.

"There's one more." He set down the canvas and picked up the last one, facing it to his chest. "This is how I imagined we'd be reunited. I didn't know how or when that would be, but all I could think about was having you in my arms again. I knew we'd find each other, whether it be in the next life or the afterlife."

Tears streamed down my face and my chest heaved. Jack turned the canvas around and there we were, perfectly painted, staring at each other with our upper halves pressed together. His hand was to my face and I mirrored him on the other side. The lower half was our bodies turning into dust, drifting away in the wind.

All I could do was wrap my arms around him and bring my

lips to his. His full, pouty lips hungrily attached to mine and the canvas dropped to the floor as he put his hands to my face, pulling me in even closer. His hands stripped off my clothes as I did the same for him. Then we backed onto the wall where he lifted me, and I entwined my legs around him. I ran my hand through his hair before his hard cock fully plunged inside of me. I bounced myself up and down, helping him with his thrusts, never parting my lips from his. He quickly stopped and carried me over to the kitchen counter, setting me down carefully before getting to his knees and pressing his hot mouth onto my throbbing clit, flicking his tongue around and instantly making me come.

"Baby," I moaned, and he continued, looking up at me and smiling as he made me come for a second and third time.

"Jack," I breathed out. "Hurt me like the night of our wedding party."

He stopped and looked at me quizzically. "No." He shook his head. "I can't."

I frowned. "Please. I'm sober. I can handle it, and if I can't, I'll use my safe word."

Jack shook his head and stood, his eyes full of concern. "Why would you want me to do that again?"

I bit my lip; I wasn't sure why. "Maybe...a mixture of curiosity and horniness?"

He smiled at me but still shook his head. "No, sweetheart. It was wrong then. I was holding onto too much anger and took it out on you. I don't want to recreate that night anymore," he explained. "But there is something I *can* do."

I perked up.

"First: your safe word?" His eyes showed that hint of darkness in him, and maybe that's all I wanted when I asked him. Maybe I felt he was being too soft on me since I returned.

"Red." I smiled.

He nodded and pressed his lips against mine. I could taste myself on him. He quickly let go of me and fisted my hair tightly in his hand.

"Get on your knees, love," he ordered, his voice gravelly and deep.

He guided me off the counter, and I quickly got on my knees. His hard cock was suddenly in my mouth, and Jack roughly face fucked me, bobbing my head back and forth with his grip.

"Mmm, fuck. You're such a naughty whore, aren't you?" he asked, keeping his pace.

He let go of my hair, and I gasped for air as I looked up at him, drool dripping all over my mouth and running down my body. He quickly slapped me and took my hair again.

"I asked you a question, sweetheart," he growled.

"Yes, Jack. I'm a naughty whore," I breathed out.

He smiled, causing my whole body to tingle with butterflies. "Get on all fours."

I turned around and got onto my hands and knees, waiting for his touch. He quickly slapped one side of my ass then the other, and I let out a yelp each time. He suddenly grabbed my hair with his hand and pulled back, making me sit up and then stand. He gripped my throat with one hand while the other still held my head back.

"You still love how rough I can be, don't you?" he asked quietly in my ear.

"Yes," I whispered, barely able to breathe with his hand pressing against my throat.

"You love the pain I give you, don't you?" he went on.

I nodded as much as I could, getting lightheaded before he

let go and I gasped for air. He was suddenly inside me, his cock deep while he pulled my hair back with one hand and slapped my tits with the other. His hand inched down to my pussy as he furiously pounded me. He rubbed my clit with fervor, forcing me to come quickly and loudly.

"Whose pussy is this, Hana?" he moaned into my ear right after my orgasm slowed.

"Yours, Jack," I breathed out.

"Say my name again, sweetheart." He was almost out of breath.

"Jack. I love you, Jack," I moaned.

His pounding grew wild as he grabbed my hips with both hands and moaned a powerful grunt, filling me with his cum.

He slowed, but my body still shook with pleasure. I needed to sit—I was drained of all energy. Jack could tell; he pulled out of me, turned me around and picked me up. He sat me down on the cloth table and wrapped his arms around me as he stood against my chest.

"Jack, I love you more than anything," I whispered in his ear.

He looked to me with the most earnest, endearing smile. "That's all I've ever wanted."

Six months ago, I had no idea what I was doing with my life. I had no purpose, no direction. I had goals, but things weren't planned out or set in stone. I didn't know who I was. I didn't know where I belonged. My life had turned into this chaotic, messy, thrilling, scary story. Trying to take my own life because I thought I would never see Jack again made me realize that all I wanted was him. And now I knew my purpose: to love my imperfect Jack, to follow him into the darkness, and to live happily ever after in our very own little twisted fairy tale.

Epilogue

Four years later.

I sat on the couch under a blanket, looking out the window at the snow falling to the ground quickly. I had set my laptop on the coffee table to take a break; the deadline for my book was quickly approaching, and I couldn't shake off the anxiety. I had written a fictional version of my life including the good, the bad, and the ugly. It felt cathartic in a way but also extremely exhausting.

I stared up at the clock that read 2:15 p.m. Jack was putting Jenny down for a nap; she was fighting them lately, and being at the house in Lake George, away from home, made her even fussier. But he always seemed to have the magic touch. She was definitely a daddy's girl. She wanted to play in the snow and watch daddy strum his guitar while he practiced some new music. Two had been a fun age so far, except for her learning to say "no" to everything I said and repeating "fuck" every time Emily was over.

"She's out," Jack whispered as he walked into the living room, tip-toeing his steps with exaggeration.

I laughed. He was exactly the dad I had hoped he would be. He was patient, silly, loving, and kind, and he spoiled her rotten. He even refused to be away from home for more than a few days at a time when he and Adam were touring. We had to tag along during their European tour when Jenny was only a few months old because Jack refused to go if we didn't.

"Let's see how many times we can fuck before our spawn wakes up." He grinned as he sat next to me before nuzzling his lips to my neck.

My phone began to vibrate on the coffee table. Jack and I glanced at each other when we realized it was the correctional facility where Michael was incarcerated. He got five years—*five* fucking years—in prison. The other women who came forward decided not to press charges— I had a feeling that Michael somehow got to them with money. Jackie's testimonial turned to shit based on her "instability." So it was all on me. Michael's lawyers made me look like an insane, slutty, unstable woman, and I'm sure my sobbing at the trial made me look guilty and unreliable and not like the actual victim that I was. It also didn't help that I admitted to trying to kill us both with the car crash. His charge was reduced to second-degree kidnapping, the court deciding there was no proof that he had sexually assaulted or abused me since we had a "dominant/submissive relationship." That was a real shocker to the court too.

He had never attempted to contact me before this. My heart started to pound in my chest while I shakily attempted to grab my phone. Jack quickly swooped it off the coffee table and held it in his hand.

"You are not answering that," he stated bitterly.

I only nodded. Why did I think it was a good idea to answer in the first place?

Jack stared at my phone until it stopped buzzing.

"He's leaving a voicemail. Let's see what this fucker has to say to you."

I bit my lip, trying not to cry. I didn't want to waste any more tears on the monster.

"Let me hear it." I held my hand out for the phone.

Jack eyed me, chewing on his bottom lip. His chest rose and fell quickly; I'm sure his blood was boiling with rage. He finally decided to hand it to me, albeit very reluctantly.

"Put it on speaker," he demanded, the scary Jack emerging

It didn't happen often anymore—he reserved it for certain sexual times, but sometimes it happened when he got angry. He never took his anger out on me anymore, thank God. I wouldn't have stayed if he did.

My hand shakily hit the button to listen to Michael's voicemail. My heart felt like it was going to jump out of my throat.

"Hana," his voice started. *"It's Michael."* He cleared his throat, and I couldn't help it—I began sobbing. *"I just wanted to let you know that I'm getting out early on good behavior. I know the trial was messy, but there hasn't been a day that's gone by that I don't think of you. I hope you can forgive me."*

Jack shook his head bitterly as the voicemail continued.

"I know you've probably moved on. I know you're still with Jack. But Hana, I've got eyes on the outside. I hope you're enjoying your time in Lake George. Just know that we will be together again someday. Someday very soon."

Acknowledgments

I have to thank everyone who has helped me during the writing and editing process.

Andrea, my editor—thank you for making my writing SO much better and helping me learn so much. Also—em dash. Was that right?

My beta readers—thank you all for hyping me up and letting me know that my story wasn't awful. You are all amazing and I appreciate you!

My ARC readers—thank you for your honest reviews, your time, and general support and love for this book.

Arianna—my very first beta reader and bestie for life. You are the best hype woman and your constant support, ideas, and brainstorming has helped me tremendously; not only with this book, but with more projects ;) Your love and friendship means the world to me and I would have probably given up on writing 5,000 times if it weren't for you.

Nick—thank you for your continuous love and support! I appreciate all of your ideas, suggestions, and comments. You have been the best cheerleader and support system. I love you so much.

To my other family and friends who have supported me along

the way—thank you! I love you all and you better not have read this book.

About the Author

Cassandra lives in Southern California. In her free time she enjoys tending to her house plants, reading, playing video games with her daughter, and laughing at cat videos with her husband.

You can connect with me on:
🌐 https://authorcassandravega.com

www.ingramcontent.com/pod-product-compliance
Lightning Source LLC
LaVergne TN
LVHW011946060526
838201LV00061B/4231